WHEN TOMORROW COMES

When Tomorrow Comes

A Novel

Jennie L. Hansen

Covenant Communications, Inc.

Published by Covenant Communications, Inc.
American Fork, Utah

Printed in the United State of America
First Printing: September 1994

94 95 96 97 98 99 00 01 10 9 8 7 6 5 4 3 2 1

Library of Congress Cataloging-in-Publication Data

Hansen, Jennie L., 1943-
   When tomorrow comes : a novel / Jennie L. Hansen.
        p.   cm.
   ISBN 1-55503-725-9 : $9.95
   1. Man-woman relationships—Utah—Fiction. 2. Cancer—Patients—Utah—
Fiction. 3. Women ranchers—Utah—Fiction. 4. Mormons—Utah—Fiction.
I. Title.
PS3558.A51293W48   1994
813'.54—dc20
94-29731
                                                            CIP

For my daughters,
Leslie and Janice Hansen

Their years at Snow College taught me
to love the Sanpete valley.

Chapter 1

"Have you told Jacey?"

"Not yet. I was hoping the matter could be settled quietly here in Baltimore without disturbing her."

Jacey lifted her head at the sound of her name and sighed. What were they protecting her from now? Ever since her family learned she had cancer, they'd protected and coddled her until she had no life of her own. She knew they meant well, but she wished they wouldn't do everything for her. If only she could convince them that she was neither an invalid nor a child.

"Dad, Jacey is the only one who can sign the contract. The will clearly states that it has to be signed in Utah, and only after she visits the property."

"She doesn't need the money or the property. That foolish old man had no business involving her. She isn't strong enough to travel across the country."

What old man? Jacey was puzzled as she sat up straighter in the wing chair where she had curled to wait for her fiancee in an alcove off the library. Before she could make her presence known, Roger's voice joined the conversation.

"We'll be flying to the west coast and on to Hawaii for our honeymoon next month. I can arrange our itinerary so that we can stop in Salt Lake to sign the papers on our way. I'll have everything ready, and there won't be a need for a separate trip."

Hawaii? There had been no discussion of a honeymoon trip.

When, she wondered, had Roger planned to tell her? And when had he arrived, anyway? Sometimes he gave her sister Anne a ride home. He probably came in through the garage with her, but obviously he was in no hurry to look up his fiancee.

"Daddy?" Jacey rose to her feet and stepped out of the alcove. Her father sat at his desk while Roger leaned one hip against a corner of the broad oak expanse. Anne stood beside the window, one hand touching a heavy brocade drapery panel. Jacey's mother was in the room too, sitting in a comfortable leather chair beside the desk. Hearing her, they all turned startled eyes in her direction.

"There you are, sweetie." Roger straightened and walked toward her. He bent to give her a quick peck on the cheek. Jacey stifled her irritation. He behaved as though he had been searching for her when she knew better. But right now she wanted to find out what mysterious papers she was supposed to sign.

"Daddy," she repeated, "I heard you mention an old man and some papers I should sign—"

"It's nothing to worry about, honey." Her father smiled. "We have everything under control. You just relax, and Roger will take care of everything."

"But I don't understand."

"It's nothing to worry your pretty little head about." Roger put his arm around her shoulder and gave a gentle squeeze.

"I don't understand why Charles made such a ridiculous will, dear." Celia Mathews spoke to her husband. "Wouldn't it have been much simpler to let your office handle the estate, rather than turn it over to some small-town lawyer who doesn't understand about Jacey?"

"Will? Mother, do you mean Uncle Charlie? Did something happen to Uncle Charlie?" Jacey stared at her mother, then turned questioning eyes to her father.

"You don't need to worry about a thing, honey. Roger will handle finding a buyer, and whatever he gets for the property he'll invest for you."

"Daddy! What about Uncle Charlie?"

"Dear, you look a little pale. Why don't you sit here." Celia rose from her chair and motioned for Jacey to take her place. When she was satisfied that her daughter was seated comfortably, she sank onto the ottoman beside the chair. "It's only been two months since you were released from the hospital, and I don't think you slept at all today. With the wedding just five weeks away, you've got to be more careful."

Roger drew a pen and notebook from his jacket pocket. "How large is this property?" he asked. "Do we need to advertise nationally?"

"No such luck, Roger." Anne strolled toward him. "Charles referred to the property as a ranch in his will, but it's really just a few acres. Jacey isn't exactly a grand heiress. The trust Grandfather left her is worth more than that few acres of Utah desert, so you'd better not plan on giving up your practice just yet."

"Cute, Anne, cute." Roger scowled at her.

"Uncle Charlie's dead, isn't he?" Jacey stared from one face to another. She thought her heart would break. "When—when will the funeral be?" She could barely get the words out. Uncle Charlie meant more to her than any other friend she'd ever had. He'd been her lifeline through her illness, her link with a happier time, and the keeper of her dreams.

"You don't have to go to any old funeral, dear." Her mother patted her arm. "Your father took care of all that."

Walter Mathews ran his fingers through his perfectly-styled silver hair. "Roger," he said, "get right on this Monday morning. You might as well take this file with you tonight." He indicated a manila folder lying on his desk with the name "Charles Mathews" printed down one side. "If everything is ready to go before the wedding, there shouldn't be much delay in Salt Lake. Jacey will be tired after the wedding, and you may have to stay over a night to give her a chance to rest."

"I'll have Marge work out a complete itinerary before she confirms our reservations."

"Well, I'm glad that's decided. Dinner has been ready for twenty minutes. If we don't move into the dining room soon, Susan will be turning in her notice." Celia rose gracefully to her feet. Elegant black silk swirled about her ankles as she placed her hand on Roger's arm.

"Anne?" Walter extended his arm to his daughter. Together the two couples moved toward the double doors opening into the formal dining room. As they passed beneath the glittering chandelier, sparkles of light danced from its crystal prisms to the older woman's gleaming champagne blonde hair and shimmered across the beaded floor-length ensemble hugging the younger woman's body.

Jacey's eyes followed the two couples, but she made no move to join them. She merely shook her head as though waking from a long sleep. She wondered how long it would be before they even noticed her absence.

She had a right to be angry. After all, how many women discover they are heiresses one afternoon and have their inheritances disposed of by their families and fiancés before dinner that same day? With their usual conspiracy to never tell her anything unpleasant, her family hadn't answered any of her questions.

Her eyes went to the folder on her father's desk. Never in her life had she touched any of the papers her father brought home from the office. Her father was the head of the most prestigious law firm in Baltimore, perhaps in the whole state of Maryland, and she understood the importance of confidentiality in his work. But that file concerned her and Uncle Charlie. She had to know.

With shaking hands she opened the folder. Her eyes quickly scanned an obituary, a death certificate, receipts from a funeral home in Manti, Utah, and Uncle Charlie's will. Her breath caught in a little sob when she read that Uncle Charlie had died six weeks ago, just two weeks after she herself had been released from the hospital. A quick glance at the will told her he'd left everything he owned to her. But the only thing she wanted was the dream they had shared for more than ten years—a dream that someday she'd visit his ranch.

Resentment filled her heart. Someone should have told her. They should have allowed her to mourn Uncle Charlie. Daddy hadn't considered it important enough to even mention to her. It was true that her father hadn't kept in touch with the uncle he considered eccentric and impractical; but Jacey had written to Uncle Charlie faithfully since she was twelve years old.

She sighed, remembering that long-ago summer when she had been sent to Longport to stay with her grandparents while her parents took Anne with them to Europe. She had been recovering from chicken pox, feeling lonely and bored—until Uncle Charlie suddenly arrived.

One day she had sat dangling her feet from the garden wall, wishing she were a princess and that a knight on a fabulous white charger would come along to rescue her from her lonely tower. The next morning she came down to breakfast to discover Uncle Charlie. His smooth pink head was bare, but a huge cowboy hat dangled from the back of his chair. He wore a white shirt with shiny pearl snaps, denim pants, and real cowboy boots.

Later she learned the boots were made of snakeskin and the hat was called a "Stetson." When she raised her eyes to his, she discovered a twinkle that immediately captured her heart. His face was round and smooth like the top of his head, and his mouth stretched into the kind of smile that had to be answered. For the rest of the summer she'd forgotten about knights and princesses and began to dream of a hero wearing cowboy boots and a white hat. The good guys always wore white Stetsons, according to Uncle Charlie. And heroes in white hats, like knights in shining armor, rode white horses. Not to church, of course; for that Uncle Charlie had a bright red convertible. But she'd felt important as she and Uncle Charlie zipped across town to attend meetings, play softball, and go to picnics. She'd been strong then, and so sure she knew what she wanted. She and Uncle Charlie had rejoiced together when her parents had sent a letter saying she could be baptized.

Too soon summer had ended, and Uncle Charlie went away. At first she'd tried to stay active in the Church; but meetings were held so far from her home that she couldn't walk to them, and her parents wouldn't allow her to take the bus by herself. Daddy didn't have time to take her to church, and then she was too ill to go anywhere. Occasionally she'd gone by herself when she grew older, but it wasn't the same without Uncle Charlie.

She fingered the heavy scar across her throat, hidden by the high collar of her dress, and wondered if she'd let illness become an excuse for not remaining active in the faith that had once filled her with such happiness. Could she regain that faith? Uncle Charlie had thought so, but now he was gone and she wasn't sure she could do it alone.

Her spirits plunged another degree. Her dreams of a hero were gone, too. Heroes in white hats didn't exist any more than knights in shining armor. She was too old to believe in heroes, yet somewhere deep inside she still wanted to.

She dropped the papers back on her father's desk, and, for the first time since cancer had been diagnosed, took a good look at her life. The time had come to stop thinking that survival was the same thing as living. Dreams had kept her alive, but if she wanted a real life she had to grow up. She'd been ill so much of her life that it had been easy to let other people take care of her while she lived in a dream world. But no more. She'd lost so much, yet somehow she must regain the independent soul Uncle Charlie had discovered and nourished years ago. Her family had stood by her through her nightmare illness, but somehow she now had to let them know she no longer needed them to wrap her in the security of their protection.

"Jacey! What are you doing sitting there? Father is waiting for you so we can begin dinner!" Anne stepped through the doorway.

"Go ahead without me. I just want to think about Uncle Charlie for a while."

"Oh, don't be silly. You can't mourn someone you never really knew."

"I did know him, Anne. I only saw him a couple of times, but he wrote wonderful letters. He was a really special person."

"He was a pathetic old man with a penchant for wearing weird clothes."

"I always wanted to visit his ranch, but Daddy always found some reason why I couldn't."

"Don't be silly, Jacey! Uncle Charles was a childish old man who would have encouraged you to actually *do* the stupid things you used to dream up. Father was furious when he discovered the things he let you do that summer while you were supposed to be resting in the country with our grandparents."

"That summer was wonderful."

"You nearly died the following winter when you came down with rheumatic fever. Father simply protected you from all that nonsense and made certain you got a good education, met the right people, and didn't exhaust yourself. Consequently you have a career with the college, and you'll soon be married to Roger."

"But I don't want—"

"There's nothing for you to worry about. As soon as Uncle Charles' property is sold, Roger will invest the money for you. With that and the trust fund Grandfather left you, you'll always be secure even if you can't work."

"What's keeping you, honey?"

Jacey looked up to see Roger sauntering casually toward her. His dark hair gleamed, and his dinner jacket showed off his wide shoulders superbly. He smiled and held out his hand as he reached her side. Dark blue eyes framed by long, dark lashes showed the proper amount of concern as he tugged her hand, drawing her to her feet to stand beside him.

"Dinner's waiting." He smiled, revealing a lone dimple in his right cheek. With one finger he lifted her chin to look into her eyes. "What's this? Tears?" Lightly brushing her cheek with his fingertips, he wiped away the tears which had started to creep down her face. "What's the matter, baby?"

"Ignore her, Roger," Anne interrupted before Jacey could speak. "She's just indulging in a little theatrics over Uncle Charlie."

"I guess she's entitled." Roger lifted one eyebrow as he pulled Jacey snugly under his arm. "You wouldn't happen to be jealous because he left his property to her, would you Anne?" Turning his attention back to his fiancee, he gave her shoulder a quick squeeze before strolling casually toward the dining room with Jacey tucked against his side.

"It's all right, sweetie. Cry if you want to; just don't let those old tears wash your pretty blue eyes away."

Jacey smiled timorously and reluctantly followed his lead.

"Why, Jacey! Is something wrong? Are you feeling ill?" Celia rose to her feet, a worried frown marring her perfect features.

"Should I call Dr. Bellows?" Walter reached for the telephone on the sideboard.

"No, no." Roger held out one arm as though to restrain his future father-in-law. "She's fine, just a little upset over Uncle Charlie."

"That's why I didn't want to tell her," Walter growled, reaching out to pat the back of Jacey's hand as Roger seated her on his right before taking the chair on her other side. "If it weren't for that nonsensical will, she needn't have been disturbed at all."

They talked about her as though she weren't even there; she might as well be invisible. But she had to tell them they couldn't protect her from missing someone or being sad.

"Daddy, I loved Uncle Charlie. You should have let me . . . "

"Now, honey, you don't need to worry about a thing. Roger will take care of everything. The rancher who owns the adjoining property has already offered to buy the place. Roger will arrange all the legalities; then, when you leave on your honeymoon, you'll only have to make a quick stop in Salt Lake City to sign the papers."

"I thought she had to actually visit the property before she could take possession or sell it," Anne interjected.

Jacey turned abruptly to look at her sister. "I get to go there?"

"Don't worry, sweetie. I'm sure it's just a technicality. Even if we do have to visit the ranch, it's only a two-hour drive from Salt Lake. We can take care of everything in one afternoon."

"But I want to—"

"Darling, eat your dinner. You mustn't lose any weight before the wedding," Celia interrupted. "I think I really must talk to Dr. Bellows about some vitamins or a food supplement. You're much too thin, and even though the neckline is high enough on your wedding dress to cover your scar, you'll still look like a bag of bones if you lose any more weight."

"Nonsense!" Roger ran his fingers down her pale blue satin sleeve. "She's beautiful. I like fragile, feminine women."

Anne made a sound which, from a less well-bred woman, might have been considered a snort. Roger frowned slightly, then picked up the gauntlet. Soon the two were engaged in a lively debate over some of Anne's feminist views. Walter and Celia joined the fray, with the discussion remaining animated until dinner was over and the last nibble of chocolate velvet crumb cake was safely stowed away.

Early in the discussion, Jacey stopped listening. Her family meant well, she reminded herself, but she was tired of being coddled, protected, and talked about as though she weren't even present. At twenty-three years of age, she had yet to be recognized as an adult. Yes, she'd been ill; but Dr. Bellows said she didn't have to worry about a relapse anymore. True, she still had to be careful; but what was there about being ill that automatically relegated her to being a perpetual child? She wasn't an invalid, either.

After dinner Walter and Celia left for the theatre, taking Anne with them.

"Now Roger, don't keep Jacey out late tonight," Celia cautioned as she shrugged easily into the black, full-length sable coat Walter held. "She's worn herself out over Charles."

"Don't worry. I'll take care of her." He leaned forward to kiss the older woman's cheek.

Jacey made her way back to the living room to curl up in a deep cushioned chair near the ornately-carved fireplace. She rested her head on her arms, and Roger followed her to stand beside her chair. Idly he picked up a strand of her long hair and ran it between his thumb and forefinger.

"Blonde silk." He smiled and she shrugged her shoulders. He insisted her hair was blonde, but she knew better. It was plain old brown, although the flickering gas flame spread gold highlights down its length. In the bright sunlight it would appear red.

Roger's gaze moved smoothly down from the pale hair between his fingers to the lace rising above the high collar of her pastel blue satin dress to her dainty gold sandals. "You look like an exquisite porcelain doll, Jacey." He smiled before his lips touched the top of her head.

"I'm not a doll." An unaccustomed surge of annoyance swept through her. She shook off Roger's hand and rose to her feet to walk restlessly across the room. Roger was as bad as her family, babying her and smothering her with effusive compliments.

"Shouldn't you be getting your jacket, sweetie?" Roger approached her, walking soundlessly across the deep pile carpet.

"I really don't want to go." Jacey looked up, pleading for understanding. "Couldn't we just stay here tonight?"

"You'll feel better once we get there. Bill and Sandra's parties are always fun."

"I'd rather not go."

"Is your jacket in your room?" Without waiting for an answer, he turned to dash up the stairs. In moments he was back, carrying a pale blonde mink coat which he draped casually about her shoulders.

Jacey let the coat drop to a chair. "I don't like wearing furs. I feel uncomfortable in that jacket."

"We've been through this before, Jacey." Roger looked sternly at his fiancee. "Your father paid a lot of money for that jacket, and he likes to see you wear it."

"What I want doesn't matter to any of you, does it?" Jacey's bitter words shocked even her own ears.

For just a moment Roger looked startled. Then, with a cheerful grin, he scooped Jacey into his arms and settled in the chair with her on his lap. For a few seconds she struggled to escape, then settled resignedly against his chest. She'd made a mess of things. Instead of standing up for herself and showing everyone that she deserved to be treated as an adult, she'd let them push her around again. Worst of all, she'd behaved like a child, confirming everyone's low opinion of her, including her own. Thinking she could prove to anyone that she was a mature, competent adult was a joke. She didn't have the vaguest idea of how to go about it.

Anne often said that women should be assertive and make their own opportunities. Well, that might work for strong, competent women like Anne; but Jacey suspected that if she demanded to be heard, she'd sound like a petulant child. She should forget about being assertive and making decisions, and remember how much Roger and her family loved her and how hard they tried to keep her safe. But dismissing her own need for independence didn't come easily, and in the back of her mind she persistently questioned why everyone else should know better than she what was best for her.

"There, honey." Roger stroked her silky hair. "We've been going too fast, haven't we? Don't worry; you don't have to do anything you don't want to do. I think you've been taking too seriously the things you've been reading about furs. You eat meat and wear leather shoes, so why should you have an aversion to furs? But if you really don't want to wear that jacket, I'll go fetch another one for you."

"No, Roger, the jacket isn't the point." If she could only make him understand how frightened she felt without any control over her own life, perhaps he would help her accept her limitations and show her how to take charge of those areas where she *could* be strong. Cancer had swept her body into a raging river where she'd been knocked and buffeted about, where all she could do was fight without ever knowing if she'd won or only reached a temporary calm. She wanted to reach out, grab hold of some part of her life, and be able to say, "This is me!" Since learning of Uncle Charlie's death, she felt as though she were headed for a black, swirling whirlpool, completely out of control, and her very identity was at stake.

"Though I feel strongly about not wearing furs myself, I really don't consider it barbaric for people who need furs to wear them." Jacey spoke carefully. Roger would soon be her husband; he said he loved her. Surely he would understand. Taking a deep breath, she tried to explain her troubled thoughts. "I'm not upset about fur coats; I'm disappointed because Father never gave me a chance to ever visit someone I cared about or even say goodbye when Uncle Charlie died. Father made those decisions, I didn't. Uncle Charlie taught me about something he called 'free agency.' He said God gave every person the right to choose his or her own path. But my family thinks that means everyone except me. I'm frightened because all the choices in my life are being made by someone else."

"You know he was only trying to protect you."

"He didn't need to protect me from Uncle Charlie. Uncle Charlie loved me."

"I'm sure he did, sweetie, but your father loves you, too. He's a brilliant and responsible man, and he has your best interests in mind. He believed your uncle was too rough for someone as fragile as you, so he did what he thought best to keep you safe. He only put off telling you the man had died because you've been through enough."

"I'm not as fragile as everyone thinks I am."

"Sh-h-h. Honey, don't upset yourself over what can't be helped."

"Roger, I appreciate my family and you. You've all made so many sacrifices to make certain I had the best possible medical attention and the love and encouragement I needed. I know I sound ungrateful, but lately I feel like everyone treats me like I were three, instead of twenty-three." She tried to get to her feet, but Roger chose not to release her. The tears that had been threatening since she learned of Uncle Charlie's death spilled down her cheeks.

"Calm down, honey. Don't cry. Your mother will be furious if you wear yourself out over this nonsense." His arms settled more securely around the slender shape he held. "You don't have to worry about a thing. I'll always be here to take care of you."

As she turned her head to protest, his mouth came down on hers. At first she resisted the insistent pressure, then realizing the futility of her actions, she ceased struggling.

"That's better," Roger smiled, releasing her. "Now, let's get moving. This party is important." Carelessly he draped the fur jacket around her shoulders as he propelled her toward the door.

Jacey sat numbly in the car beside Roger, who whistled an accompaniment to the car radio, seemingly unaware of the despair consuming her. Once again she was going where Roger and her family wanted her to go, wearing what they had decided she should wear, and despising herself for meekly going along. She wished she had the strength, backbone, or whatever it was called to either accept her life the way it was or stand up to everyone and change it.

Jacey chided herself for indulging in this little impromptu pity-party. She'd stop thinking about herself, she vowed, concentrate on remembering that Roger loved her, and begin doing everything she could to make him happy. The least she could do would be to smile and act happy. After all, the party they were going to was important to Roger.

She greeted their host and hostess politely despite her lack of enthusiasm. Roger kept his arm around her waist as they slowly circled the room and he made a big production of showing off his "beautiful fiancée, Walter Mathews' daughter." Jacey's high-heeled shoes pinched her toes, and she struggled to find the words to respond to those who wished them well. But even when she found herself tongue-tied, she smiled graciously.

Almost an hour later, Roger led her to a chair and insisted that she rest for a while. He then excused himself when he spotted an important contact he wished to talk to privately.

Jacey disliked large, noisy parties where everyone wandered

around with glasses and plates in their hands, talking too much and too loudly, performing a balancing act as they tried to eat with their fingers or from toothpicks. The noisy chatter and laughter seemed particularly annoying tonight. After a few minutes she left the chair and made her way to an out-of-the-way window seat where she curled up to wait for Roger. She could see him busily circulating among the beautiful and important people gathered at this penthouse party. He looked relaxed and comfortable, while she kept glancing at her watch, wondering how soon they could leave.

Jacey's mind wandered far from the exclusive suite where the party was being held, even as her eyes seemed to focus on the music and laughter around her, and a polite smile hovered on her faintly pouting mouth. Her thoughts centered on that magical summer with Uncle Charles when he had taught her to swim, ride a horse, and to play cowboys and Indians. Best of all had been his hair-raising tales of the wild West and the pioneers who had settled that faraway land. His stories were always full of fearless cowboys, stalwart pioneers, wonder horses, and brave, faithful sweethearts.

Suddenly her eyes focused on Roger. He stood a little apart from the group of men he had been talking with moments before. Beside him a tall woman with long, outrageously curly red hair smiled directly into his eyes over the rim of her glass. The neckline of her slinky silver dress plunged nearly to her navel and her hemline hovered near the top of her thighs, displaying a shocking amount of bare skin. Laughing at something Roger said, she slid a hand up his dark jacket sleeve. He tapped her nose teasingly with one finger, and his laughter joined hers. Their pose appeared provocatively intimate.

They're having fun, she thought absently, then brought herself up short. *Isn't this the moment when I'm supposed to be consumed with jealousy?* Carefully she reviewed her feelings as she watched the pair. Nothing. She felt nothing. And that was the saddest thing of all.

"Maybe you ought to just let this one go by."

"Excuse me?" Jacey looked around to see who had spoken. For just a moment she'd imagined it was Uncle Charlie's beloved gravelly voice she'd heard. No one stood close enough to have spoken. A wave of embarrassment swept over her; she'd let her imagination carry her away. But still she found herself wondering what Uncle Charlie would have thought of Roger Blake.

Roger was tall enough, slim, and had dark curly hair, but she couldn't imagine him as the hero of one of the old man's tales. In fact, she couldn't begin to imagine him riding a horse or leading a wagon train, let alone rescuing a lady in distress. Actually, she had a hard time imagining Roger even getting his hands dirty. But why was she imagining him as a pioneer, anyway? Frontier skills were hardly requisites for a successful law practice.

Jacey's thoughts took a grim turn. Roger might look terrific in a three-piece business suit or a tuxedo, and no way could he be considered a sissy, but he definitely wasn't white Stetson material. According to Uncle Charlie, heroes were committed to truth and honor. But Roger hadn't been truthful or honorable—and neither had her family, she thought resentfully as she remembered all they had kept from her, and the way they persisted in doing what was "best" for her without once considering her preferences.

Glancing up, she noticed that Roger and the woman were still together, though their conversation seemed to have taken on a more serious tone. Glumly she twisted her engagement ring around her finger. The two-carat diamond gleamed as it caught the light. Jacey couldn't recall clearly how she and Roger had managed to get engaged. Roger was the son of one of her grandfather's boyhood friends, a child who had arrived so late that his parents were contemporaries of his playmates' grandparents.

Roger and Anne had been classmates at the prestigious private school where they had both been sent as eager five-year-olds, and they had both been accepted into her father's law office together almost twenty years later. The two had fought and competed with each other as long as Jacey could remember, and Roger had been like a big brother to her all those years.

Through all of Jacey's illnesses Roger had brought her dolls and storybooks, and later candy and roses. He'd pampered and teased her; then, before her surgery six months ago, he had suddenly promised her they would get married as soon as she was strong enough. She had awakened hours later with tubes in both arms, thick bandages on her throat, a whispery voice that grew raspy when she tried to make herself heard and completely disappeared when she got upset—and a huge solitaire on her finger.

Instead of feeling as delighted as her whole family appeared to be, she felt confused and disoriented, wondering how she had managed to sleep through Roger's proposal. When her mother began talking about a June wedding, she found herself wishing they'd all go away and let her go back to sleep. Then she had been violently ill. Not a very auspicious beginning for their engagement.

Sitting there at the party, Jacey wished she had the courage to give the ring back to him. She momentarily froze, then admitted that the thought had been at the back of her mind for a long time. She didn't love Roger. Deep inside she'd always known it, but she had never considered that Roger might not love her. But as she lifted her eyes once more to the man she was engaged to marry, she knew with dreadful certainty. Roger loved the little girl he'd petted and spoiled for twenty years, but he wasn't in love with the woman she'd become. He didn't even know her.

All the way home, Jacey wondered what she should do about her discovery. She should talk to Roger—but what could she say? Then he was telling her good-night, and she hadn't said anything. As she closed the front door behind her, she berated herself for being a coward.

She moved down the hall and noticed a light under the library door. She peeked in to see her father with his head bent over a thick law book. He looked up and smiled.

"Hi! It's getting late. You'd better get up to bed."

"Daddy, I'd like to talk to you."

"You look tired; we can talk another time."

"But Daddy . . . " Jacey twisted her hands in the folds of her dress.

"If you're concerned about this stunt your Uncle Charles pulled, you can forget it. Roger is a good attorney, one of the best. He'll straighten everything out."

"I'd like to visit Uncle Charlie's ranch."

Walter went on as though his daughter hadn't spoken. "I can understand Charles' concern that you receive the benefits from his property, but he knew you were ill and in no condition to be

concerned with disposing of it yourself. I'm tied up with a complicated case right now, or I'd straighten it out for you myself; but
Roger will do fine. You're lucky to have that young man."

"Daddy, Roger . . . I don't think I should marry him."

"Now, don't you worry about Roger. All he wants is to take
care of you."

"But we don't love each other."

"You've gotten yourself worked up over Charles. Go to bed
now; everything will be fine in the morning. You just need to rest."

"You don't understand . . . " Jacey looked at her father. He'd
already dismissed her and returned to his book. She'd never make
him understand. Her footsteps dragged as she left the room and
made her way up the stairs.

Mechanically she began to undress. She hung her dress in the
closet, then seated herself before her vanity mirror to brush out her
hair. As she stared at her own wide, gray eyes in the mirror, she
wondered why she couldn't make her family listen to her. This
wasn't the first time they'd disregarded her wishes and assumed
they knew what was best for her. But today was the first time she'd
acknowledged her frustration.

She hadn't objected when her father chose a nice, safe, boring
career for her. She'd accepted his excuses for not visiting Uncle
Charlie. She'd even agreed to marry the man he decided was right
for her. But could she give up forever the dreams she and Uncle
Charlie shared?

She really did wish she might see Uncle Charlie's ranch just
once. He had told her so much about it in his letters that it had
become more of a home to her than the one she had lived in for all
of her twenty-three years. Its stucco walls and warm carved oak
paneling had become part of her dreams. The thought of selling
Uncle Charlie's ranch to some big rancher, who could never care
about it the way she did, brought a painful lump to her throat.

She longed to be strong and courageous like Uncle Charlie's
pioneers. But she wasn't, she was weak and afraid. She drew the
brush carefully through her hair and watched the odd colors wrap
around the bristles. Her shoulders slumped. Even her hair lacked
the gumption to be something definite.

No one took her seriously. She dreamed of taking a stand and being treated as a real person, but she didn't know how to make herself heard.

Frowning, she caught her reflection in the mirror. *Even my appearance is wishy-washy.* She saw her not-quite blonde hair with its streaks of rich brown and honey as an outward indication of her inability to be decisive. She thought her pouting mouth, tiny puckish nose, and elfin features looked childish and immature rather than pretty. Even her eyes lacked strength, the way their gray tint changed to pale blue or a whimsical green with every mood swing. Her height was about average, but her small bones made her appear tiny. Even her figure looked frustratingly average.

Worst of all was the scar. At least it wasn't average. It extended from one side of her throat to the other in a long, raised ridge. The doctor had assured her that a plastic surgeon would eventually help it to fade to a pencil-thin white line, but right now it stood out raw and ugly, and had to be constantly hidden beneath ruffles, scarves, or turtleneck sweaters. Mother, of course, had provided her with an entire wardrobe designed to conceal it.

Sighing resignedly, Jacey reached for her nightgown, a confection of flowered pink brushed nylon, covered with ribbons and lace. A tiny ruffle edged with more lace circled her throat. With its pink pearl buttons, ruffled yoke, and long sleeves, the floor-length Victorian gown made her look about ten years old. Catching sight of her reflection, Jacey burst into tears.

Minutes later, a knock sounded a quick tattoo on her bedroom door. Before she could react, the door opened and Anne strolled into the room.

Taking one look at Jacey's tear-streaked face, Anne hurried to her side. "Are you sick? Should I call mother?"

"No!"

Anne's reflection in the mirror revealed her surprise at the vehemence in her little sister's voice. Her eyes narrowed and she looked thoughtful for a moment. Then, not meeting Jacey's eyes, she asked, "Did Roger . . . ?"

Blushing furiously, Jacey shook her head vigorously.

"Good grief! You're not crying over Uncle Charles, are you?"

"No . . . yes . . . I don't know. It's so confusing. I'm so tired of being treated like an invalid or a child. I dread going back to my boring job. I hate my clothes, my hair, my whole life. Mother and Father make me want to scream! Sometimes I almost hate . . . " Jacey paused, looking guiltily at her sister.

"Me." Anne finished the sentence quietly. She appeared momentarily stunned by the younger woman's outburst. "I know I haven't been very pleasant to live with lately. I came in here to apologize and let you know I'll be moving into my own condo before you and Roger return from your honeymoon."

"No, not you. Roger." Jacey looked at her sister defiantly. They'd been close once, in spite of the six years' difference in their ages.

"Roger? I thought you loved Roger. He's adored you since you were a baby. Jacey, you're wearing his ring. You're going to be married in five weeks."

"I care about Roger," Jacey said carefully. "But I don't love him. There's something important missing in our relationship. Tonight at the party I watched him talking to a pretty, red-haired woman. They looked happy together." She noticed her sister's eyes narrow. "She flirted with Roger, and they both seemed to sparkle."

"You were jealous. Roger needs a good talking to."

"No, I wasn't jealous—and I felt guilty because I wasn't. I just felt sad, because all my life I've dreamed of a gallant knight or a romantic hero in a white hat falling in love with me, and I realized that Roger isn't my hero. I don't love him and he doesn't love me. He's only marrying me because he's kind."

"It won't hurt his chances for becoming a full partner in Dad's law firm, either."

"He'll be senior partner some day with or without me, Anne."

"Sorry, forget I said that." Anne stared pensively at her sister. "You don't have to marry Roger. You could break the engagement."

"Oh, sure." A touch of bitterness underscored Jacey's response. "Who would listen to me? Over and over, I tell Roger and Father I won't wear furs, but they override my protests and I wind up wearing them anyway. Mother won't even let me pick my own clothes. If I tell Roger I won't marry him, he'll just pat me on the head and turn around and order the champagne."

Anne paced between her sister's bed and the window. She too

was ready for bed, attired in short, navy blue satin pajamas, but there was nothing childish about her appearance. Jacey wished she were more like Anne, strong and self-confident, a woman prepared to take charge of her own life. She slumped back down on her bed and watched her sister run her fingers through her short-cropped pale hair. Anne's long legs stopped abruptly and she twirled around.

"This isn't a whim, is it? Something you'll change your mind about next week?" Anne demanded.

"No. I think if I were going to fall in love with Roger, I would have by now. I'm positive he doesn't love me either. He treats me like a child or a pet. There's no sparkle when he looks at me like I saw when the woman at the party flirted with him—or even that alert, alive glow he radiates when he fights with you."

Anne watched her sister narrowly, seeming to search for something. When Jacey remained quiet, Anne began making plans. "All right, it looks like you need some breathing space, some time to be sure you want to marry Roger. You also need to get out from under Daddy's thumb and away from Mother's fussing. A little independence will do you good. So this is what we'll do. I'll contact a friend in Switzerland I handled some legal work for last summer, and arrange for her to forward your mail. As long as Father thinks you're resting at her sanitarium, he won't tear up the country looking for you. You can hole up at Uncle Charlie's ranch until you get it out of your system and decide what you really want to do."

Chapter 2

Jacey glanced at her rearview mirror. Rats! The maroon truck pulling a horse trailer was still right on her bumper. Carefully she pressed a little harder on the gas pedal, nudging the speed of the little red convertible up to twenty miles per hour. The obviously unhappy truck driver didn't seem impressed by her burst of speed. Her knuckles gleamed white as she gripped the steering wheel. With her bottom lip caught between her teeth, she negotiated the sharp curve of the narrow mountain road. Granted, the drop-off on her right wasn't exactly a sheer cliff; but the steep incline from the road to the stream below didn't invite taking chances, either. She would never have agreed to drive Uncle Charlie's car if she'd known this awful road lay between his attorney's house and the ranch.

The mountain to her left rose sharply from the edge of the highway. She didn't dare raise her eyes from the road to see just how high it towered. She wished she had more experience behind the wheel. Though her high school had automatically enrolled all seniors in a driver's education course, her parents had allowed her little opportunity to practice. Other than brief trips to friends' homes within the neighborhood, her driving experience consisted of traveling the ten residential blocks to and from the nearby college where she first attended as a student, and later became employed four days a week as a research assistant in the medieval history department. Narrow, winding mountain roads had definitely not been a part of the curriculum.

The driver of the fancy maroon and chrome truck and trailer behind her signaled his impatience by tapping his horn once again. Clearly he couldn't pass her due to the continuous blind curves, but he had no qualms about sounding his annoyance.

When a narrow dirt road appeared following a particularly harrowing curve, Jacey pulled off the pavement with a sigh of relief and let the horse van pass. Instead of appreciating her action, however, the driver stuck his arm out of his open window to crudely gesture his opinion. Behind the truck, four more cars and a panel truck picked up speed and hurried by. Her face reddened with embarrassment and anger as she realized how many people her hesitant driving had inconvenienced.

When the road had cleared and she appeared to have the narrow canyon to herself, she began slowly backing the car toward the pavement. As her rear tires touched the asphalt, she heard a loud noise and slammed on the brakes in time to see a motorcycle roar around the blind curve and rush past scant feet from her car. She shook uncontrollably as she realized it was too dangerous to risk backing directly into traffic.

Peering ahead, she could see that the little dirt road dropped sharply toward a small stream. A narrow plank bridge stretched across the stream to allow the dirt road to continue along the mountainside. Perhaps on the other side of the stream she could find a place to turn around. With one foot on the brake, she inched her way down the steep trail and approached the bridge, which appeared to be nothing more than rough logs laid side by side. The closer she got, the more leery she became of crossing it. She stopped the car and glanced from left to right. On either side of her, deep grass extended from the road to thick brush alongside the stream.

Surveying the scene, she decided it might be safer to turn the car around on the grass than to try crossing the bridge. She didn't like the looks of the rough, weathered logs or the absence of rails. She turned the steering wheel and began a careful circle, designed to bring the little car back to the road and point it toward the highway.

Midway through the curve, the car gave a sudden lurch, and

the rear passenger side dipped precariously. Perhaps she was driving too slowly. Applying more gas did no good. Jacey could hear the wheel spinning, but the car had stopped moving.

Trying to go forward only seemed to make the car tilt more. She put the car in park, scanned the area for snakes (but with so much tall grass they could be hiding anywhere), took a deep breath, and cautiously climbed out. After only a couple of steps, she felt water squish above the soles of her sandals. Doggedly she proceeded toward the back of the car. Tears filled her eyes and her lip quivered when she saw how deeply the tire had sunk into the mud. Where the tires had crossed the lush, deep grass, the tracks looked like twin ditches, filled with muddy water rising halfway up the hubcaps.

She retraced her steps and slipped back inside the car. For long minutes she sat staring straight ahead, then tears began to trickle quietly down her cheeks. What could she do? She had no idea how far she might be from a town, and she didn't know anyone to call even if she could get to a telephone. Briefly she considered walking back to the road to flag down a passerby, but the thought of encountering another belligerent driver terrified her.

Jacey moaned in frustration. She had let someone else talk her into doing something she wasn't sure she wanted to do, and once again she was unhappy with the results. Anne had made reservations, helped her write notes to her parents and Roger, packed her clothes, and driven her to the airport so quickly that Jacey had been over Kansas before she had even caught her breath. She hadn't even been competent enough to run away by herself—and just look at the mess she was in now.

Just as Anne had promised, Uncle Charlie's attorney met her at the airport in Salt Lake City and drove her as far as his office in Payson. The morning had passed in a blur as the friendly, lanky Westerner explained the terms of the will, gave her directions to the ranch, turned over the keys to the bright red convertible sports car which had been her uncle's, and suggested she stock up at the corner grocery store before starting out. He'd informed her that she had two definite offers for the property. Both of Uncle Charlie's next-door neighbors, a Mr. George Lindquist and a Mr. Lee Kitsu, had made offers. Also, because of the stream running through the property, a local mink breeder was preparing a proposal.

Armed with a portfolio of papers, a beautiful spring mountain morning, and the passenger seat full of groceries, Jacey's spirits had soared. It had been a heady experience to feel confident and in charge.

The euphoria was gone now. Daddy and Roger were right; she did need someone to take care of her. Her head touched the steering wheel as she examined her options. She could leave the car and walk until she found a house or a town where she could ask someone to call Daddy. Or she could stay right where she was and hope someone would come along to rescue her eventually. "Of course, this is where my hero riding a wild mustang and wearing a white hat should suddenly appear," she muttered gloomily. "Fat chance!"

An unfamiliar bellow accompanied by the sound of snapping brush brought Jacey's head up. Her heart pounded as she turned to watch four white cows plod through the deep grass toward her. Each step they took created a wet sucking sound as their hooves slogged through the mud hidden beneath the grass. She had always liked animals, but these seemed awfully large and menacing.

With a squeal of alarm, Jacey slid to the center of the car seat as one cow stuck its head inside the car, only inches from her face. Feeling a wet snuffle against her shoulder, she turned her head quickly to find herself eye to eye with another cow. She scrambled to her feet, her heart pounding. Anxiously she looked at first one cow, then the other. Then, to her horror, she realized that the other two cows had their heads buried in the grocery bags sitting on the passenger seat. As one cow lifted its shaggy white face, calmly chewing on half a dozen stalks of celery, the other shook her head impatiently in a vain attempt to dislodge a pair of filmy panty hose which had become stuck to her wet nose. A scream of outrage erupted from Jacey's throat as she lunged to rescue her stockings. She'd never been strong enough to oppose her family, but she certainly didn't intend to let a cow intimidate her!

"Well, I'll be . . . " George stopped in amazement, square in the middle of the bridge, at the sight before him. Charlie Mathew's old red convertible rested up to its fancy spoked hubcaps in the grass and mud right before him. But instead of old Charlie sitting at the wheel grinning back at him, there stood the prettiest young woman he had ever seen. Only she wasn't grinning at him; she was standing on the seat yelling at a bunch of cows, and carrying on a tug-of-war with one of the beasts.

George stared in amazement at the riot of golden curls bouncing with every swing of her head. On second thought her hair wasn't really gold, but more brown with gleaming lighter streaks and burnished tips. From this distance he couldn't see her eyes, but he suspected they would be a golden hazel, warm as sunshine. However, he wasn't too far away to notice long, slender legs beneath the white shorts hugging slim hips, a tiny waist, and . . . He swallowed convulsively as his eyes noted the remainder of her attributes. A cotton knit pullover in flaming pink drew his attention as its delicate owner fought the recalcitrant cow.

He shifted uncomfortably against the back of the huge plow horse he rode. She had to be the prettiest woman he'd ever seen. He hadn't even met her yet, and already he had the oddest feeling that she could wipe out the loneliness he'd walked with since he was ten years old and his parents died. With his grandparents and Charlie gone too, he didn't have anyone now except his sister. He'd thought a lot lately about getting married and starting his own family, but until this moment he hadn't seen one woman who struck the kind of sparks this woman did. He could hardly wait to meet her.

Slowly the stunned expression left his face and a scowl took its place. The car was Charlie's old car; that meant the driver had to be the woman who couldn't be bothered to come to the poor old man's bedside as he lay dying. Charlie's niece!

He felt cheated. It wasn't fair for Charlie's black-hearted niece to look like an angel. It wasn't fair that he'd have to be the one to rescue her, either. Slapping his denim-clad legs against the flanks of the big horse, he started toward the red convertible.

"Shoo! Yi! Git! Come on, move!"

Jacey froze in place, the disputed panty hose dangling from her fingers, as the biggest man and the biggest horse she had ever seen began chasing the cows back toward the creek. Their bawling complaints barely registered as she stared dumbstruck at the gigantic duo. Gray striped denim coveralls, immense brown boots, a slightly crooked baseball cap, and a mud-colored horse big enough to pull a beer wagon swam before her eyes. Moments later, horse and rider stopped beside the little car. Craning her neck, Jacey looked up at her rescuer and smiled tentatively.

He sat there silently for an uncomfortably long time, a frown marring an otherwise ruggedly attractive face. He appeared to be a year or two under thirty and about the same size as Roger's favorite pro linebacker. Jacey had time to notice the firm jaw and the straight, wide mouth with little lines at the corners which looked like they might be more accustomed to smiling than frowning, though that was probably wishful thinking. His eyebrows were thick and dark, darker than the light brown hair she glimpsed curling slightly against his neck beneath a battered purple cap with JAZZ written on it in big gold letters. But his eyes, whose intense blue depths should have been sunny and inviting, were instead bleak and accusing.

Hesitantly Jacey pushed a tangled mass of curls away from her face. "Hi! I'm Jacey Mathews." She held out her hand. "Thank you for chasing the cows away."

"The road's up there." He ignored her hand and nodded his head toward the highway.

"I know." She tried smiling brightly.

"Then what are you doing down here in the mud?"

"Well, I . . . " How could she explain?

"Women drivers!" He didn't even try to disguise his disgust. At least he impugned all women drivers rather than singling her out exclusively.

"You should have brought your fancy chauffeur, or at least a nursemaid."

Jacey's back stiffened. He had no right to judge her. She struggled to maintain her dignity as she admitted she had made a mistake and swallowed her pride to ask his assistance in getting back to the road. "Will you help me?"

The big man continued to stare.

At first she wondered if he had heard her, then she feared he had heard, but chose to ignore her plight. Would he leave her stranded in this desolate place? For some reason he seemed to have taken an instant dislike to her. Of course, it might not be just her; maybe he didn't like women period. But some instinct told her it wasn't all women, just her specifically he didn't like.

Removing his cap, he scratched his head as he stared off into space. Then, slamming his hat back onto his head as though he had reached some decision, he muttered, "I guess I don't have much choice. Haul your butt out of there and let's get this thing back where she belongs."

Tears hovered in her eyes as Jacey carefully stepped out of the car on the side away from her reluctant rescuer and water flooded her open-toed sandals. He needn't be so rude. She stood watching helplessly as he slid from the horse's bare back before reaching into her car to shift it into neutral. Minutes later he located a rope in the trunk of the car, which he stretched from the car's front axle to his horse and back. The sight of his muddy coveralls as he rose from the ground, where he had lain on his back to fasten the rope to the axle, filled her with guilt.

After checking to make sure that all the knots were tight in the makeshift harness circling the horse, he moved to the back of the car. She watched him gather an armful of brush and sticks, which he shoved in front of the tire most deeply mired.

"Get back here and push!" His gruff order startled Jacey.

"Me?" she stammered.

"It's not my car, princess. You won't dissolve if you get a little mud on you."

Biting her lip as much to keep back tears as to prevent a protest of his rude treatment from rising to her lips, she slopped her way to the back of the car to take her place beside the bossy male already bending to lift the back bumper. Calling an order to the horse, he, like the big animal, settled his massive shoulders lower and began to push. Jacey almost forgot to push as she watched the ripple of muscles tighten and strain against the fabric stretched tautly across shoulders and thighs, scant inches from her own sweating body. Feeling an uncomfortable heat, she hastily averted her eyes and forced herself to concentrate on pushing against the slowly-moving car.

Knowing her puny effort wasn't really helping much, she strained harder against the red metal beneath her hands. She failed to see any good reason why the man should insist she push, since she obviously couldn't accomplish much. Surely he could see she wasn't big enough or strong enough to push a car. As she took quick little steps to keep from falling behind, a bare toe peeking through her sandal connected with a heavy stick submerged in the wet muck. Sharp pain ripped through her foot, her grip slackened, and her knees began to buckle. The car rolled away from the tips of her fingers and she crashed to her knees in the mud. She flung out her hands in a vain effort to cushion her forward fall, but it did no good. A scream rose in her throat and died as mud cut off the sound.

Sprawled full length, she raised her eyes in time to see the exasperating man send a contemptuous glance her way before easing the car onto solid ground.

Somehow she knew she wasn't going to get any assistance from him. Silently he worked the ropes loose which held her car tethered to his horse. She spit mud and grass from her mouth and swiped an arm across her face. Gingerly she rose to her knees, then eased her way to her feet. She glanced down, then choked back a cry as she surveyed the mud and debris clinging to her skin and clothes. Her once-white shorts were now indistinguishable from the rear end of the big horse. Her wet, slimy shirt was no longer pink and it stuck to her body. The mud caking her arms and legs was drying rapidly, leaving her skin feeling as though cracks were forming on its surface. She swung her head to free her face from the wet hair sticking to it, and became aware of the chunks of mud clinging to the swaying strands.

Slowly lifting one foot, then the other, she sucked in her breath as a sharp stab of pain let her know she'd likely lose a toenail. Ignoring the pain as best she could, she limped toward the car. Her mind went blank until she glanced up to see the big man standing with both hands planted firmly on his hips, watching her slow progress. A wide grin stretched from one side of his handsome face to the other, sending a curl of red hot anger spiraling dangerously from somewhere deep inside her.

She had never hit anyone before in her life, but suddenly something snapped deep inside her and she wanted to rip that taunting smile off his face. She wanted to see him bleed. He represented all the people who had made her feel helpless and inferior. With an unladylike snarl, she launched herself at his considerable bulk. Her fist missed its target as she swung at his face, landing harmlessly on his broad chest, to be followed by another wild swing.

"Don't laugh at me," she sobbed. "I did the best I could and now my clothes are ruined and I'll get Uncle Charlie's car all muddy. I'm sick of people who think they know everything. You're mean and hateful!" As her fists rained uselessly against his chest and she gave way to near-hysteria, his smile disappeared, then his heavy arms reached effortlessly around her. He swung her into the air, then marched resolutely toward the bridge with her screaming and kicking in his arms.

"This should cool you off and clean you up," he muttered before dropping her casually over the side.

As the icy water closed over her head, Jacey gasped with shock, swallowing a huge mouthful of water. Desperately scrambling for the surface, her head broke free only long enough to take in a gulp of air before she lost her balance and slipped under again. Her arms flailed against the water as she tried to propel herself toward the shore. Her knees scraped against the rocky bottom, and she rose to her feet in water that barely reached her knees. Shivering, she stood still for a long minute and struggled to catch her breath. Hearing a sound, she raised her head to see her tormenter wading toward her with one hand extended. He wasn't smiling now, but Jacey wasn't fooled. Underneath he still laughed at her. No one in her entire life had ever treated her so badly. She hated him.

Jacey ignored the hand, making her own way toward the bank a little further downstream. Clutching a handful of willows, she pulled herself from the water. The man fell in step behind her as she made her way back to the bridge.

"Are you okay?"

She ignored him. Looking neither right nor left, she marched toward the red convertible. The sooner she got back in her car, the sooner this nightmare would end.

George stopped on the bridge. He watched Charlie's niece walk away. She held her body rigid as she moved toward her car.

Her face was carefully blank, her eyes unseeing. She shuddered as her slender body sought to shake off the shattering cold of her dunking. He shouldn't have done it. He and Lisa had been swimming in that hole since they came to live with their grandparents when they were kids; but he should have remembered that Charlie's niece was a city woman, unaccustomed to cold mountain streams. He'd better make sure she had a sweater or blanket to wrap herself in.

An uneasy feeling crept over him when he noticed the way her wet clothes clung to her slim body. A strong urge to kiss her pain away rattled him with its intensity. He shook his head to dispel the unwanted thought and reminded himself that this woman happened to be Jacey Mathews. And Jacey Mathews happened to be the cold, calculating, mercenary woman who had hurt his best friend.

His eyes narrowed. Her movements appeared awkward and a stab of guilt made him wonder if he'd hurt her. Yes, she definitely limped as she made her way up the dusty trail toward her car. Squinting his eyes, he could just make out the trickle of blood making its way down her leg from a scratch on her thigh. She seemed to be favoring her right big toe as she walked, too.

A couple of swift strides brought him even with Jacey as she reached the side of the convertible. Glancing down, he saw that her knees were scraped and the big toe of her right foot was turning dark, while blood oozed from the nail which hung halfway off. He hadn't meant to hurt her. Shifting uneasily, he put out his hand to touch her shoulder.

"I'm sorry," he tried to apologize.

She shrugged off his hand as though she couldn't bear his touch. She turned slate gray, venom-filled eyes in his direction briefly before slipping into the driver's seat of the little car. Her hand reached for the ignition key.

"You can't drive like that," he said.

"I can and I will." She turned the key and the car roared to life. He leaned forward, placing both hands on the door.

"Your foot is injured and you're too upset to be safe on the road."

Her lip curled and sparks seemed to shoot from deep jade eyes.

Her foot hit the accelerator and the car shot forward, leaving him stumbling in the dust. The rear end of the red car fishtailed slightly as it shot onto the pavement. It turned a corner and was out of sight in seconds. She never looked back.

George clenched his fists in exasperation. He'd have to ride Clyde back to where he'd parked the truck, get the horse loaded in the trailer, and follow Ms. Mathews to Charlie's place to make certain she got there in one piece. He just hoped she wouldn't run her car into a mountain before she got there. In spite of his own reservations about the woman, he had promised Charlie he'd help her when she came. He hadn't expected to have to make good on that promise, however.

The mountain road was behind her, and she found herself approaching a small town before the first sob shook her aching body. Carefully surveying the few shabby businesses, she failed to see any indication that there was a doctor in the town, so she drove on.

The next town was a little larger, but she decided not to even look for a doctor. She stopped in front of an old storefront sporting a blue and orange pharmacy sign and went in. As her eyes adjusted to the dark interior, she stifled her disappointment. This wasn't anything like the gleaming white-and-stainless-steel pharmacy back home. The aisles were cramped and narrow. The shelves were a combination of old wood and tacky peg-board. They were crowded with kitchen gadgets, plastic wading pools, packets of garden seed, canvas shoes, men's heavy socks, over-the-counter remedies, and feminine sanitary supplies. Gingerly she picked her way past a heap of garden hoses and irrigation shovels to where she could see boxes of gauze and tape. She selected a tube of disinfectant and a bottle of Tylenol. In the back of the store she could see a small, glass-enclosed cubbyhole where a tall, thin man in a white smock, apparently the pharmacist, stood talking to a customer in baggy jeans and a cotton shirt which didn't quite meet over a large silver belt buckle. Unlike the pharmacist, whose balding pate was crossed by a dozen hairs carefully combed from one side of his head to the other, the customer wore a billed cap perched over long, stringy hair. She hadn't been aware that she was staring until the man winked broadly, a speculative gleam in his eyes.

Feeling flustered and somehow insulted, Jacey made her way back to the front of the store where a middle-aged woman bustled about, flicking a feather duster across several lawn chairs. As she approached the wooden checkout counter, the woman hurried over.

"My goodness, what happened to you?" She stared at Jacey's crumpled, still-damp clothing and the dried trickles of blood on her legs.

"I . . . uh . . . fell." Jacey stumbled over the words. She didn't know what to say. She couldn't tell this woman that a giant had attacked her without making a bigger fool of herself than she already felt.

"Well, here, let me help you. You can't walk around like that."

"It's okay. I can do it," Jacey stammered, taken aback by the clerk's offer of help.

"Nonsense! Come along."

The woman, who introduced herself as Anna Peterson, led Jacey to a tiny rest room. "Can you get your sandal off all right?"

"Yes," Jacey responded, but she bit down on her bottom lip as she tugged the wet leather away from her swollen toe.

Mrs. Peterson handed her a wet cloth, and soon all traces of blood were wiped away. The motherly woman showed her how to smear disinfectant on her knees, then helped bandage Jacey's thigh and toe. The woman clucked sympathetically over her injuries and demanded to know when she had had her last tetanus shot. Startled, Jacey reported that her shots were all current, then practically had to create a scene before the busy little woman would accept the twenty-dollar bill she left on the counter to pay for her purchases.

Returning to her car, she discovered she'd left her sandal in the store. She couldn't drive barefoot; she remembered her driving instructor saying that was illegal or something. She'd have to go back. She hopped inside and quickly discovered there was no way to get her bandaged toe back inside the sandal. Mrs. Peterson scurried down the aisles looking for a solution to her problem, and a few minutes later Jacey returned to the car with a sandal on one foot and an oversized fuzzy slipper on the other. She sat in her car, eyeing a telephone booth farther down the street. Should she call

Daddy? He'd send Roger to get her. Mother would fuss and Dr. Bellows would make a house call. But at least she'd be safe from unfriendly strangers. And bored. And helpless. Besides, not all of the strangers had been unfriendly. She'd been frightened and hurt, but she'd coped. She'd come this far, so she might as well go on. Turning the key, she pressed the fuzzy slipper against the accelerator.

Twenty minutes later, she pulled off a narrow rutted road to pass beneath a pole arch festooned with antlers. A mailbox beside the driveway carried Uncle Charlie's name in faded lettering. At long last she was home; she'd reached Uncle Charlie's ranch, realizing the dream that had sustained her for so long.

Each pothole jarred her spine as she followed a twisting dirt lane to where it ended in front of a small log house nestled under a dozen strangely-twisted junipers and a couple of sentinel pines. This couldn't be the place; it looked nothing like what Uncle Charlie had described. But she was tired, her toe throbbed, and she couldn't go any further.

Jacey stared forlornly at the small, unpainted cabin with its sagging porch and narrow windows. No green lawn broke the dull, dusty gray which encompassed the house, trees, a couple of shaky sheds, and the entire vista stretching toward a gray-green mountain slashed with pink. It was far from the gracious ranch house Uncle Charlie had described in his letters, but somehow it fit him; and while it wasn't at all what she'd expected, she sensed a welcoming warmth. She'd walk up to the door and knock. If no one answered, she'd try the key.

Glancing around, she noticed for the first time a battered blue pickup truck and horse trailer parked near one of the sheds. A giant mud-colored horse stretched its neck across a pole corral fence a few feet from the truck. An uneasy premonition shot along her spine even before one door of the truck opened and a familiar figure stepped out and started toward the convertible.

Gauging the distance to the cabin, she wondered if she could beat him to the door. She flung open the car door and made a mad dash, running as fast as her stiff body and odd footwear would allow.

"Stop right there! Don't move!"

Horrified, she glanced behind her to see him approaching in long, loping strides, his face grim. He waved a heavy shovel in his upraised hand. Terror lent wings to her heels as she struggled to outdistance him. Then she stopped short as a new terror rounded the cabin and streaked toward her, its small evil head extended on a skinny neck with a streak of red wobbling underneath, and its heavy, awkward body ending in long, vicious, curved claws. Before she could scream, the man behind her streaked past to meet the animal's attack with the flat of his shovel. Deftly he pushed it toward a small mesh wire enclosure. With the bird or beast or whatever safely ensconced behind a locked gate, the man strode back to where Jacey sat in a heap on the top porch step. She couldn't move. Every speck of energy had deserted her. In all this open space, how had she stumbled onto that man's house?

George stared bemused at Jacey's limp form. Her arrival couldn't have been worse if he'd planned it, which should have been a highly satisfying triumph for him. He knew what she had thought when she turned and saw him with the shovel. That should have at least amused him, but he found himself feeling sorry for her instead. She looked so much like a bedraggled kitten, or worse yet, a kicked puppy. He wanted to pick her up and snuggle her in his lap. Somehow the thought of settling her in his lap and cuddling her aroused feelings that had nothing to do with comforting a stricken kitten.

"That was just . . . " He cleared his throat and started again. "That was just Gus. Charlie's had that old turkey for years. He's not too friendly around strangers."

Slowly Jacey raised her head. This was Uncle Charlie's ranch—her ranch. Her green eyes sparkled with unshed tears. "And what is your name? You seem to be another turkey who's not too friendly around strangers."

He winced as her sarcasm bit. He removed his cap and twirled it absently between his fingers, all the while staring at her eyes. What color were they, anyway? Out by the creek they'd looked blue, then black, now green.

"George. George Lindquist. I live next door." He nodded his head to the south, wishing he could back up and start all over with this woman.

"Well, George," she drawled, mimicking his husky tone. "Why don't you pack up your big horse and get your butt off my property!" Rising to her feet, she found the added height of the porch brought her eye-to-eye with him. There was no mistaking the animosity sparking between them.

"Because, your majesty, he's not my horse. He's yours. I was only exercising him, and his name is Clyde."

Jacey stared blankly as the big man turned to walk away. His long strides carried him quickly to the blue pickup truck. She was still clutching the porch post as he roared down the lane, trailing a thick cloud of choking dust.

"Why do other women get to meet Sir Galahad on a faithful charger or John Wayne in a white hat, while I have to run into Farmer George on a Clydesdale?" she moaned with more than a touch of self-pity before she turned to open the door to her new home.

Chapter 3

Jacey scanned the room from the doorway. It was as raw and masculine as the man who just left in a cloud of dust—like nothing she'd ever seen before. The corner of her mouth twitched. George Lindquist was like nothing she'd ever seen before, either. She had wished to be treated like a real person. Well, George had certainly treated her like a real person, all right—one he didn't like. He'd been rude and abrupt; but in a way, he'd granted her wish. He hadn't pampered her, and he'd made her angry enough to stand up for herself.

A wide stone fireplace against the north wall caught her attention. In front of its gaping mouth sat a big cushioned rocking chair. Its arms and rockers appeared to be polished slabs of pine. She could see Uncle Charlie sprawled in that chair, reading late into the night. An ache in her heart reminded her he'd never sit there again. A matching sofa leaned against the western wall. The cushions of both pieces of furniture were covered with a faded orange-and-brown, loosely-woven fabric. A coffee table and two end tables rested on the rims of ancient wagon wheels. The western motif didn't surprise her. Uncle Charlie had loved anything western.

Overhead, another wagon wheel, suspended from the ceiling by black chains, bristled with lightbulbs. Over the fireplace a scruffy stag head lifted a magnificent rack of antlers. On the floor a shaggy piece of brown fur, which she suspected might have once been a bear, covered a section of the stone hearth. A pair of pheasants with long tails dragging across the pine paneling were mounted on the wall behind the sofa. Uncle Charlie must have thought they lent western authenticity to the decor, but they gave her the same uncomfortable feeling her fur coat did.

A battered pine bookcase stood near the window, its shelves overflowing with paperback books. She recognized titles by Louis L'Amour, Zane Gray, and Tony Hillerman along with a few church books. She and Uncle Charlie had shared a love of books, and she looked forward to exploring his collection more thoroughly.

The house puzzled her. It didn't resemble the ranch house Uncle Charlie's letters had led her to expect. Where was the oak staircase? The large cool rooms? The hand-crafted kitchen cupboards? This house didn't bear much similarity to Uncle Charlie's description, but it fit her uncle better than the one he'd described on paper.

Sucking in her breath, Jacey took two steps toward the other end of the room, where a shiny black monstrosity occupied a large square section of stone flooring. She knew it was a stove, but it looked as if it had come straight off the set of *Little House on the Prairie*. She hoped it wasn't the only source of heating and cooking in the cabin.

She reached out to touch the dusty surface of a round pine table. Four straight-backed chairs surrounded it. Pine cupboards graced the south wall, with a small sink set in the middle of the butcher-block counter tops, directly beneath a small paned window. She supposed the cupboards could be considered "handcrafted." She rubbed her fingers across their highly shellacked surface, admiring the wood grain. Once they were dusted, they would be beautiful.

She breathed a sigh of relief to see an old, but strictly conventional refrigerator against the opposite wall.

Wandering through an arched doorway between the refrigerator and sofa, she discovered a small spartan bedroom consisting of an oversize pine bed, a five-drawer chest, and a battered desk. She looked at the bed longingly, but rest would have to wait a little longer. She smiled at the sight of a white Stetson hat hanging on one bedpost, and wished Uncle Charlie were there. One whole end of the room was a clothes closet. Peering inside the pine doors, she felt a lump rise in her throat at the sight of western-cut shirts, a fringed leather jacket, and a familiar pair of snakeskin boots, now much worn and scuffed. They probably weren't even the same pair she remembered from so long ago.

Jacey opened a door at the other end of the bedroom and discovered a most amazing bathroom. The fixtures were a bright Valentine red except for the toilet seat lid, which appeared to be made from discarded lumber, reminiscent of an old outhouse lid with the grinning face of a big bear burned right into the wood. The walls were papered with pages from a Victorian era mail order catalog. The huge red bathtub stood on curved claws several inches above the floor. It looked big enough to hold George. A blush crept up her cheeks as a picture of George relaxing in the depths of that monstrous tub flitted through her mind.

Getting herself firmly under control and relegating that accursed man to the depths of Hades, she returned to her car to begin hauling her suitcases and supplies into the house. She bemoaned the sorry condition of her groceries as she put them away in the refrigerator and cupboard. Discovering that one cupboard door concealed a microwave oven lifted her spirits somewhat. She didn't have a clue as to how to operate that monstrous stove, but a microwave she could handle.

Much later, she stretched full-length in the red tub, basking in the luxurious feel of hot water easing the aches and pains from her body. Her mind felt too numb to take in all that had happened to her in the past forty-eight hours. Without Anne making the arrangements and inventing a cover for her, she would never have succeeded in leaving Baltimore. Since being on her own she'd had to be rescued twice, but somehow she didn't feel as though she'd come off the loser—well, not completely, anyway. She'd found Uncle Charlie's ranch and moved in. So what if she was all alone and a long way from her family, the night was getting cold and she didn't know how to start a fire, and nothing was like she expected? This might be her only chance to be really free, and she intended to make the most of it.

She giggled when she remembered that it was just two nights ago she'd argued with Roger over wearing a fur coat; now she was living in a house where a fur coat decorated her floor and stuffed animals cluttered her walls.

"They will just have to go," she mumbled as her eyelids slowly closed.

She awoke from a jumbled dream where she remembered a grinning face topped by a purple Jazz cap looking down at her from above the fireplace, and the knifelike sharpness of cold water closing over her head. Shivering in a tub full of cold water, she turned on the hot water tap and hurriedly washed and rinsed her hair before reaching for the comforting warmth of a heavy terry towel. She quickly blew her hair dry before tumbling into bed to toss restlessly, disturbed by a malevolent demon chasing her with an irrigation shovel.

George shut off the feed auger. His chores were done, and it was time to get over to Charlie's place to feed the old man's stock. His pulse accelerated as a picture of Jacey came to mind. He didn't want to think about her, but he'd found thinking of anything else since he'd left her the night before nearly impossible. It annoyed him that he'd dated half a dozen women in the past year, but not one of them had caught his attention the way she had. He'd like to get married and have a family, but he wouldn't let himself fall for someone as irresponsible and money-hungry as his former brother-in-law. Lisa had made a big mistake, and he didn't intend to follow in her footsteps.

Maybe if he hurried, he could be finished and gone before the pesky woman woke up. But why should he do the work while she slept? Because Jacey Mathews wouldn't crawl out of bed before noon, and by that time the chickens would scratch their way out of the run, Gus would beat his feathers off trying to get out of his cage, and the cats would come looking for him. He didn't need Charlie's cats moving onto his place. No, those were just excuses. The truth was that he owed her an apology, and this time he was going to make her listen.

He stopped at the house long enough to pull off his coveralls and let Lisa know where he'd be, then he headed for his pickup truck. He grumbled as the truck lurched up Charlie's lane. He knew Charlie had meant to smooth out the potholes and order a few loads of gravel, but his first heart attack had interrupted those plans. It had interrupted all of Charlie's plans, but it hadn't stopped his dreaming. George clenched his jaw, remembering all the long months the old man had worked on that fool saddle, and how every morning when he'd stopped by Charlie had handed him a letter to mail to Miss Jacey Mathews of Baltimore, Maryland.

Charlie's letters were never answered. Years earlier, when George had been a rebellious teenager, he'd resented the letters some little girl back East was forever sending his pal; but when his friend became old and ill, the letters stopped. Just when Charlie needed them the most. Toward the end, when everyone knew Charlie wasn't going to make it, George had tried calling Jacey on the telephone, but his calls were always answered the same way: "Ms. Mathews is sleeping and cannot be disturbed," or "Ms. Jacey is unable to come to the phone." Once a man's voice had come on the line to order him to stop his annoying calls. He'd tried to explain about Charlie and been told the family was in touch with the hospital and were being kept abreast of the situation. And no, Jacey would not visit him; the idea was unthinkable.

Charlie had died dreaming of Jacey's coming to visit him. He'd even extracted a promise from George that when she came, he'd give her the saddle and do everything possible to help her. Well, he'd help her, all right. He'd buy the narrow strip of ground and send her on her way with cash in her pocket. But before she went, he'd make sure she saw Charlie's little farm up close. He'd rub her snooty nose in it. She couldn't be bothered to visit the old man while he was alive, but she'd appeared fast enough when she learned someone was willing to pay cash for those few acres.

The truck jolted through the last hole; he swung it behind Charlie's red convertible and shut off the engine. Early morning silence filled the air as he stared at the little car. He had a sudden picture of Jacey standing on the seat arguing with a cow, Jacey walking toward him drenched in mud, and he grew warm remembering the feel of her in his arms just before he tossed her into the creek. He shouldn't have done that. He couldn't remember one other time in his whole life when he'd ever done anything so mean to a woman. What was it about Jacey Mathews that had him wildly overreacting to every move she made? She wouldn't listen to his apology yesterday, and she probably wouldn't today. He'd wind up paying for his impulsive action by giving her too much for Charlie's farm. He climbed out of the truck and headed for the cabin. Anger dogged his steps. All right, he'd pay for his stupid stunt. But by darn, Ms. high and mighty Jacey Mathews would do a little paying, too.

Jacey awoke to the sound of heavy pounding. She reached for her favorite emerald green robe, and quickly pulled it on before stumbling to the door. Groggily she jerked the door open to tell whoever was making so much noise to go away, then stopped cold. It was true, then; he really existed. The man nightmares are made of stood on her front porch.

George caught his fist in mid-swing as the door flew open. His eyes widened and his throat went dry as he looked into baby blue eyes which were rapidly changing to green as he watched. He stared at the tousled mane of curls before him. Was he imagining, or was it the glint of early-morning sun which added a hint of fiery red to the gold-and-taffy color of her hair? Her feet were bare, and he guessed she didn't have much on under that velvety green bathrobe, from the way she'd pulled the belt tight and clutched the lapels together with one hand. His voice came out harsher than he'd intended.

"Get some clothes on. It's time you started tending your own stock!"

"What?"

He might have known. Jacey Mathews considered herself too good to do farm chores. Well, this would be one time her social position wouldn't protect her from getting her dainty little hands dirty.

Jacey stared uncomprehending at the baffling man standing on her porch glaring at her. Taking a tighter grip on the door, she contemplated slamming it quickly before the crazy man could inflict any more torture on her.

As though reading her thoughts, he reached out one arm to brace the door open. Jacey's heart raced, and she felt something akin to claustrophobia as his big body moved closer. He wasn't wearing the coveralls today. Instead his hips, much slimmer than the coveralls had led her to expect, were encased in faded 501s. The coveralls, however, certainly hadn't led her to underestimate that chest or the rippling muscles of gigantic biceps generously highlighted by a much-too-tight tee shirt. She licked her suddenly dry lips. A flickering flame leaped in the blue eyes carefully watching her every movement, and she stepped back nervously. Her isolated position and the sheer size of the man standing before her sent a frisson of alarm straight through her.

"I don't know what you mean." Was he crazy or was she? He was big and powerful and they were alone, but it really wasn't fear as much as fascination she felt.

Her voice sounded to George's ears like a sanatorium attendant trying to placate a madman or a mail carrier trying to escape a pit bull. She clutched the top of her robe tighter about her throat and shifted her weight to her back foot like she expected to run for her life. *She thinks I'm loony,* George thought in disgust.

Slowly he shook his head. "Didn't Charlie's lawyer explain to you that along with this little piece of property, Charlie left you some animals? Animals have to be fed."

George watched as her bottom lip sagged, causing her mouth to form a delightful little 'O.' Her eyes grew round and misty green. His pulse took up a woodpecker beat.

"Uncle Charlie died more than six weeks ago." There was no mistaking the horror and regret in her voice. "They must all be dead by now."

He fought the urge to put his arms around her and offer comfort. He had to remember how callous and self-centered she really was, and how she had hurt a dying old man.

"Of course they're not dead. You've already met Gus and Clyde. The others are all around here someplace, too. I've been feeding them." He meant to sound soothing, but his voice came out harsh and abrupt. He'd had trouble speaking normally since the minute he'd laid eyes on Jacey Mathews.

"You? You fed them?"

She needn't look so surprised. He didn't appreciate her assumption that he would let dumb animals starve to death. What kind of man did she think he was? Of course, he had a pretty good idea what kind of man she thought he was. That she had such a low opinion of him rankled, even though in all honesty, he'd done nothing to deserve a better opinion.

"Yes, I've been feeding them, but now you've come to claim your inheritance you can feed them yourself." He abruptly turned to walk away, automatically ducking as he reached the doorway. His head barely cleared the sill.

"I don't know how." Her voice followed him, and he sensed more than heard the panic in it.

"I know you don't. That's why I came to show you. I'll be in the barn when you're ready."

"I'll hurry," she whispered in a breathless little voice, and her face lit up like he'd crowned her "Days of '47" queen.

He pulled the door shut behind him and stomped across the porch. Rats! He was committed now. It would have been simpler to do the chores himself for the few days she'd be here. He should have kicked himself the moment he'd gotten the brilliant idea of making her do it.

Racing to the bedroom, Jacey pulled on the first clothes that surfaced as she searched through her unpacked suitcases. She knew the cranberry red stretch pants and ruffled cream blouse weren't exactly ranch wear, but they would have to do. She peeled off the thick bandage from her toe and substituted an adhesive bandage so she could get her foot into canvas deck shoes. Grabbing her brush, she hurriedly pulled it through the tangles of her hair, then dashed for the door.

Uncertain which shed was supposed to be a barn, she hurried toward the largest one. Peering inside, she found George calmly sitting on a large metal can, a long-haired black cat draped over one shoulder and an obviously pregnant calico purring in his lap as he gently stroked her brightly-colored coat. A flock of little brown chickens scurried around the barn as she approached. When she stepped through the door, George jumped to his feet, brushing the cats to the floor. They ran a few feet then looked back, meowing plaintively.

"They're mousers, so they only need a little dry feed and fresh water." George led Jacey to where their feed was kept. Reaching into another bag, he brought up a can of grain. "Give old Gus a can of this. Then scatter another can around for the chickens through there." He pointed to a low door which opened at the back of the barn to a fenced enclosure where several more of the little brown chickens were pecking at the dirt and ruffling their feathers in the dust.

"They're cute, but aren't they awfully small chickens?" Jacey asked while tossing the grain on the ground as instructed.

"Bantams!" George responded, his eyes on the smooth fit of her tight red pants. No two ways about it, Jacey Mathews was a distraction. He wondered if she'd deliberately chosen the red pants to keep him off balance. Probably not; more likely she bought all her clothing in some fancy boutique and wouldn't be caught dead in work clothes. Well, she'd ruined one outfit yesterday, and he had a hunch her red pants and prissy blouse wouldn't fare much better today. He'd show her around, and as soon as she complained about getting dirty, he'd raise his offer a bit and write out a check. She'd be gone before the ink dried.

Suddenly becoming aware of the puzzled expression on her face, he remembered she'd asked about the chickens. He cleared his throat and launched into an explanation. "Banty hens are a small variety of chickens. They're just like other chickens, only littler. They lay pretty good eggs, but you have to use twice as many of them as you would the regular kind. Charlie liked them, thought they were better to look at and a little smarter than leghorns."

Jacey nearly dropped the feed can. She couldn't believe George was actually explaining something to her. He must have been surprised himself, because he promptly frowned and started toward the big turkey's cage. Warily she approached Gus's wire cage, too. The old bird gobbled threateningly when she reached through the wire to dump the feed into his dish. She withdrew her hand quickly before he had a chance to attack it. Secretly she thought the turkey and George were a lot alike. They both were big, cocky, and attacked without warning—but she'd keep her opinion to herself. She wanted to stay here as long as possible, and the only way she could do that would be to learn all she could about taking care of the ranch. George appeared to be the only person available to teach her.

Seeing a hose lying on the ground, she followed it to its source near a metal water trough. She filled water dishes for the chickens and the cats, then let the trough fill, though she couldn't see Clyde anywhere. When she finished, she looked up to see George watching her. She couldn't decipher his expression, but it left her feeling uncomfortably like a bug under a microscope. She recognized the metal rings and leather straps in his hand as two horse halters. Evidently Clyde wasn't her only horse.

"Do you want to see your horses?"

"Oh, yes!" She couldn't hide her excitement.

George jerked his head in the direction of the hill behind the cabin and started walking. She trudged beside him, taking two steps to his one, across the rough pasture land to the crest of a small hill. From that elevated point she spotted the silver gleam of water. At the foot of the hill, a small stream wandered through a carpet of green. Unlike Uncle Charlie's house, this was all she'd dreamed of. Willows hid her view of the water in a couple of spots, and beyond the grassy meadow the mountain began its sharp ascent, with brush and the twisted cedar clinging to its side. The stream disappeared into thick shrubbery at the mouth of a small canyon. Near streams or the many irrigation ditches the land looked lush and green, while every spot higher than the water was dusty and covered with gray brush.

"Over there."

Her eyes followed the line his big hand indicated. Clyde towered over his smaller partner as they grazed side by side in the deep grass. In the distance she saw three darker spots lying in the shade of the willows.

"They have all the food and water they need right now, but in the winter they have to be fed hay and grain. The horses need to be exercised regularly, too." Not waiting for a response from the woman beside him, George began walking slowly toward the horses.

Jacey trailed behind, wincing when her sore toe accidentally bumped against small rocks or depressions in the ground. George reached into his pocket before extending the flat of his hand toward the horses with a generous chunk of carrot resting on his palm. Clyde lumbered toward the proffered treat. His flowing fetlocks, mane, and tail shimmered in the early morning breeze. The mare minced skittishly, more cautious and dainty in her approach. Slowly George extended his other hand toward her as

Clyde helped himself to the first treat. As the mare nosed his hand, he slipped the halter over her head.

Throwing up her head, the mare attempted to jerk away, but George didn't allow it. He patted her nose and whispered in her ear until she calmed down. Moments later, she rubbed her long face against his shirt and nuzzled his pockets, looking for more carrots.

Jacey's spirits plummeted. Cats and chickens were no big deal; she could take care of them. But she'd never be able to control the horses. They were nothing like the pony Uncle Charlie had rented for her that magical summer. Clyde was huge, and the little mare was frighteningly high-spirited. Neither one would pay the least bit of attention to her.

"Do you ride?"

Startled, Jacey realized George was speaking to her. She didn't want him to know the horses intimidated her. Slowly she nodded. "A little. Uncle Charlie taught me years ago, but I haven't been on horseback since." As she moved toward the palomino, George handed her a carrot. She held it on her palm the way Uncle Charlie had taught her and offered it to the pretty golden horse. She stifled an urge to giggle as rubbery lips snuffled and blew against her hand. The horse appeared to be checking out the donor before accepting the treat. Jacey stroked upward to scratch behind the perky ears; the mare nuzzled against her hand and she took hope. Maybe she *could* ride this horse—not yet, of course, but after they'd had time to become friends.

"She needs exercise. She hasn't been ridden for a while. Jeremy Kitsu rides her when he's home, but once the rodeo season starts he isn't around much. Besides, he has his own string to work. He got married last winter, so there hasn't been much time to ride the lady—and I'm too big," he added ruefully as he glanced down at his over six-and-a-half-foot, well-formed body.

"Is that her name? Lady?"

"Not really; I just call her Lady. Her name's Li'l Trigger on her papers." Removing his cap, he scratched his head before continuing. "Old Charlie bought her when she was just a few weeks old. Because she's a runt the owner didn't want her, even though she comes from good stock. He knew she'd never be big enough to show or work cows, let alone use for breeding. He figured she wasn't good for anything other than being a pet for kids, but Charlie wanted her. He said she looked like a smaller version of his childhood hero Roy Rogers' horse, Trigger."

Jacey laughed, remembering Uncle Charlie's fascination with the old cowboy movie heroes. George shared her amusement for several seconds, then apparently remembered he didn't like her. His smile disappeared. "He bought her for you," he snapped. "You never came, so Jeremy broke her, and they both petted and spoiled her while they waited for you to claim her." Without warning, his hands settled around her waist and he swung her on top of the mare. "You're here now, so the least you can do is ride the stupid horse before you sell her."

Digging her hands into the horse's silvery mane, Jacey hung on as the horse danced in a circle. Her heart pounded and the ground seemed a long way off. She doubted she'd be able to control the mare; it had been eleven years since Uncle Charlie taught her to ride. She bent forward and whispered conciliatory words in the mare's ears, praying that she could hang on. Gradually the horse calmed, and Jacey relaxed her fierce grip. Trepidation turned to pleasure when she discovered the horse responded to the pressure of her knees. She had never ridden bareback before. It was exhilarating. She could hardly believe she was riding a real horse. If only Uncle Charlie could see her. Or George. How silly; George *could* see her. Her excitement was promptly deflated when she saw that George was holding the reins in his hand. At once she felt like a child riding a pony at a supermarket opening.

The feeling left abruptly when George handed her the reins before turning to Clyde. He grasped the huge draft horse's mane, swung himself aboard, and headed across the pasture. Jacey watched his broad back in shock. She'd expected a patronizing remark, and instead he'd turned Lady over to her. She straightened her back and grasped the reins tightly. She could ride Lady by herself. George thought she could do it, and she would. She nudged the horse with her knee; Lady fell in behind the bigger horse, and together they moved off toward the cattle.

The cows rose to their feet as the riders approached, and Jacey stared in amazement. These cows were nothing like the white cows which had frightened her the day before; neither were they the reddish-brown and white hereford cattle she had expected. They looked like something out of an old western movie with their long horns and stringy, bony bodies.

"I didn't think there were any longhorn cows left! Aren't they dangerous?"

A deep, throaty chuckle erupted from the man beside her. "Not unless you try to milk them, and since two of them are steers and the lone cow is due to drop a calf in a few weeks, there's no milking involved. When the calf arrives, it will take care of any necessary milking."

George's amusement encouraged Jacey to wonder if he might be in a good enough mood to answer a few questions. She really didn't know anything about running Uncle Charlie's ranch, and she knew even less about this man who calmly sat astride a massive Clydesdale with his long legs hanging below the horse's belly, like an overgrown kid on a pony.

"Uncle Charlie told me in his letters about rounding up strays. Are these cows the strays he meant, or are there others somewhere?"

"These are the only cattle Charlie ever owned, but all of his animals were strays in one way or another."

George looked at her strangely, but he'd answered, so she'd try another question. "My uncle's attorney said the ranch is almost thirty acres. I know how much an acre is in square yards, but I can't visualize how much land is thirty acres. Can you tell me where Charlie's ranch starts and ends?"

George gave her a dark look she couldn't fathom before pointing to his own fence line, then Lee Kitsu's. "Everything between those two fences is yours. The fence on the end separates your land from government land, and the road is the boundary on the front."

"You know a lot about my uncle's land and animals. Did you know him well?" If she got him to talk about Uncle Charlie, he might tell her about himself and agree to help her until she learned her way around.

A scowl darkened George's face, and his bushy brows lowered as he appeared to debate answering her question.

"Yeah, I probably knew him better than most. We were close friends."

"Tell me about him, please."

George rubbed his chin thoughtfully before answering. "What do you want to know? How much he was worth? How fast you can unload this place? Did he leave a secret stash of gold or bonds? I hate to disappoint you, but Charlie didn't leave you a fortune. He was just a lonely old dreamer with a soft spot for kids, who never stopped hoping a certain selfish, spoiled brat would find time someday to come out here and play cowboys with him!"

"Do you mean me?"

"Do you see any other gold-digging, pampered princess around here?"

"You weren't his friend. No friend of Uncle Charlie's could be so hateful and mean to someone he loved."

"A love you certainly didn't return!"

George kicked Clyde's flank, startling him into a thundering trot. He regretted his outburst before Clyde had taken ten steps. He'd let his temper get away from him again; he hadn't had this much trouble keeping a rein on his emotions since high school. He wasn't sure whether his anger was directed at himself or at Jacey. He'd expected her to weasel out of actually doing any work and to complain about the dust and dirt, but she hadn't said a word even when Lady drooled down her bright red pants and took a nip out of the lace on her blouse. She hadn't seemed to even notice.

All morning, she'd acted like Charlie's little farm was the most exciting place she'd ever been. George had started to believe her happy, innocent act, then she'd spoiled it all with her sly questions. Instead of losing his temper, he should have slapped a check in her hand. Dealing with her directly wasn't working. He'd avoid her in the future by negotiating with Charlie's attorney.

Jacey stared after George. He was the most exasperating man she'd ever met. Maybe not more exasperating than Roger—or Daddy. He thought she'd neglected Uncle Charlie and let him down. Maybe she had, though it wasn't intentional. Uncle Charlie had evidently shared his plans with George for Jacey's visit, but had stopped short of explaining why those plans never materialized.

She followed George at a slower pace, letting Lady pick her way along a well-worn trail back toward the barn. She considered telling him about her illness, but she didn't want to. George's pity would be more unbearable than his animosity.

Her anger began to rekindle as she reviewed in her head everything this retreating mountain of opinionated male, leaving her to eat dust, had said. How dare he assume she was a fortune hunter and a "spoiled brat?" He knew nothing about the years she had faithfully corresponded with Uncle Charlie, or the special bond they had shared. He'd judged her without knowing anything about her. She touched the fingertips of one hand to her throat and remembered the gray-haired volunteer who had sat beside her bed, reading Uncle Charlie's letters over and over to her. Sometimes, after listening to the letters, she'd dreamed of the pictures they painted for her—the sparkling streams, the clear blue sky, grass as high as a cow's belly, and the inevitable cowboy smiling beneath his white hat. When the reality of pain was more than she could handle, she had escaped to the dream Uncle Charlie had given her.

"That big jerk doesn't know my family either," she muttered under her breath as she wiped away the tears streaming down her face. "He should just try changing Daddy's mind about anything! He'll never know how badly I wanted to come, because I'll never tell him. He can think anything he wants to." She swallowed back a sob and knew in her heart that she really *did* care what he thought.

As she approached the barn, she could see Clyde standing with his nose lowered into the water trough. Carefully she wiped away all signs of her tears before her oafish neighbor could see her red, swollen eyes. He already had such a low opinion of her that she didn't want him to think she was a crybaby, too. She bemoaned the fact that she cried so easily, and hoped Dr. Bellows was right when he told her that her weepiness was a temporary problem.

At first she didn't see George; then she spotted someone leaning against his old blue pickup truck parked in the shade of one of the pine trees. It definitely wasn't George. It looked like a woman. Sliding from the mare's back when she stopped next to Clyde, Jacey's legs felt shaky. She stood for long minutes leaning against the little horse's flank. Across Lady's back she watched the strange woman unfold her arms and start around the side of the truck. Tall and wearing faded blue jeans with a cotton shirt knotted at her waist, she moved with elegant ease. A long, thick blonde braid swayed below her waist as she walked. Jacey watched the woman open the passenger door of a white sports car parked behind George's truck. When she straightened a minute later, she was balancing a baby on her hip.

A smile lit Jacey's face and she started toward the corral fence to meet her visitors. From the corner of her eye she saw George emerge from the barn. Her steps faltered as she watched his long, sure stride cover the short distance to where the woman and baby waited. He reached out to take the chubby infant in his big hands. His rumbling laughter blended with the baby's chortling squeal of delight as he faked tossing the baby in the air, then lowered the infant to his broad shoulder where the child made a swift grab for the purple cap.

Jacey didn't understand the heavy weight that pressed against her chest. The bright sun seemed to dim. What was the matter with her? She should be halfway across the yard by now, instead of standing in one place watching them talk to each other. She was too far away to hear their words, but they appeared to be arguing. Before she could force her feet to carry her forward, George returned the baby to the car and held the door for the woman to get in. He leaned forward, his head on a level with the woman's for several minutes, then backed away. Without a glance in Jacey's direction, he climbed into the truck and started the motor. Both vehicles moved down the driveway, leaving a cloud of dust in their wake.

As she walked toward where the two vehicles had sat, Jacey watched the trail of dust until long after the cars were out of sight.

"He's married! I never even considered he might be married. He's not only a jerk; he's a *married* jerk!"

Chapter 4

Carefully placing the last dish back in the cupboard, Jacey gave a big sigh, then wiped her nose. Sniffing miserably, she glanced around at the spotless room. It was as clean as she could get it, and she had done it all herself in spite of her cold. She'd never been permitted to do much housework at home, and she felt certain that Susan, her family's housekeeper, could have done it faster and more efficiently. But it gave her an unaccustomed sense of accomplishment to know she'd managed without help.

The cabin was beginning to feel like home, yet the room lacked something. It needed curtains and pillows, and a new rug would be nice. She glanced around, then frowned when her eyes lit on the stag head. This was her home now, and she didn't want any dead animals hanging on her walls. She wanted that stag head down!

There might be a ladder in one of the sheds; she would look as soon as she felt a little better. Her feet dragged as she made her way out the front door. Settling on the top step, she leaned her aching head against the porch pillar. If she were home, back in Baltimore, Dr. Bellows would give her something soothing for her throat, and mother would insist that she stay in bed. The thought of laying her head on smooth sheets suddenly seemed inviting. She contemplated going back inside and crawling into her big pine bed; but if she went to bed now, she'd have trouble sleeping tonight.

She had been here four days. Every day had been spent scrubbing and cleaning the house, feeding and befriending the animals, and exploring her ranch. The days had been full, but the nights were long and lonely. They were cold, too. The little fires she'd lit in the fireplace with bits of wood she'd found didn't keep the cabin warm all night, and she hadn't yet figured out how to start the stove. That was something else she'd work on as soon as she got rid of her cold.

The ranch wasn't very big—nothing like the miles and miles of open space Uncle Charlie had described so vividly in his letters— but Jacey didn't mind. If it had been a large working spread with hundreds of cattle, she wouldn't know what to do with it. Glumly, she admitted she didn't know what to do with the few acres and animals she did have. Gus scared her half to death, and she hadn't been able to coax Lady close enough to put a halter on her.

As she wiped her running nose again, she lifted her face to gaze at the fields and mountains surrounding her. She knew that the land south of hers belonged to George Lindquist. Just thinking about him made her mouth tighten and her anger boil. It was his fault she had a miserable cold. She'd been fine until he tossed her into the creek her first day in the Sanpete valley. Working herself to exhaustion each day, then lying awake half of each night because she was unaccustomed to being alone, had nothing to do with it.

Another wave of homesickness washed over her, and she found herself wishing she were back in her own room with her mother bringing her hot drinks and Dr. Bellows popping in to check on her. Roger would bring her huge bouquets of red roses, and Anne would pick up a dozen new paperbacks for her. And Daddy . . .

Drat! She didn't want Daddy deciding whether or not she should go to work or back to the hospital! And she didn't want Roger's roses or her mother's fussing. She was doing just fine. It was just this stupid cold. Once more she glared in the direction of the Lindquist ranch.

In the field that ran parallel to her pasture, a herd of thirty or forty white cattle grazed. The stream meandering through her pasture continued through George's property. She assumed that the clear running water which originated in the government-owned canyon above her property was the reason George had offered for her land. She had read enough history to be aware of the vital role water played in the settlement of the west—a role which hadn't lessened with time.

In the distance she could see a dozen long, low buildings. They looked like exceptionally long horticultural nurseries, except they didn't appear to be made of glass.

"Barns sure don't look like barns around here," she complained. George's barns didn't look any more like barns than the shed on her property did. Barns were supposed to be big, red two-story affairs with hay lofts and rounded roofs. She sniffed. Her throat was sore. Here she was, thinking of everything else and trying not to admit that a sore throat terrified her. The threat of a strep infection had limited her activities since her bout with rheumatic fever. A strep infection now would mean she'd have to go back home, and she didn't want to give up her new-found independence. Not yet.

She should go into town and call Anne. If she didn't, Anne would probably be out here checking on her by Friday. She slowly got to her feet and went inside to change into a short, straight skirt with slit pockets in front and patch pockets in back, and a matching red-checked shirt. She tied a red scarf around her throat, slipped into white sandals, picked up her handbag, and grabbed her car keys. Halfway to the door, she remembered her pill. She swallowed it with a glass of water and made a mental note to ask Anne to get her prescription refilled and send it on to her.

Jacey was ready to step into her car when she saw a plume of dust approaching along the dirt lane. Was George coming to see her? For just a moment her spirits lifted, than plummeted as she remembered a long-legged blonde. She didn't care if he was married, she told herself vehemently. In fact, she felt sorry for the poor woman; she didn't like George anyway. She wasn't going to take any more of his insults, and she wouldn't let him intimidate her with his huge size. Her chin lifted stubbornly as she waited to confront the obnoxious man.

It wasn't George Lindquist's truck that stopped beside her bright red convertible. As the dust settled, two strangers stepped from the once-white king cab pickup. Sun glinted from the silvery streaks in the older man's hair; deep grooves lining his cheeks failed to detract from his rugged, sun-bronzed good looks. His jeans were faded, and he wore a blue plaid flannel shirt. On his head sat the white western hat of her dreams. The younger man appeared to be barely out of his teens and was dressed similarly to the older man. Their faces betrayed a duplication of features, leading Jacey to guess that they were father and son.

Though the father appeared self-confident and interesting, the son exuded cockiness as he swaggered toward Jacey. His eyes raked her from head to toe, leaving her feeling disgusted and annoyed. She shuddered and sneezed twice.

The men introduced themselves as Calvin Walker and his son Todd. Todd's leering visual appraisal irritated Jacey, making her glad that his father wasted no time getting to the point.

"Miss Mathews, we understand you are the new owner of Charles Mathews' little farm. Over the years I've made more than one offer for this place, but Charles always said he wanted to live out his life here. I understood that, so I never pressed. Circumstances have changed now. This place isn't big enough to farm; farming isn't a life for a woman alone anyhow, especially a little eastern girl accustomed to city ways. I'm offering to top any other offers you've had."

Jacey sneezed and searched her pockets for a handkerchief before answering. With her eyes and nose running, she felt at a great disadvantage. "I'm sorry, Mr. Walker. My ranch isn't for sale."

"Oh, come now; I've been in touch with your attorney. Mr. Blake told me early Monday morning that you two were getting married in a few weeks and are hoping to have the matter settled so you can sign the papers by the end of June. If you're hoping for a better price, you're kidding yourself. I've already offered more than Lindquist or Kitsu."

"Roger had no right to tell you anything," Jacey gasped, hurt anew that Roger had ignored her wishes. Her mind spun. Roger wouldn't have known until Monday evening that she was gone. Her father had told him to start arrangements immediately to sell her property, and he'd certainly done it. She was glad Anne had had the forethought to have Jacey give her sister limited power of attorney. Remembering Anne's assurance that only she could act for Jacey, and that the property could not be sold without Jacey's signature, gave her courage. "Roger Blake is not now, and never has been, my attorney. Furthermore, he never will be. He's no longer my fiance, either." A sniffle ended her angry outburst.

"Okay, lady. Take it easy. I didn't mean to upset you. Sounds like you've had a fight with your boyfriend and my timing is bad. I'll come back when you've settled down. Think about what I said. I'll give you top dollar. Your place is ideal for my purpose."

"And what is your purpose?" Jacey asked, ice dripping from her voice as she moved closer to her car. She didn't want them to see how scared she was; they might contact Roger again, and he'd discover where she'd gone.

"Mink, ma'am. I raise mink."

How could Roger even consider selling her property to a mink breeder? Jacey slid into her car before responding. "Don't bother to come back. I won't be selling to you—ever." Her voice shook instead of sounding strong and confident as she wished. The engine roared to life as she gave the key a vicious twist. In spite of the sound, she heard the crude epithet Todd used as she pulled away.

"Their hats probably aren't even real Stetsons," she muttered as the dust billowed in her wake. Her struggle not to cry added strain to her already sore throat. Fear pushed the gas pedal to the floor as she admitted to herself that if she didn't get a long way from the two men, she might be coerced into selling her ranch.

When she reached the highway, she decided to go to Ephraim since it was closer, rather than back to Moroni. She hoped the town might be a bit larger than the one where she'd stopped to buy bandages for her leg. As she followed the two-lane highway past the cemetery and into town, she realized that the town was just as small, or nearly so. It didn't take long to traverse the short Main Street which boasted a couple of tiny motels, a Ben Franklin variety store, two miniature grocery stores, a drug store, a malt shop, a bank, several service stations, and a handful of other businesses. She began to relax as she toured the sleepy little town.

There were homes on Main Street, too. The houses tended to be rectangular in shape, with their long sides parallel to the street.

Many were made of stucco or old rough-sided brick. Their evident Scandinavian architecture reminded her of Uncle Charlie's description of his house. He had been a frequent visitor to this little town; had he admired the houses so much that he'd built an imaginary house to impress her? Impulsively she decided to drive around and see the places he'd described so vividly to her.

Turning up a side street, she passed a post office and found herself in the middle of a small college campus she identified as Snow College. She found the sprawling, tree-shaded lawns and old stone buildings juxtaposed with modern brick ones, just as they'd been described to her. She watched a small group of college girls scurry across the street, noticed clusters of students sitting on the lawns or congregating in entryways, and smiled at the usual campus lovers snuggling together on a dormitory lawn. It was an appealing campus, but it lacked the emotional impact she experienced a few minutes later when she passed an elementary school. Wistfully she thought of her derailed plans to teach small children—a plan her father had squelched, fearing her exposure to children's illnesses. A wave of rebellion swept through her. She'd write the college in Baltimore and resign. She had a degree in elementary education, and it was time she used it. She wouldn't tell her father until after she found a teaching position in an elementary school somewhere. Maybe here. She reached for another tissue and discovered the box empty. She needed to stop stalling, make a few purchases, and call Anne. After returning to Main Street, she decided to place her call from a pay phone she'd spotted near the Snappy Service Thriftway sign. She checked her watch and allowed for the time difference. Anne should be back from lunch and in her office. She just hoped she'd be lucky enough to catch her sister alone.

Luck was with her, and she soon found herself assuring Anne that she just had a spring cold and that it was nothing to worry about. It took nearly fifteen minutes and a promise to see a doctor to convince her sister.

"I'm going to talk to Dr. Bellows about a supply of cold medication that will be compatible with your prescription."

"No, Anne. He might tell Daddy where I am."

"Don't worry. Dr. Bellows can keep a secret. Anyway, I

already checked with him before I let you take off for Utah."

"You didn't tell me that."

"I had to make certain you wouldn't be in any danger." Anne's words irritated Jacey. Anne had helped her get away, but in many ways she was as interfering and bossy as the rest of her family.

"Since you're talking to Dr. Bellows anyway, would you ask him for a refill of my prescription?"

"Sure. By the way, Dad was pretty angry when he got your letter. He hasn't stopped insisting that you should come home. He says you can rest here as well as in some fancy sanatorium halfway around the world. He tried to call you and was told patients do not have telephones in their rooms in order to protect their privacy."

Jacey laughed. "What if he sends someone to check on me?"

"Lisel is resourceful. She'll think of something. Mother is worried about you being so far from Dr. Bellows, and Roger doesn't believe you've really broken your engagement. He insists you're tired and upset over Uncle Charles' death, and that you only meant to postpone rather than cancel the wedding, in spite of your returned ring in his pocket."

Anne reported that their mother had cried and worried over whether or not it was too late to cancel the invitations and back out of the hotel reservation. She, too, insisted that the engagement hadn't been broken, and announced at frequent intervals how wise she'd been to pick out Jacey's gown early and have it safely hanging in her daughter's closet. It was such a relief not to have to worry about fittings during this trying time. Of course, if they had a September wedding instead of a June wedding, it might be necessary to make a few alterations if Jacey lost any more weight, and she would certainly need to pick up a few more items for Jacey's trousseau and change the color scheme.

Jacey sighed. "I knew no one would believe me. They'll keep right on planning the wedding until I give in. They won't even notice it's not what I want; they'll just congratulate themselves for doing what's best for poor Jacey."

"You haven't changed your mind? You still don't want Roger?"

"I haven't changed my mind." She considered telling Anne

about George. But what could she say that wouldn't bring Anne rushing out here to her rescue? She couldn't tell Anne he'd shouted at her, thrown her in the creek, or even that he'd turned over the animals to her. And she couldn't tell her he had the bluest eyes she'd ever seen, muscles she couldn't keep her eyes away from, and on the few occasions he'd smiled, his smile had made her forget everything else.

Anne moved on to another subject and became her usual efficient self. "Uncle Charles had a small account at the bank in Ephraim. That money is yours, and I've arranged to have the account changed to your name, but you need to go in and sign a signature card and get a checkbook. Don't use your checkbook or credit cards from here."

"All right. Anne, two men came to the ranch today. They want to buy it and they said they'd talked to Roger. If they talk to him again, he'll know I'm here."

"I'll talk to Roger and show him the power of attorney you signed, so he won't contact them again. I've already taken all the papers concerning the ranch from the firm's files and locked them in my own safe. I'll send you a box of things you might need, including some Swiss postcards. Mail one off once in a while through my friend. That should keep everyone from getting suspicious."

Jacey sneezed and searched for her already damp tissue. "I'd better hang up, Anne. I need to buy orange juice and tissues."

Before hanging up, Anne's voice changed slightly. Jacey picked up a hesitant undertone that sounded nothing like her confident sister.

"Since you won't be here to attend Judge Terrington's party next weekend, and it is important to Roger's career, as well as to the firm, I agreed to accompany him. You don't mind, do you?"

"Of course not; I just hope you won't be too bored."

Anne made a little strangled noise before going on. "I'm sure I won't be bored. Now, go find a doctor immediately; then go back to Uncle Charles' place and get some rest."

After hanging up the telephone, Jacey stopped at the bank. A helpful cashier helped her transact her business, then told her the number to call to have a telephone installed. She also pointed out the location of the town's only doctor, informed her that Charles Mathews' ranch was in a great location because both the Kitsus and Lindquists were lovely neighbors, and invited her to church on Sunday. At the doctor's office, a nurse performed the strep test and told Jacey to call back later for the results. By the time she finished purchasing a few groceries, she felt so exhausted she could hardly keep her eyes open on the drive back to her ranch.

As she approached the dirt lane, she found herself worrying about the visitors she had left behind that morning. She realized belatedly that she should have stayed until they were off the place, but she had been so angry she hadn't stopped to think. She got angry all over again when she thought about Roger, who should know how she felt about furs, even discussing selling her ranch to mink breeders. He hadn't intended to even discuss it with her; he would simply take the highest bid, no matter what they wanted to do with her land. Thank goodness she'd broken their engagement. And since Roger had scarcely crossed her mind in days, she'd obviously made the right decision. She wished she could dismiss a certain rancher from her mind as easily.

The yard was empty of vehicles, much to Jacey's relief. The mink breeders were gone, and she hadn't seen George since they'd ridden the horses. She was glad George had stayed away. She sensed that being around him wouldn't be wise. If she couldn't get him out of her head, then being around him could be dangerous. Anyway, he didn't like her and he had a wife, so she was being foolish to keep expecting to see him at every turn.

She hefted a grocery bag in her arms and carried it into the house. By the time the groceries were put away, she felt too tired to even crawl into bed. With a glass of orange juice and a fresh box of tissues, she made her way to the sofa where she curled up with her legs beneath her to sip the juice. When the juice was gone she set the empty glass on the floor, leaned her head back to rest a moment, and fell asleep.

She awoke several hours later with a stiff neck and the afternoon almost gone. From the cramped angle where she lay, she slowly opened her eyes to find herself eye-to-eye with the stag head.

"You've got to go," she muttered. "First thing tomorrow I'll look for a ladder."

She stood up, then stopped. An unfamiliar sound came from outside. She hurried to the kitchen window to peek out. In the distance she could see George on a dirt bike, riding along the fence line separating her pasture from his field. He stopped frequently to check posts and wires. The posts were strangely mismatched in height and thickness, like those all over the valley. Accustomed to neat, precise fences where all of the posts looked uniformly alike, she found a humorous appeal in their nonconformity. Curious about George's actions, she made her way outside to the porch. With one hand she shaded her eyes against the setting sun. A smile threatened to break free as she watched the incongruous sight of the big man astride the little motorbike.

From behind her, there came the scuffle of rapid footsteps. Twirling around, her hand went to her throat, where a gasp died before it could become a full-fledged scream. In the back of her mind she half expected to see Todd Walker, but instead she faced two identical little boys. Their black hair had been clipped in a style reminiscent of the Beatles, and mischief danced in their black eyes set off by almond skin. Both were wearing blue jeans, scuffed sneakers, and white T-shirts.

"Hi!" they said in unison.

"Hi! Where did you guys come from?" She hadn't heard a vehicle other than George's bike.

"We came from our house." They pointed to a grove of trees to the north. "You can't see it because the trees are in the way," one child explained while the other asked, "How come you're staying in Charlie's house?"

"It's my house now. Uncle Charlie doesn't need it anymore, so he gave it to me."

"He died and went to heaven," one boy pronounced. The other solemnly nodded his head in agreement.

"Are you Jacey? I thought Jacey was a little girl, but you're a grown-up lady!"

She loved them already; they recognized her as an adult.

Jacey sank onto the porch step to be more on their level. The calico cat settled in her lap while the black one wrapped itself around a small boy's leg. "The last time Uncle Charlie saw me I was a little girl, but we wrote letters to each other while I was growing up. We didn't get to see each other because we lived so far apart, and I was very sick."

"Will you still play with us?"

"I think I would like that." She smiled at the boys, then sneezed. The startled cats ran for the barn. She dug in her pocket for a tissue and wiped her eyes and nose.

"Are you still sick?" one of the boys asked.

"No, I just have a cold. I took a little dip in the creek a few days ago." She sent a glare toward the man she could see coming closer on his noisy little bike.

"You shouldn't go swimming yet! Mom said we have to wait until all the snow is melted on the mountains. Even in the summer it's awfully cold."

"Your mother is right; it was awfully cold." She smiled at her two small visitors. "You know my name, but I don't know yours."

"I'm John Hyrum Kitsu." The closer twin thumped his chest before pointing to his brother. "He's Joseph David Kitsu."

"We're nine years old and I'm the oldest," the other added.

"Ten minutes! Just ten minutes!" John objected to Joe's claim of seniority, which started a minor scuffle.

A few minutes later John looked up at Jacey to ask, "Are you going to let the sheep go through?"

"What sheep? Go through where?"

"Our sheep," Joe answered. "Every spring Charlie lets us open the gate between our pasture and his so we can take the sheep up into the mountains for the summer."

"Then in the fall they come back through again," John added. "Dad will come talk to you tomorrow."

"I'll have to think about it." Jacey glanced nervously toward George's pasture, remembering his herd of white cows. Uh-oh; she certainly didn't want to get caught in the middle of a range war between cattle and sheep ranchers.

"Uh, Jacey," John started hesitantly, "Gus is driving Uncle Charlie's car."

"He's *what?*" Jacey jumped up and started toward the car.

"He's not really driving it," Joe clarified. "He's just sitting there."

Jacey stopped short. The big gobbler occupied half of the front seat of her car. How could she possibly get him out? Eyeing the boys suspiciously, she asked, "How did Gus get out of his cage?"

"We opened the gate," the boys admitted proudly, then looked hesitant when they saw the expression on her face.

"Uncle Charlie said he's not an ordinary Thanksgiving turkey."

"He's special."

"Uncle Charlie said Gus is an attack turkey."

"If he's locked up, he can't protect you."

"Who's going to protect me from Gus?" Jacey glared at the big bird, who voiced his disapproval of the approaching trio.

Both boys waved their arms and shouted at the turkey. He didn't budge from the car, just extended his neck and gobbled and hissed. Jacey retreated to the house to get a broom. Returning, she gingerly approached the car to poke the broom at the turkey. Angrily Gus jumped to the top of the door and gobbled more ferociously, frightening Jacey and the boys back to the safety of the porch.

Together they considered various options for capturing the turkey. But Jacey soon suspected she was doomed to being stranded in her house and running footraces with the dumb bird every time she went to the barn to feed the chickens.

"I know," Joe suddenly shouted, taking off at a run with John right on his heels. "We'll be right back!"

Jacey stared at their disappearing backs, then stepped into the house for a fresh supply of tissues before returning to the porch to await their return. She didn't have long to wait.

"Oh, no!" she groaned, eyeing the unmistakable figure approaching with one small boy gripping each big hand. "Why is it that every time I need John Wayne, I get George Lindquist?"

He didn't glance her way once as he marched toward the car. Ignoring the frantic gobbling, George reached down with one leather-gloved hand to swiftly upend the angry tom. Toting the heavy ball of feathers by its feet, he carried Gus to his cage. After locking the bird in, he moved back to where Jacey clung to a porch pillar.

"Thank you." Jacey had to swallow hard before she could get the words out.

"He's used to running around free, but if you can't control him, keep the gate locked."

It wasn't her fault Gus got loose, and she certainly didn't ask George to catch him. Before she could defend herself, a violent sneeze shook her slight frame.

John looked from Jacey to George, then knowingly announced, "She went swimming before all the snow melted."

George's head swung from the earnest child's face to the young woman struggling to mop her eyes and face with paper tissues. A guilty flush climbed his ruddy cheeks.

"You kids run on home," he ordered. "It's getting dark, and your mom is going to be looking for you."

Obediently, John and Joe waved goodbye to Jacey and promised to return soon to play with her.

Jacey waved, but before she could think of a way to send George on his way too, he grabbed her arm and hustled her inside the house.

"Get to bed," he ordered abruptly. I'll bring you something hot to drink." He gave her a none-too-gentle shove toward the bedroom.

In her room, she had pulled her nightgown out of her drawer and started to unbutton her blouse before her mind kicked into gear. Obeying was an ingrained habit. Stopping dead still, she rebelled. She'd go to bed when she wanted, not when someone else ordered her to! She wouldn't undress while George was in the house, either. She'd wait until he left, then soak in a hot tub. She might even read awhile before going to bed. She sneezed to punctuate her decision.

Turning abruptly, she marched into the bathroom to turn on the hot water. When a sudden sneeze racked her frame, she dislodged a tray of toiletries and sent the contents flying. She paused to wipe her streaming face and began gathering up the tubes and jars. As she reached for a wet cloth to wipe up spilled shampoo, she heard George's steps behind her. She whirled to face him. How dare he follow her into her own bathroom!

George stepped through the door with a steaming mug in one hand. He had an unobstructed view of the bathroom and Jacey bending over to pick up something. *Jumpin' goose feathers! What have I got myself into?* Her short skirt barely covered the essentials, and he figured he'd better backtrack immediately. He took a nervous step backward just as she turned to face him. Her face looked pale, and her eyes were like deep navy pools.

"What are you doing? I told you to get into bed." The words sounded like they came from a bear with a toothache.

"What do you think I'm doing? I'm getting ready to take a bath," she snapped back.

"It's too cold in here to take a bath."

"I'll take a bath if I want to." Jacey placed her hands on her hips and gave him a baleful glare. She made it clear she wouldn't back down.

George's size might intimidate most people, but Charlie's niece didn't seem impressed. He'd botched things on every front since meeting her, and now she was sick and he could only blame himself. He'd like to make amends, but the fool woman took exception to everything he said or did.

He didn't like the suspicious way she eyed him as he carefully sat the hot cup down beside the sink before reaching for her. "You're going to bed *now*. Being wet and chilled isn't going to help your cold." He took her arm and turned her toward the bedroom.

"Take your hands off me." Jacey twisted away.

He took a step and his feet started to skid. Intent on propelling Jacey toward the bedroom, he hadn't seen the puddle of shampoo. With a powerful lurch, he struggled to right himself. The backs of his legs struck the side of the tub. He grasped wildly for anything to hold onto, and his arms swept everything in their path to the floor as he tumbled backward into the steaming water, sending a tidal wave splashing across the room.

Jacey staggered backward when the water hit her. When her back made contact with the plank door, she stopped. Her mouth opened, but no sound came out. She could only stare at George in Uncle Charlie's big red tub.

"He does just fit," she said breathlessly, surveying the well-muscled torso before her. His wet shirt appeared almost invisible. Backing away slowly, she edged toward the door.

"Are . . . are you all right?" she whispered hoarsely. When he only stared back in return, she glanced nervously down her own front to where the water had splashed, wetting her own clothes nearly as much as George's. Embarrassed, she turned away.

"You're beautiful, Jacey."

She couldn't believe either the words or the gentle voice coming from the depths of the cavernous red tub. They scared her more than when he shouted. George shouldn't be here, and he shouldn't be saying things that made her feel trembly inside. She backed carefully out of the room and made a dash for her closet to pull out her heavy robe. Before she could pull it on over her wet clothes, George reached her side and took it from her grasp.

"Take off the wet things first."

She stared at him dumbly, not moving.

"You can't go to bed in wet clothes," he admonished gently.

"I'm not undressing until you leave." She crossed her arms across her chest. He didn't move or say a word.

Her body shook—whether from cold or some unfamiliar emotion, she couldn't tell. She raised her eyes slowly to his face and felt trapped by his gaze. His head inclined fractionally toward hers, and they both seemed to hold their breath until the movement continued. Soft as a summer breeze, his lips touched hers, hesitated, then settled firmly to stir up a whirlwind of feeling.

Jacey sighed, then suddenly stiffened as she remembered the woman with the golden braid and a baby on her hip. Was she George's wife? The chatty bank teller had referred to the Lindquists as plural. She quickly stepped backward, frantically reaching for her robe. Turning her back, she wrapped it around her shivering body. This time George didn't try to stop her.

"I didn't mean to embarrass you." George's voice held an apologetic note. "Lisa tells me often enough that I'm too impulsive and that I should think first before I act."

"Is Lisa the woman who was here a few days ago?"

"Yes. I should have introduced you, but she was in a hurry and only stopped to make sure I'd be home in time to watch Ashlie while she went grocery shopping."

Jacey's teeth chattered and her shoulders sagged. She'd been right; the blonde woman was George's wife.

"Get into bed. I'll bring you something hot to drink." He spoke quietly before leaving the room. He closed the door softly behind him.

What should she do? Anne wouldn't be standing here with her teeth chattering, wondering whether or not to undress and climb into bed. With a defeated little sob, Jacey scrambled out of her wet clothes and into her nightgown. She pulled the quilt up to her chin just before George tapped twice on the door then stepped inside.

She watched wide-eyed as he walked toward her with a steaming mug. He placed it in her hand, bent over to gently kiss her forehead, then walked out of the room again without uttering a word. Jacey heard the front door click and the lock slide into place.

Chapter 5

Jacey crawled out of bed with the first streaks of morning light. She'd gotten little rest. It was impossible to sleep when the memory of last night's encounter with George wouldn't leave her alone. Every time she closed her eyes she saw his wet shirt clinging to well-muscled shoulders, and his kiss haunted her. How could she let a married man kiss her? It went against everything she believed in. With a grimace she ran her fingers through her hair, as if intent on pulling out every strand—and her confused thoughts with it.

Roger had kissed her, and she'd never felt like this. Why George? She didn't even like him, and she was certain he didn't like her either. Besides, she had no use for women who chased married men, and even less for men who cheated on their wives!

She stumbled into the bathroom and groaned. The room looked like a herd of rampaging buffalo had run through it. Cautiously avoiding the pool of shampoo on the floor, she made her way to the tub to release the now-cold water. It took several thick bath towels to wipe up the puddles of water on the floor, and another to wipe the mirror. She had to stretch flat on the floor to reach the shampoo bottle, which had been kicked under the claw-footed tub. She found the bar of soap behind the toilet, and her favorite lipstick lay crushed by a muddy boot heel.

As she scrubbed out the big red tub, she couldn't help remembering the way George had looked sitting in it. Once again she saw shock register on his face, observed the way his wet clothes clung to his skin, and relived the moment she realized he was watching her. A tear rolled down her cheek, and she dashed it away with her fist. *Stop thinking about him,* she ordered herself sharply. If she got out of the bathroom, out of her bedroom—better yet, out of the house—she'd forget sooner.

Jacey returned to the bedroom to dress. She didn't own one outfit suitable for doing chores. Wiggling into bicycle shorts, she vowed to buy some jeans as soon as possible.

In the kitchen she found her bottle of lemon juice and a squeeze bottle of honey sitting on the table, reminding her of the hot drink George had prepared for her the night before. She winced at the memory. She left them sitting on the counter and took from the refrigerator a carton of orange juice, then opened a bag of mini-muffins which she popped into the microwave. It wasn't much of a breakfast, but she didn't feel very hungry.

The cats were waiting for her when she reached the barn. They meowed and wove their way between her legs as she made her way to their bag of feed. After scattering grain and watering the chickens, she hunted for eggs. She found six. Gus was next. She scooped up his can of feed and carried it to his cage.

"You dumb bird," she scolded as she carefully poked the feed through the old turkey's wire enclosure. "You have no idea how much trouble you've caused. If you had stayed in your cage where you belong, Johnny and Joey wouldn't have brought George here. And if George hadn't come over last night, I wouldn't have made such a big fool of myself."

Gus gobbled disdainfully.

"You may be a tough old bird, but you're going to be the main course for an early Thanksgiving dinner if you don't straighten up."

With water in the creek and plenty of grass in the pasture, Jacey decided the horses and cows didn't need any attention from her. She picked up the bucket of eggs and returned to the house.

The moment she stepped through the door, the offending stag head caught her attention. Her head ached, her nose felt stuffy, she hated George, and she despised her own weakness. The stag head became the final straw.

"You're history!" she frowned at the thing. "The only thing I dislike more than you," she told the head, "is Gus. And George," she amended, while a little demon in the back of her head reminded her that she had a strange way of disliking someone. Angrily she turned about and headed for the two sheds she hadn't yet explored.

Opening the door to the shed closest to the house, she discovered it was half full of chunks of wood, all cut to an appropriate size for use in the fireplace or stove. A small stack of coal gleamed in one corner. She felt like kicking herself for not searching the sheds sooner. She still didn't know how to light the stove, but she'd figure it out. She'd burn her house down before she'd ask George to help her again. She picked up an armful of wood and carried it to the cabin before going on to the other building.

The second shed yielded a surprising array of tools, along with shovels, paint brushes, hoses, a couple of western saddles shrouded in canvas, and much to her surprise, a snowmobile. Finally she spied an aluminum ladder—just what she had come for. Promising herself she would explore the contents of the building more thoroughly later, she picked up the ladder and maneuvered it out the door.

By the time she had the ladder in place next to the fireplace, she felt hot and sticky. Her uncombed hair felt plastered to the back of her neck. She leaned her head against the ladder and considered going back to bed. No, she'd rest after she'd accomplished her objective. She'd toss that mangy stag head out, just the way she'd tossed out all those silly thoughts about George!

Jacey placed one foot on the ladder, then the other. When she reached a height where she could look the ragged beast in the eye, she stretched out her hands. She didn't want to actually touch the animal, so she tugged at the base. Nothing happened. She tugged harder and lifted the head an inch or so. Its weight surprised her, and the ladder wobbled as she struggled to dislodge the trophy from the wall. One more hard pull should do it.

George stood in the doorway admiring the spandex-clad view. Jacey must have been too busy doing whatever she was doing to hear his footsteps cross the porch. She certainly didn't give any indication that she had noticed his arrival. He grinned when she bent a little further over the top of the ladder. The ladder tilted slightly, and his grin disappeared with an angry roar. Jacey started, and the ladder teetered precariously. He knew it had been a mistake to shout the moment the words left his mouth. He leaped forward to grab her around the waist. The ladder toppled to the floor as he lifted her clear.

"Good grief, girl!" George thundered. "You could have been hurt. Don't you ever think first?"

"Let go of me!" She kicked at his shins.

George looked down at the woman struggling to free herself from his hold. For long seconds their eyes met, and he felt an urge to pull her closer. Mesmerized by the green fire in the depths of her eyes, his head started to descend. Then something behind the flame stopped him. It wasn't really fear, but something more akin to pain. Anger and confusion were there, too.

Opening his hands, he allowed Jacey to step back. She stared at him wordlessly. They both swallowed hard before looking away. A loud rap on the door sounded before either could speak. Right behind the hammering came the excited shouts of two little boys.

George schooled his face to hide his disappointment. Of course he shouldn't be disappointed; he should be grateful his neighbors' interruption had prevented him from making a bigger fool of himself.

Jacey turned to the open doorway in time to see John and Joe scamper into the room. They were a few steps ahead of a young cowboy who stood in the doorframe, smiling expectantly at the room's occupants. Jacey gasped. Here was a real cowboy, perfect in every detail save one: he was short. He twirled a white hat in his fingers, definitely a Stetson. His checked western-cut shirt, sporting pearl snaps, stretched tautly over a muscular chest; on his feet gleamed elaborately-stitched cowboy boots with tiny blunted spurs; and his slim hips were encased in denim jeans held up by a tooled leather belt complete with dazzling silver buckle. Leather chaps rode low on his hips and rippled with a masculine grace down the sides of his pant legs. Jacey's eyes flew to his face where teeth, brilliant enough for a toothpaste commercial, flashed a bright smile. His dark eyes sparkled, and a wavy lock of shiny black hair fell across his forehead.

He wasn't quite like the cowboys she'd watched on T.V. None of them had been Oriental. She had read a story once about a black cowboy, and she knew some of the best cowboys were actually Indians; but an Asian cowboy had never crossed her mind. Could there be such a thing as a Japanese cowboy?

"Jeremy Kitsu." The grinning cowboy extended his hand toward her.

Jacey stammered her own name as their hands touched. The strength of his grip surprised her, and his eyes sparkled knowingly with laughter. One thing was for sure. He might be short, but he was certainly real. She watched in awe as Jeremy greeted George with an enthusiastic handshake before turning back to her again.

"Dad is busy this morning, so I volunteered to see if Monday would be all right with you for moving the sheep. The Dynamic Duo," he flashed a teasing grin at the twins, "said they had already talked to you about it."

Jacey looked hesitantly from Jeremy to George, but got no help there. She didn't know what to do. Were sheep and cattle ranchers still at odds with each other? She certainly didn't want to get caught in the middle of a range war in her own house. The men seemed to be on fairly good terms with each other, but would she be upsetting some delicate balance if she agreed to let the sheep go through her property? The twins said Uncle Charlie had allowed it, so it must be all right. She hesitated a moment longer, then agreed that Monday would be fine.

"Do you and Lisa want to come along?" Jeremy turned to George. "I've got a big gelding you'll love, and Lisa can ride Honey." Bouncing his attention back to Jacey, he continued. "Do you want to ride Trigger Lady, or would you rather I brought a mount for you?"

Jacey didn't know what to say. The exuberant cowboy assumed she would accompany them on the sheep drive, but she knew nothing about sheep. She wasn't an experienced rider. She probably couldn't even catch Lady. Before she could get an answer out, she heard George say, "Come on, Jacey. I think you'd enjoy it."

She wanted to go, but should she? Would she become fatigued and hold everyone up? On the other hand, she might not ever get another opportunity to do anything so exciting. "I'd like to go, if you don't think I'd be in the way."

"We'll catch Lady for you," a small voice volunteered.

"We can saddle her, too," the other child added.

"That won't be necessary," George rumbled as he scowled at the two youngsters, who had righted the ladder and were now perched on the top rung laughing down at the adults. "I have to come over anyway to give her the saddle Charlie left with me."

George had the saddle Uncle Charlie had made for her? But why?

"Get down from there!" Jeremy warned his brothers as the ladder swayed. George lifted Joe in his powerful arms while John hastily stood up to crow, "I'm bigger than George."

"That's what you think, pipsqueak." George swung him down too and tickled him thoroughly before tossing him on the sofa beside his brother.

"Let's go visit Gus," Joe yelled as he headed for the door with John on his heels.

"Don't you dare let him out!" Jacey called after them.

"Behave yourselves or we'll leave you home on Monday," Jeremy added.

"I've got to get back." George turned to Jacey. "I've got a feed delivery coming this morning. I just came over to check on your animals and see if you were feeling better, but I see you fed them yourself and you're . . . " He stopped, turned around, and took two long strides toward the stag head. Reaching up, he unhooked the wire anchoring it to the wall. "Where do you want this thing?"

"As far from me as possible," she answered with a shudder. "And those two dead birds can go with it," she said, pointing to the pheasants over the sofa.

Chuckling, Jeremy plucked them off the wall and followed George out the door. Eyes as full of mischief as those of his little brothers sparkled at Jacey as he turned to say, "'Til Monday."

Jacey watched as George dropped the stag head in the back of his pickup. Jeremy tossed the birds in, too. She couldn't believe that neither man had argued with her. They hadn't told her the trophies were valuable or made her feel guilty because Uncle Charlie had cared for them. All she'd had to do was say she didn't want dead animals on her walls, and George took them away. Jacey felt like singing.

The two men conversed briefly before George climbed into the cab of his truck and roared away in a cloud of dust. Jeremy almost doubled over with laughter, and Jacey wondered what was so funny. She had an uneasy feeling that Jeremy's laughter had something to do with her. She watched him slap his hat against his leg, then settle it on his head as his little brothers ran up to join him.

Three horses stood tied to the corral fence. Jeremy quickly tossed one of his little brothers into a saddle while the other twin scrambled up the pole fence and leaped into a saddle by himself. Jeremy placed one booted foot in a stirrup, and with all the grace of every western movie star Jacey had ever watched, swung his other leg across the ornate saddle that glistened with silver trim. He and his brothers were halfway down the lane when it hit Jacey. What had she done? How could she be so stupid? Had she really agreed to go on a sheep drive with George . . . and George's wife?

Suddenly feeling extremely tired, Jacey's shoulders slumped. She should have gotten a prescription from the doctor yesterday, instead of waiting for Anne to send one to her. Perhaps a hot bath would soothe her. She made her way to the bathroom to soak for half an hour in steamy hot water. She only had to remind herself once not to think about the last occupant of the tub. She scrubbed every inch of her body and washed her hair. With her blow dryer in one hand and a pick in the other, she tamed her unruly curls, then swallowed another glass of orange juice and a couple of Tylenol tablets before crawling into bed.

It was past lunch time when she awoke, feeling decidedly better. She opened a can of chicken noodle soup to heat in the microwave and selected one of Uncle Charlie's paperbacks to read. She was just finishing chapter two when she heard a vehicle outside. A quick peek out the window revealed the insignia of the telephone company blazoned on the side panel of the truck.

It didn't take long to connect cable to a pole outside and string the necessary lines. She couldn't imagine how Uncle Charlie had gotten along for so many years without a telephone, but he'd never wanted one. The few times he'd called Jacey, it had been from a

pay phone. Soon a jack was installed, and the telephone she had
arranged to lease was in place. She tried out her new phone by
calling the doctor's office to get the results of her throat culture,
and was relieved to find it was negative for strep.

As the telephone company truck prepared to leave, a large
brown panel truck lumbered up her lane. She signed for two big
packages from Anne which the delivery man left on her front room
floor. Jacey didn't wait for him to reach his truck and drive away
before she was tearing at the boxes to see what Anne had sent.

Anne must have air expressed them to Salt Lake City to have
gotten them here so quickly. When Jacey couldn't break the
packing tape by hand, she got a knife from the kitchen. The larger
box held clothes, her small CD player with a dozen of her favorite
disks, the decorative pillows from her bed, pictures of her family,
an old and much-loved teddy bear, and dozens of small mementos
and knick-knacks she had treasured over the years.

Turning her attention to the smaller box, she noted the seals
indicating it was fragile and highly insured. The knife slipped
smoothly through the tape. Pushing back the flaps of the heavy
carton, she lifted out several handfuls of packing peanuts to reach
a small leather case. Setting it aside for the moment, she moved
more packing material until she unearthed a larger leather case.
With a spurt of happy laughter, she unzipped the case to find that
her laptop computer had arrived safely. She searched further in the
carton for her printer and a box of disks.

Satisfied that everything had survived shipping, she opened the
small case to discover several refills of her prescription, a bottle of
cough syrup, an antibiotic, and a prescription bottle nearly as large
as a pint jar which rattled when she shook it. Taped to its lid she
found a note from Dr. Bellows. "When life gets tough, take a
couple of happy pills. Good luck." She laughed, remembering the
arrangement she and Dr. Bellows had when she was a little girl,
stubbornly refusing to take any more "nasty medicine" until he
secured her cooperation with a little bottle of "happy pills." He'd
told her to take two M & M's after each dose of the nasty
medicine.

A knock sounded on the door, startling Jacey. Extricating
herself from the contents of her packages took a few moments. In

her struggle she knocked over the little leather case, sending its contents rolling across the floor. Another tap sounded on the door and she scurried to open it. George must have forgotten something. Why she expected to see George on the other side of the door, she didn't stop to question. She flung open the door and words failed her. Instead of George, she found herself face to face with the young blonde woman she had watched from behind Lady's back the day George acquainted her with her chores.

Jacey's cheeks flushed as she eyed her visitor. She felt like slamming the door in self-preservation. The beautiful woman eyeing her thoughtfully stood at least four inches taller than Jacey, and while Jacey's bones were fine and delicate, her visitor looked as though she could model for Nordic ski wear.

"Hi! I'm Lisa Lindquist." She held out her hand in a firm gesture as though she shook hands every day. Self-consciously Jacey began to extend her hand, then realized she still clutched the huge pill bottle. Flustered, she sat it on the top of the bookcase and extended her hand again. Lisa shook it with a grip strong enough to make the smaller woman wince.

"I, uh, I'm Jacey Mathews. George mentioned you." That came out sounding stupid.

Carefully withdrawing her hand, Jacey gestured for Lisa to come in. Feeling embarrassed and ill at ease, she watched her guest pick her way to the rocking chair, twice stepping over pill bottles. Jacey rushed to pick up the scattered containers, which she stuffed back into the leather case before seating herself on the sofa.

"Some of my things just arrived. I was unpacking." Jacey felt she had to explain the clutter. Silently she added, *In spite of the way it looks, I'm not really a sloppy pig and I don't steal other women's husbands.* She felt ill at ease and wondered what to say, but Lisa didn't seem at all uncomfortable.

"George said you had a cold. I thought I'd stop by and see if you needed anything, and if you were feeling better, ask if you'd like to drive to Manti with me. I need new jeans; everything I own is a bit too snug since Ashlie was born." Her beautiful cornflower-blue eyes dimmed for just a moment.

Feeling uncertain as to whether she should agree to go with

Lisa, Jacey waved her arm at the clutter heaped in the center of the room. "I should put this away."

"Come on," Lisa smiled. "Women can clean up messes any time, but it isn't often I can persuade George to watch the baby so I can get out for a few hours. Of course, Ashlie is a very good baby, and I can take her almost anywhere, but sometimes it's nice to go somewhere without her. She really isn't much fun to take shopping yet."

Without quite knowing how it happened, Jacey found herself securely strapped into Lisa's white sports car with the windows open, allowing the wind to whip her curls into tangles of rioting color as they flew down the narrow two-lane highway. Several times she glanced at Lisa, but couldn't think of anything to say.

Long before they reached the outskirts of the small town, Jacey could see a huge revival-style castle, complete with towers sporting bell-cast roofs. A golden figure perched on one of its two towers.

"What is that?" she asked, staring at the strangely beautiful structure.

"That's the Manti temple."

"Uncle Charlie told me about it once a long time ago, but I guess I forgot. I've seen pictures of the Salt Lake temple, and I've passed the Washington D.C. temple quite a few times. This one doesn't look much like either of them."

"The most well-known temple is the one in Salt Lake City," Lisa explained, "and the Washington temple looks like a modernized version of it, but there are actually quite a few different styles. This is one of the oldest, and it was built with a great deal of sacrifice by the Scandinavian pioneers who settled this valley over a hundred years ago."

"Your ancestors, I'll bet."

"Yes," Lisa laughed. "Grandpa never let us forget that we came from good, strong Swedish pioneer stock."

"I don't think I descended from pioneers, but my grandmother was a Mormon. She didn't talk about it much, and I don't remember her ever going to church."

Lisa looked at her strangely. "Charles Mathews was an active member."

"I know. He took me to church with him when I was a little girl and we both spent a summer with my grandparents at their vacation home in Maine. I was even baptized, but it was so long ago I don't remember much about the Church except the wonderful pioneer stories he used to tell me."

"Your parents aren't members?"

"No."

"You should go to the pageant next month if you like pioneer stories. It's held right there on the temple grounds." Lisa waved a hand casually toward the hill where the temple stood.

They were in Manti now, and Lisa zipped through the sparse traffic. Jacey was delighted with the mixture of architectural styles, and was particularly entranced with Victorian and Queen Anne houses sitting next to simple adobe homes or two-story frame houses boasting half a dozen dormer windows. She felt slightly disappointed when Lisa parked the car in a small parking lot in front of a nondescript modern brick-and-frame structure.

"Add two inches to your waist size and four to the pants length you usually buy," Lisa instructed as she held up a mammoth pair of Levis for Jacey's inspection. Lisa must have read skepticism on her face because she burst out laughing. "Really. You take them home, throw them in the washer and dryer a couple of times, and the fit is perfect."

Half an hour later the two young women loaded their purchases into Lisa's car, and the tires spun as Lisa tore out of the parking lot. On the drive to Manti, Jacey had been so relieved that Lisa didn't seem inclined to talk about George, that she had scarcely paid attention to the way she drove. But now, as the car flew down the highway, eating up the miles between Manti and Ephraim, Jacey found herself clutching the armrest with a white-knuckle grip. Lisa's driving didn't inspire confidence. She liked Lisa and had enjoyed their shopping excursion, but riding with her was an experience Jacey wouldn't want to repeat. She closed her eyes as the car swooped around a sharp curve.

With a squeal of brakes and the unmistakable odor of burning rubber, the car suddenly shuddered to an abrupt halt. Thanking Detroit and Congress for seat belts, Jacey jerked forward, then slammed back against her seat. She braced herself for the sound of shredding metal. Instead she heard the bleating of sheep.

She couldn't believe what she saw. A sea of jostling, bleating, dirty white sheep filled the road.

"Sheep!" She heard Lisa explode. "They'll slow us down, and George won't ever babysit for me again." She pounded her fist against the steering wheel, then slowly let the car creep forward.

"Shouldn't we wait until they're out of the way?" Jacey protested mildly.

"That could take forever, and I promised George I'd be back by five." She continued to inch the car forward.

Feeling indignant on Lisa's behalf, she mentally berated George for his inconsideration. After all, shouldn't a man be happy to watch his own child without making his wife feel guilty for leaving her in his care?

Jacey kept watch out the window. The ugliest sheep she had ever seen completely surrounded the slow-moving car. They had recently been sheared and looked naked and skinny without their wooly coats. The lambs were cute, though, as they jumped and cavorted about with amazing energy. She wished Lisa would stop and wait for the sheep to pass instead of driving through them. She noticed several men and a young girl on horseback who appeared unconcerned by the presence of the car in the middle of their flock. A couple of small black and white dogs patrolled the sides of the road, keeping their charges in line.

Jacey heaved a sigh of relief when they finally emerged from amidst the sheep to face an open road once more. Lisa's foot immediately hit the gas pedal.

"Jacey, do you mind if we stop at my house first to see if Ashlie is awake? It's time for George to start on his chores, and he doesn't like to take the baby with him."

"No, I don't mind," Jacey lied as her heart sank. She really didn't want to see George in his own home. She didn't want to see him with Lisa and Ashlie either, a little voice whispered, which she immediately shushed.

Lisa followed a tree-lined lane which seemed faintly familiar. When Jacey caught a glimpse of a house through the trees, she swallowed a gasp of dismay. She knew this house, inside and out.

The central portion of the house revealed its Scandinavian

origins, being rectangular with the long side facing the driveway. The stucco had been scored to look like brick and rose two stories high, with four dormer windows overlooking the front of the house. A wide veranda stretched the length of the house, its pillars serving as supports for the balcony fronting the upper story. At either end, a one-story addition had been added to provide a pleasing blend of the old and the new. The extension on the right obviously housed a double garage. The house touched a special place in Jacey's heart, bringing a lump to her throat.

"I knew you'd like it."

She started at the soft, gravelly whisper in her ear, then shook her head to clear away the sound. This wasn't the time to imagine Uncle Charlie speaking to her. But why had he written to her in glowing detail about George's house? Had he wanted to impress her and thought she'd find his cabin lacking? He needn't have worried; she loved the cabin. Her only regret was that he wasn't there to share it with her.

The car stopped with a lurch as Lisa slammed on the brakes. "I'll just be a minute," she called as she gave her car door a shove. Jacey watched her race up the front steps and disappear inside the house.

Jacey was relieved that she wouldn't have to go inside where she might see George. She pulled a paperback out of her handbag to read while she waited. A light tap sounded on her window, and she swung around to face the very person she had hoped to avoid.

"Come on out," he invited. "Lisa's minutes stretch into hours. Since you're here, perhaps you'd like to see my place?"

Jacey glanced toward the house.

"Lisa is feeding the baby. It'll take her half an hour or more."

Reluctantly Jacey opened the car door. She was glad George was once again covered from neck to ankle in coveralls. She walked beside him around the side of the house to where a narrow gravel path led through a small grove of trees in the direction of the barns Jacey could see from her house. It was a good thing she had on low-heeled shoes. Her nose twitched as a pungent odor drifted her way. Before she could ask about the smell, George slipped a wire loop from around a fence post and led her through a gate into a huge open space. Jacey stood still. As far as she could see were birds. Gawky, white, ugly birds.

"What are they?" she gasped.

"Turkeys."

"No, Gus is a turkey. These are . . . are . . . " She stammered, at a loss for words. Glancing up at George's grinning face, she suspected he was playing some kind of joke at her expense.

"They're turkeys, all right. White turkeys. Old Gus is a bronze turkey. I raise nearly 40,000 turkeys each year. Sanpete County is one of the top ten turkey-producing counties in the United States," he added proudly. "People don't just eat turkey for Thanksgiving dinner anymore. With today's emphasis on low fat and watching cholesterol, health-conscious people are eating more turkey."

Jacey stared helplessly at the big man beside her. He was serious. Those birds were really turkeys—and that made George a turkey farmer. From somewhere deep inside, a smile made her mouth twitch, then laughter burst forth in howling peals. She laughed until tears streaked her face. When she saw George's grin change to a scowl, she tried to control her laughter.

"What's so funny?" His voice came out in a defensive growl.

"Nothing, really." She hiccupped as she tried to swallow the laughter threatening to erupt again. "Only, Uncle Charlie told me his closest neighbor was a big rancher who runs thousands of head of stock. I thought a ranch meant cattle, and that you owned a big cattle spread; I didn't realize he meant *you* are big, and your stock consists of thousands of—*turkeys*."

A sheepish grin lifted one corner of George's mouth, sending Jacey into peals of laughter again. Unconsciously she leaned her head against his arm. "I feel so silly. I've been worrying about a range war between your cattle and Kitsu's sheep."

Laughter rumbled from deep in George's chest. "Lee Kitsu raises turkeys, too. His sheep are a sideline, just like my Charolais cattle are for me. We both raise hay, too."

"Isn't it kind of strange that all of the animals around here are white? White cows! White sheep! And now, white turkeys!"

"Not quite all of the animals are white," George chuckled. "Kitsu's son, Jeremy, keeps a string of horses he hauls around to rodeos. They come in all colors. Then there are your animals. They're certainly different."

Her eyes met his laughter-filled ones. He moved closer and wrapped his arms around her. It felt so right to be in George's arms. He was a pretty exasperating man at times, but at least he didn't ignore her. Jacey stiffened. No, George didn't ignore her, but he should. Her face turned hot as she remembered that they were standing right out in the open where anyone could see them, including George's wife. A few short steps away in their home, Lisa sat feeding their baby. Jacey's muscles tensed, and she struggled to free herself.

George felt her struggle and wondered if he'd crushed her. She wasn't very big, and in his enthusiasm he may have hugged her tighter than he'd meant to. He opened his arms, and Jacey stepped away as though she'd been scalded. She wouldn't look him in the eye as she backed away. "I need to go home," she stammered.

"Did I hurt you?"

"No. I—I have to go home."

His chin jutted forward and his mouth tightened to a grim line as he watched Jacey back away. "I'll drive you," he told her brusquely. He'd lost his head for a minute there. Jacey had that effect on him. With all he knew about her, he was as big a fool as Charlie.

"No, I can walk or wait for Lisa." Misery shone in her eyes as she continued to back up.

"Nonsense, I'll drive you." Taking her arm, he propelled her rapidly toward his pickup truck. The sooner she got off his property the better. She couldn't have made it clearer that she considered herself too good for a turkey farmer. He'd thought their laughter was shared, but it wasn't. She'd been laughing *at* him. He'd learned long ago to ignore the jokes people invariably made about turkeys and turkey farmers, but Jacey aroused in him a painful sensitivity that left him emotionally raw.

Jacey felt sick as she leaned her head against the passenger door. She was falling in love with George, and she hated herself for it. She reminded herself that she had just broken up with one bossy man, and she didn't need another one. This one wasn't available, anyway.

George wasn't bossy the same way Roger was, a voice in the back of her head argued. Roger steam-rolled right over her and never noticed that she even had an opinion. George at least left her the option of disagreeing.

She'd come west with her head full of dreams and landed smack in the middle of trouble. George wasn't the cowboy of her dreams; he was a turkey farmer. And he was married. If she couldn't remember that, she'd better go back to Baltimore.

Chapter 6

Jacey moped around the house the next day, reading, sleeping, and getting over her cold. Her thoughts strayed frequently to her big neighbor. Thinking of those few occasions when she had been in his arms had the power to start her pulse beating faster and warmth to flush her skin. Repeatedly she reminded herself that he belonged to someone else, and that on less than a week's acquaintance she was utterly foolish to fancy that she might be falling in love. Besides, her future was too uncertain to become involved in a relationship that would only make things more difficult. That thought always brought a heavy ache to her heart.

On Sunday she decided her cold was gone and she no longer had an excuse for hanging around the house feeling sorry for herself. Today would be a good time to get in her car and explore the valley. But the telephone rang before she could act. She picked it up to hear a child's voice ask, "May we ride to church with you?"

"Church?"

"Mom said we had to find a ride because Dad went to an early meeting, and she and Sam are going to a missionary farewell in Moroni."

"We don't want to go to Moroni, so will you take us?" An almost identical voice joined the conversation from another extension.

"I don't know where you go to church." Jacey tried to prevaricate.

"We'll show you!"

"Thanks! We'll be at your house in a few minutes." Two clicks in her ear told Jacey both boys had hung up. She looked around the room in dismay. Church? She hadn't been to church in a long time. Her family didn't attend church, and they'd treated her earlier interest in religion as a childish whim that she would outgrow. She'd once loved attending church, but after Mother and Daddy returned from their trip they didn't have time to take her; then she'd become ill. Well, it might be nice to visit Uncle Charlie's ward. She'd been denied the opportunity to attend his funeral; perhaps going to church would be a way to say good-bye.

Dashing to the closet, she grabbed the first dress she came to. Darn, she should have remembered to buy more pantihose; and had Anne forgotten to pack her pink heels? The twins arrived long before she was ready. She dumped her jewelry box on the bed and let the boys search for her tiny gold hoop earrings while she french-braided her hair. Her keys decided to play hide-and-seek in the bottom of her handbag, and she felt flushed and only half put together as she ushered Joe and John into her car. She pulled the seat belt across them both, and wondered if that was legal.

Shyness struck Jacey fifteen minutes later when she peeked into the crowded chapel. She hesitated as the sound of a familiar hymn revived a flood of memories. The meeting had already begun. She considered turning around and quietly leaving, but two small hands clasped hers and tugged her into the chapel. Pulling her along like a reluctant trophy, they led her to a row of metal chairs set up at the back of the room.

It was a relief to sit down. Heads slowly turned back to the chorister, and Jacey began to relax. Then, two rows ahead, she saw him. She hadn't given a thought to running into George at church. Lisa sat beside him with Ashlie on her lap. The bright Sunday morning dimmed, and Jacey wished she hadn't come.

She tried to concentrate on the service. It brought back warm memories of the meetings she'd attended with Uncle Charlie, and she felt a longing to recapture the way going to church made her feel then. A young girl spoke first about the need for everyday honesty, and Jacey glanced uneasily at the back of George's head. He'd kissed her—and that didn't strike her as being honest with Lisa.

She listened to a returned missionary use Book of Mormon stories to illustrate his points. She didn't know much about the book, but it seemed to be full of heroic stories such as Uncle Charlie used to tell her. She'd seen a Book of Mormon in Uncle Charlie's bookcase. When she got home, perhaps she'd start reading it.

The words to the closing hymn were new to Jacey, but they touched her in a way she didn't understand. *Because I have been given much, I too must give.* She glanced up to see Ashlie's pale hair peeping over George's shoulder. Her eyes were closed and her little mouth trembled with each deep breath she took. A wave of sadness overtook Jacey. George might think a few kisses were unimportant, but he was wrong, and no matter how attractive she found the man, she'd stay away from him from now on. He had certainly been given much; he should take the words of the song to heart and give his family his whole heart in return.

"We have to go to Primary now," John whispered.

"Relief Society is that way." Joe pointed down the hall.

"But where will we meet after . . . ?"

"You don't have to wait for us."

"Dad will take us home."

Jacey watched two dark heads disappear in the crowd. Alone, she didn't know where to go or what to do. She saw Lisa smile and start toward her. She didn't want to talk to Lisa. She didn't want to see George.

Blindly she turned toward the chapel doors. She almost reached them before someone called her name. Startled, she stopped. Thank goodness it wasn't Lisa. The lady from the bank smiled and expressed her delight that Jacey had decided to come to church.

"We're always happy to have new people in our ward. My husband is ward membership clerk, and he'll need to send for your records. Come along and I'll introduce you right now." She took Jacey's arm and propelled her toward a small man in a brown suit. Jacey couldn't have described him if her life had depended on it. Her attention kept straying to the Lindquists, standing a few feet away and chatting with another young couple.

George glanced her way, and Jacey struggled to concentrate on the questions the clerk asked her. From the corner of her eye she saw George check his watch, shuffle a stack of books he held in one hand, glance down the hall, then after another glance in her direction, hurry away. Once he was out of sight, she bid the clerk a hasty farewell and dashed out the door.

She breathed a sigh of relief as she drove down the highway. She'd done the right thing, and she'd go on doing the right thing. If she carefully avoided George and Lisa, pretty soon she'd forget this silly fascination.

Just as she hit the first chuckhole leading to the cabin, she remembered. Tomorrow she'd be spending the whole day with them while the Kitsus moved their sheep. Did she dare refuse to go? If she stayed on Uncle Charlie's ranch, it would never do to be rude to her neighbors. How could she back out without appearing unfriendly to the Kitsus?

Back at the cabin, she donned her new jeans. A glance in the mirror convinced her that Lisa did know how to buy them. They fit like a TV commercial. None of her blouses seemed quite right for what she had in mind, so she slipped on one of Uncle Charlie's shirts still hanging on one side of the closet. Uncle Charlie hadn't been a big man, but his shirt was still much too large for Jacey. She solved the problem by knotting the long tails around her waist. A pair of soft leather calf-length boots and Uncle Charlie's hat completed her ensemble. The hat fit surprisingly well, but perhaps that was because Uncle Charlie had no hair and she had so much.

She stuffed her pockets with carrots, apple slices, and a handful of sugar cubes before leaving the house for the pasture. Over her shoulder hung Lady's halter and a lead rope. Clyde ambled over immediately to sniff her hand and help himself to the apple she offered him. Lady trotted toward her, stopping ten feet away to warily eye the extended hand. Slowly, one suspicious step after another, the mare moved toward the offered treat. Stopping a few feet away, she stretched her nose toward Jacey's hand; her reach fell short by several inches. She shook her long head, then reached again.

Jacey held her breath, waiting for the right moment to slip the bridle over the little mare's head. She was so close, just another inch would do it. Telling her muscles to get ready, she willed Lady to come closer. Unfortunately, Clyde chose that moment to rub his big head up and down Jacey's back, nudging her forward in an attempt to let her know he'd like seconds.

As Jacey tripped forward, Lady lunged backward, twirled about and with her tail flying high, tore madly across the field.

Disappointment welled up in Jacey's throat, but undaunted, she determined to try again. Turning to the big plow horse, she patted his nose and fed him an apple chunk. As she leaned her forehead against his lowered head, her eye caught the movement of the other horse as she made a wide circle, bringing her back toward her mistress.

Keeping her back to the approaching horse, once again Jacey nearly forgot to breathe as she waited to see how close Lady would come. She didn't have long to wait. On delicate legs, the mare minced toward her. Jacey felt Lady's breath blowing against the back of her neck and wondered if she dared turn around. Before she could move, her hat went flying from her head and the horse took off on another wild gallop. Once again the little palomino ran like the wind, and once again her curiosity drew her back.

After repeated attempts, Jacey finally coaxed the little mare to eat an apple from her hand, and even managed to pat her neck, but she couldn't get the halter near the shy creature. As a last resort, she released the lead rope from the halter and tossed it around Clyde's neck. The docile beast cheerfully followed Jacey up the hill and plodded slowly toward the barn. As she had hoped, the mare followed close behind. As both horses lowered their heads to the water trough, Jacey slipped behind them to close the corral gate. She'd done it! She hadn't succeeded in getting a halter on her horse, but at least she had brought her in from the field. A wave of jubilation swept through her, wiping out the fatigue of her long, dusty walk.

She rewarded each of the horses with sugar cubes, patted their noses, and crooned soft words of praise. They could stay in the corral overnight. It would be easier to catch the mare in the morning without so much space to run around in.

From a ridge on the other side of the fence, George watched Jacey patiently trying to catch her horse. He could make it easy for her, but he decided not to interfere. He still smarted from her brush-off two days ago. Grinning at the antics of the canny little mare, he applauded Jacey's unrelenting determination. Silently he congratulated her ingenuity in securing the horses in the corral, where the mare would be ready for tomorrow's ride. Of course, he could have wandered over and helped her; but he figured she ought to learn to handle the horse herself.

Pensively he watched as the trio disappeared over the hill. He had never before been so attracted to a woman as he was to Jacey. Her unusually husky voice had the power to send shivers along his spine each time she opened her mouth. It was becoming increasingly easy to forget she was the same spoiled, self-centered girl who had neglected Charlie Mathews over the years. He'd expected her to be brash and cocky, but instead he sensed a vulnerability that tore at his heart.

Right to the end, the old man had sworn that his Jacey would come; but she hadn't. He'd made excuses for her, said she would come as soon as she could. On Christmas Day, he'd found Charlie with his head buried in Lady's mane, his shoulders shaking with sobs. All he would say was that something terrible had happened. Not even when the old man lay dying in a lonely hospital bed did she come. She hadn't called or sent a card. She hadn't come for the funeral, either.

Could he have misunderstood Charlie? Had the "something terrible" been something that had happened to Jacey, rather than her failure to arrive? George's jaw clenched as he recalled how quickly she had appeared once he and Lee Kitsu both submitted bids to purchase the narrow strip of land which separated their two farms.

His anger switched to a different but equally strong emotion as he recalled his first glimpse of her, standing on the front seat of the red convertible, her hair glistening in the sun as she argued with a cow over a pair of panty hose. His heart softened as he saw her timid entry into the chapel that morning with the Kitsu boys. She'd looked lost and vulnerable.

One minute he wanted to teach her a lesson for her callous placement of pleasure over an old man's dream; the next minute he wanted to hold and comfort her. Regret filled his heart as he blamed himself for her cold. He shouldn't have dumped her in the creek. Until he met Jacey, he'd thought that kind of impulsive behavior was far behind him. He'd never stop feeling guilt each time he remembered her wet, bedraggled figure limping away from him with her back straight and blood trickling from her scrapes. If she were the spoiled socialite he'd thought her to be, that should have sent her screaming back to the city. Instead, she'd exhibited an inner strength of which she seemed totally unaware.

This morning he'd had a strong impression that she was afraid of him. It was his own fault. He'd been giving her mixed signals, and he couldn't blame her if she'd become as skittish as Lady. But he was becoming more and more uncertain as to what signal he did want to give her.

He wondered how much longer she would stay before heading back east. A stab of pain flitted through his chest as he thought of her leaving. What was the matter with him? He wanted her to leave. Of course he did.

"Tomorrow." He spoke out loud. "Tomorrow, I'll stay beside her as we move the sheep. I'll be friendly and get to know her better, ask some questions, then I'll be able to see if under that beautiful exterior is the cold-blooded little witch I despise—or an entirely different woman." Silently he added, *If that doesn't work, I'd better go jump in Salt Creek myself!*

"Alarm clocks are entirely unnecessary around here," Jacey grumbled as she awoke at five the next morning. She could hear the little bantam rooster crowing away as he did every morning at daybreak. Gus's bossy gobble joined in, and Jacey jumped out of bed.

She splashed water on her face and wished for a shower before attempting to untangle her hair. The big tub was great, but at times she longed for the fast efficiency of a shower. She spread lotion on her face and arms, then pulled on a pair of her new jeans, added a pale blue shirt of Uncle Charlie's and a darker blue bandanna around her throat, slipped into her boots, and jammed Uncle Charlie's hat on her head. When she finished dressing she stopped in the kitchen for a quick glass of orange juice, then hurried to the barn.

Gus greedily gobbled his food and Jacey hurried back to the house. Halfway across the yard, George's battered pickup truck stopped beside her.

"Hi!" he called cheerfully as he unfolded his long legs and

stepped out of the truck.

A streak of lightning zigzagged its way up her spine as she looked all the way up from the pointed toes of brown riding boots, along an amazing length of pale blue denim clinging lovingly to long, long legs and well-muscled thighs, past slim hips, to a huge expanse of solid chest covered by a thin cotton shirt. Her eyes bravely continued their upward climb to a face which looked devilishly handsome beneath a pale gray Stetson.

"Oh, my!" she whispered. All she could think of were the words to an old Dolly Parton song, "Why'd you have to come in here looking like that?" It was going to be a long day. The resolve she had made while lying awake last night to be friendly, but aloof, with George would be awfully hard to stick to, even with Lisa riding beside him.

"Speaking of Lisa, where is she?" Surprised to hear herself ask the question out loud, she just hoped that was all she had said out loud.

"Lisa isn't coming," George responded with a grin. "She decided to stay home with Ashlie."

"Oh," Jacey's face brightened for just a second, then she felt her heart plunge to the bottom of her boots. Grasping for something to say, she quickly asked, "Would you like some breakfast? I haven't eaten yet."

"No, I've had breakfast, but you go ahead. I'll get your saddle out while you eat."

"All right."

Jacey gulped down a bowl of cold cereal while waiting for the toaster. She leaned over the sink to wolf down a couple of slices of toast dripping with honey. When she finished she tossed her pill in her mouth and swallowed it with the last of her orange juice. Spying the brown pharmaceutical jar of "Happy Pills", she poured a generous amount in her hand and dropped them into her shirt pocket. She had a strong hunch she'd need happy pills before this day ended. A pearl snap closed the pocket and Jacey ran for the bathroom to brush her teeth and add a light coat of lipstick to her mouth.

George hesitated before walking into the house. Jacey had left the door standing open, she must have meant for him to come inside. He stepped through the doorway just in time to see her shake a pill into her hand, then pop it into her mouth as though she had done it a thousand times before. He froze when he saw her reach for a larger bottle. From it, she dumped a whole handful of brightly colored pills into her pocket. A frown creased his forehead as he saw the row of brown drug containers on the cupboard shelf. Beside them was a small zippered leather case and behind that he could make out a box of sugar cubes and a couple of candles.

George's hands turned sweaty. He remembered Lisa saying something about their new neighbor and drugs. What had Lisa said? That when she first met Jacey she seemed flushed and jumpy and there were pill bottles all over the floor. All the way to Manti, Jacey had been almost in a trance; but later she'd seemed perfectly all right, and they'd had a good time shopping together. Here was something else he'd have to find out about.

"I'm ready." Jacey re-entered the room.

George's heart skipped a beat as he looked at the pretty young woman stepping into the room. A clip anchored beneath her hat caught back her bright hair. She wore new jeans that fit just right topped by a blue shirt and matching bandanna. A faint frost of lipstick made her lips look damp and her eyes held a sparkle of anticipation.

Who was this girl? His mind demanded some answers. What kind of woman could ruthlessly cut off an old man who loved her, then show up to claim his estate, pop drugs like candy, and still make him think she was as innocent as Ashlie?

"Ready to try your hand at putting a saddle on Lady?" he asked aloud. The words came out more brusque than he had intended. He clenched his fists at his sides. He had to get some answers. Before this day ended, he intended to know once and for all whether Jacey was the best actress and liar he'd ever met in his life, or the sweet young woman he wanted to get to know a whole lot better. He felt himself drawn to Jacey more each day, but he wouldn't make the same mistake Lisa had. He wouldn't let himself get involved with someone who put money and pleasure ahead of responsibility.

"Just a minute." She hurried to the open cupboard door and

grabbed a handful of sugar cubes. "I gave some sugar to Lady yesterday; she seemed to like it. Maybe I can coax her to come to me with some today."

"You won't need that." George's voice sounded a little strained to Jacey's ears. "Sugar isn't really good for horses."

Jacey tucked the sugar cubes into her pocket anyway as she followed George out the door. At the barn, he scooped up a few oats in a bucket, handed it to Jacey, and together they approached the corral. She couldn't hide her amazement when the little horse ran immediately toward her, pausing only briefly before plunging her nose into the bucket. She wished she'd known about oats yesterday.

George handed Lady's bridle to Jacey, and without any fuss the little horse let Jacey slip the bit between her teeth and buckle the strap.

Glowing with pride over her accomplishment, she turned a heart-stopping smile George's way where he perched on the top pole of the corral. His mouth went dry, but he managed to wave one hand toward the saddle straddling the fence beside him. One smile nearly did him in. That didn't bode well for the rest of the day.

Jacey reached out one hand to stroke the beautifully detailed leather. Tears came to her eyes. She remembered the gray-haired lady reading from one of Uncle Charlie's letters about a special saddle he was making for her. She remembered his invitation for her to come West to collect her saddle as soon as she could "shake that bunch of medicos holding you captive." The saddle was a loving reminder that Uncle Charlie had cared.

George hadn't expected her emotional reaction to the saddle. He remembered the long painstaking months, as fall turned to winter, that the old man had spent working an intricate design into the leather, and how depressed he had seemed when the saddle sat unclaimed under his Christmas tree. Bitterly he remembered the morning two months later when the paramedics were carrying him from the house; his last words were to beg George to make certain Jacey got her saddle. Well, she had her saddle now, and by darn, she could put it on her horse herself.

"Swing it over her back and buckle the cinch underneath." He waved his hand toward Lady.

Lifting the saddle and swinging it onto the horse's back turned out to be harder than it sounded. With Lady tied to a fence post, Jacey boosted the saddle as high as she could reach and twisted toward the mare. Lady side-stepped. She hefted it again. The saddle weighed more than Jacey had expected, and she had trouble lifting it as high as Lady's back. After a dozen failed attempts to saddle up, she leaned dizzily against a post, breathing heavily.

"Need some help?"

"No!" She didn't know what made her refuse his offer. She didn't know what to do next, but one thing was for sure, she didn't want George to do it for her. She was through sitting back and letting other people make life easy for her. The saddle and the horse were gifts from Uncle Charlie, part of the dream they'd shared. She had to do this herself.

Watching the two horses nose at the empty oat bucket, she suddenly had an idea. She returned the saddle to the fence, then picked up the bucket and placed it far enough outside the corral that Lady would have to stretch her neck through the poles to reach it. She dropped several sugar cubes into the bucket, then scrambled to the top of the corral fence. She didn't care what George thought about using sugar cubes! As soon as the mare reached for the bucket, Jacey dropped the saddle onto her back, then jumped down to fasten the cinch.

As she turned to smile triumphantly at George, he didn't know whether to congratulate her or prick her bubble. He could show her the horse was trained to kneel on command. Even a child could saddle Lady in two minutes flat. She seemed so proud of her accomplishment he put off saying anything. She was like a kid, so darn happy about every little thing she learned to do.

"What's the matter with me?" he chided himself as he went about checking to be sure she'd cinched the saddle properly. He'd never before in his life sat by and allowed a woman to struggle so physically hard. And it had been difficult. He hadn't missed the perspiration running down the sides of her face or the way she'd stumbled toward the fence. She'd probably kill him when she discovered how easy the whole operation could have been. Yet he couldn't shake the feeling she'd fought some great battle there in the corral, and had he done the chivalrous thing, she would have lost the war.

The clatter of hooves had both of their heads turning to watch three horses approach the corral. Jeremy, seated on a sturdy brown mustang, tossed the reins of a big buckskin to George. His teeth flashed in a proud smile as he turned to the rider on the other horse.

"This is my wife, Nga." He introduced the tiny raven haired beauty sitting astride a sleek black horse. Her long hair swirled, thick and straight, to within an inch of the horse's back. Instead of jeans she wore a heavy, split riding skirt with a beaded, long-sleeved shirt. Leather gloves protected her hands. From her child size boots to her Aussie rolled-brim hat, she was a picture of elegance.

"Hi!" she smiled shyly at Jacey.

Jacey returned the greeting with a smile. Not waiting to see if George would help her mount, she hastily used the fence as a mounting block. George checked her stirrup length before mounting his own horse. Soon all four were cantering up the hill behind the cabin.

"Dad and the boys will meet us with the sheep where we plan to open the fence," Jeremy shouted over the drumming of hooves.

As they approached the fence the two men rode ahead, and Jacey watched them release the wire from a pole and fold it back like a gate.

"I'm not sure what to do when the sheep come through," Jacey admitted to Nga as they caught sight of the slowly approaching sheep.

"Jeremy say not to worry. I too not know what we do. He say stick with him. Everything okay." She smiled her confidence in her young husband's instructions.

Jacey and Nga talked briefly while they waited and Jacey discovered the other woman loved horses as much as she did. The young Asian was new to the West too, and, like Jacey, had already fallen in love with the mountains, the sparkling clear air, and the tiny Sanpete County towns.

The men rejoined them just as the sheep began pushing their way through the opening in the fence. An older version of John and Joe rode up and introduced himself as Lee Kitsu. Jacey discovered there were three more Kitsu boys, two teenagers and a third who was away on a mission. The teenagers, with the twins, waved from the far side of the sheep. Lee explained that without dogs to help them, they would have to spread out to surround the herd or they'd stray.

"You two ride ahead to open the gate," Lee called to George and Jacey as he wheeled his horse and rode after a ewe headed the wrong way.

Jacey volunteered to stay and let one of the others go, but Jeremy overruled her by leaning over to hug his bride and announce he could only handle one greenhorn at a time. Nga blushed and pushed him away.

Jacey could feel George watching her as they circled widely to avoid startling the sheep. She couldn't read his expression, but sensed that he struggled as deeply as she to understand their strange attraction. She wished she could avoid looking at him, or at least stop fantasizing about those big arms holding her securely as they rode off into the sunset. Drat! She was doing it again. She had always been a dreamer, but at least her dreams had always been pretty harmless before. *There is nothing harmless in dreaming about a married man,* she reminded herself severely.

Attempting to change the direction of her thoughts, she asked George why Nga had a noticeable accent, while she couldn't detect any trace of an accent in the voices of any of the other Kitsu family members.

"The Kitsu family has an interesting history," George began. Neither Lee nor Jeremy would mind if he shared the story with Jacey, and it might encourage her to talk with him. She'd been behaving like a skittish colt all morning and he didn't want to start right in demanding some answers until she relaxed and appeared a little more receptive.

"The first Kitsu arrived in San Francisco ten years before my ancestors left Sweden," George began. "Being Japanese, instead of Chinese, he wasn't welcome in China Town. He took up with a Polynesian girl some sailor had abandoned, and together they headed for the goldfields. Eventually, they made their way to Salt Lake where they joined the Mormon Church."

George steered Jacey around a clump of brush then picked up

his story. "Their only son went to Hawaii on a mission for the Church. There he met a Japanese girl and brought her back to Utah. Lee's grandparents were both fourth-generation Americans, but they spent World War II in a detention camp, while Lee's father served in Army intelligence. When the war ended, he brought home a Japanese war bride and they settled here in Sanpete County to raise Lee and his sister. Lee met his wife, Miki, at Brigham Young University. Her family has been in America almost as long as Lee's family."

Jacey listened intently to George tell the Kitsu family story. Gradually she relaxed. The sun warming her skin felt good, and she enjoyed riding Lady. She encouraged George to continue talking. "Is Nga from Japan?"

"No, Nga isn't Japanese. She was born in Vietnam, but her family left there after the war. After years in a refugee camp her family settled in eastern Canada. While vacationing in western Canada she met Jeremy when some friends took her to the Calgary Stampede. She and her parents are converts to the Church and she has a really strong testimony. Their shared commitment to the gospel is helping them both adjust to their cultural differences."

George spurred his horse ahead and Jacey watched him open a gate for the sheep to pass through. She envied Nga being so much in love with Jeremy she'd left her family and country to be with him. She looked tiny and shy, but she knew what she wanted and had the courage to take it. Jacey admired that. George turned around and smiled, and Jacey thought her heart would break. She'd never have the chance to discover whether her feelings for George might grow that strong. And she was being foolish to think about it. She could change the kind of person she was, but she couldn't change the fact that she had nothing to offer a man like George. She should be thankful he was married and nothing could come of her infatuation.

After the sheep passed through the gate, Jacey managed to put a little distance between herself and George as she followed along one side of the herd. The sheep didn't seem to be in any hurry. They stopped frequently to snatch bites of grass or drink from the tiny stream. Occasionally one would wander away and others would begin to follow until a rider would haze them back toward the herd. Once when George suddenly appeared beside her, she asked, "I thought a group of sheep was called a flock, and a group of horses or cattle was a herd, so why do you always refer to the sheep as a herd?"

"I don't know." He scratched his head and grinned. "It might have to do with the way we take care of sheep. In some places shepherds lead sheep; here sheep herders herd sheep."

"Do you have any animals besides your turkeys and cattle?" Jacey gave vent to her curiosity.

"Not right now. My sister and I both had horses when we were kids, but Grandpa sold them after we grew up. He had a couple of milk cows, a pig or two, and some chickens, but after I took over I didn't want to bother with them. How about you? Do you have a pet back home?" If he could turn the conversation back to her, he might learn answers to some of the puzzling questions he had about Jacey Mathews.

"Mother never allowed animals in the house. She said they carried too many germs, but when I was twelve I spent the summer at my grandparents summer home in Maine and Uncle Charlie rented a pony for me to ride."

Ahead a couple of sheep turned off the path. "I'll get them," Jacey called. Her cheeks flushed and her eyes sparkled as she urged her horse to cut off the strays. George swallowed his disappointment. She'd barely started to talk about her former life, but it was a start. He'd watch for another opportunity.

Jacey had plenty of time to look around and absorb the lazy warmth of a June mountain morning as the sheep and riders made their way up the canyon until it opened into a small green valley. Here the riders fell back, letting the sheep drift and graze. Joe and John jumped down from their horses to give a personal farewell to a couple of bum lambs they'd bottlefed earlier in the year. Jacey climbed stiffly from the saddle to join them.

"May I touch it?" she asked Joe of a lamb he was hugging.

"Sure. See how soft he is." He patted the springy wool.

Crouching by the lambs, she patted one and soon found the other one begging for attention too. She laughed at the sheer joy of the capering little lambs.

"If they don't have mothers, aren't they kind of young to leave by themselves?" she asked the boys.

"Naw, they eat grass now, so they're better off with the other sheep. Mom says if they stay around the house any longer, she'll turn them into Sunday dinner." Seeing Jacey's shocked expression, the twins giggled before assuring her their mother wasn't really serious about the threat. Jacey joined their laughter and felt more alive than she had for years; in fact, she hadn't enjoyed herself so much since that summer with Uncle Charlie. A cloud darkened her day. This would end just as that summer had. Anne could only keep her secret for a short time. Daddy and Roger would discover her whereabouts any day and when they did, one of them would come get her. She'd have to go back some day; she'd always known that. There were tests she'd have to undergo at the clinic in September. She only hoped there would be time enough to learn to take charge of the part of her life left to her by the cancer.

George stood a few feet away, one arm resting on his saddle horn. His eyes followed Jacey as she cuddled the lambs and laughed with the two little boys. This woman just didn't add up to the same picture as the one he had gleaned over the years of Jacey Mathews. Had his own feelings for Charlie Mathews colored his reaction to the old man's precious niece?

He had only been ten and Lisa eight when their parents were killed in an automobile accident. Their grandparents took them in, but George had been constantly at odds with his grandfather. The stubborn old man lived by rigid principles, which he expected his grandson to observe. The summer George turned fifteen a neighbor decided to leave the valley and shocked George's grandfather by selling most of his farm to Lee Kitsu, and the remaining thirty acres and his little cabin and outbuildings to Charles Mathews.

To say grandfather disapproved of Charlie was an understatement. He didn't like his new neighbor's flashy clothes, his 'toy car', or the way he seemed to collect strays, including a gangly, awkward, half-grown boy with rebellious ideas. He considered Charles a bad influence on George. George, however, had immediately loved the old man who always had time for him, never criticized, but who encouraged him to dream big dreams. Charlie talked about Jacey constantly, and George had been jealous of his friend's adoration of the little girl.

At first George had been secretly glad the girl never came to visit, but as he grew older he ached for the old man who continued to plan for her big visit, which never happened.

George's heart turned over as he watched Jacey touch the tip of her nose to the lamb's little face. It didn't add up. She stood, brushed off her jeans, then patted John's shoulder before returning to her horse. She seemed to genuinely care about people and animals, and she didn't act spoiled and hard as he'd expected. Just the opposite. There was an air of wonder about her. She gave the impression she was seeing the world for the first time, or at least after a long separation. He couldn't see any reason for her to pretend to be anyone other than who she was, so why hadn't she ever come?

Jacey's backside ached and she dreaded the ride back. She wished she could stay all day in this beautiful, peaceful little valley. Hearing the jangle of bridles, she looked up to see the Kitsu family leading their horses and walking toward her. She wondered if Nga might be sore too, but her graceful movements didn't betray any stiffness.

"How are you doing?" Concern laced Lee's voice. "This is kind of a long ride for someone who isn't accustomed to riding."

"I'll be all right, but I'll admit I'm looking forward to a long soak in a hot tub." She laughed ruefully as she clumsily attempted to mount her horse again.

"You go ahead," George spoke to Lee and his sons. She hadn't heard him come up behind her. He placed one big hand on her shoulder and continued to speak to the others. "Jacey ought to walk the stiffness out a bit before she gets back in the saddle. I'll walk with her for awhile."

Jacey didn't want to be alone with George. She already felt too conscious of him standing close beside her. It was downright dangerous. No matter how many times she reminded herself he wasn't the man of her dreams, she continued to be drawn to him like she'd never been to any other man. Certainly not to Roger.

Before she could remount or think of an excuse to keep Joe and John with her, the whole family rode away, leaving her alone with George. Awkwardly she began walking. She didn't want the

Kitsus to get too far ahead.

The first few steps were the worst. Her legs didn't seem to want to cooperate at all. George broke the silence.

"This isn't much like what you're used to. Do you miss the city?"

"Not really. Sometimes I miss some things, like ordering pizza, mother's garden, and a big library, but I love Charlie's ranch. I'd like to stay here forever."

George wondered if she spoke the truth. Would she really be happy and was she seriously considering staying? "Don't you miss the social life you're accustomed to? There's not much night life in the Sanpete valley."

"Nightlife doesn't interest me much."

"What does interest you?"

"I like to read and I enjoy quiet dinners." She patted Lady's neck. "And I like animals, especially riding Lady."

George stopped in the middle of the trail. He reached out a hand to halt Jacey. "Why didn't you come see your uncle when he was ill?"

Her hand toyed with the scarf at her throat and she gazed past him as though seeing something else. "I didn't know he was ill." Moisture added an extra shine to her eyes.

"But he wrote to you almost every day until he became too weak to write."

"He never told me."

"What about the messages I sent you?"

Her eyes widened and she appeared hurt and confused. "I didn't get any messages." He sensed she was telling him the truth. But if no one told her, why not? Not knowing had hurt her.

"I'm all right now. We could ride again." She didn't want to continue the conversation. Her problem with her family was something she had to work out herself.

"Are you sure?" George looked down at her with a look she could easily interpret as tenderness; that tore at Jacey's heart. Gently he reached for her hand. She knew she should pull her hand free, but she didn't. For several minutes they stood quietly with her small hand resting in his big one.

George lifted Jacey's hand. He could see where small blisters had formed at the base of two of her fingers. He brought the hand to his mouth and brushed his lips over the tender injuries. Her eyes mirrored shock and she tugged to free her hands, but he didn't release her. Instead his arms closed around her and he pulled her closer.

For just a second, she felt the delicious warmth of leaning against his solid chest, knew the thrill of watching his mouth descend toward hers. Then, just as her traitorous mouth moved to meet his, she remembered. Lisa! She jerked away, taking several stumbling steps backward.

"No! Don't touch me!" Panic swept through her and she dodged behind Lady. She'd been weak and pliable too long. Her weakness hadn't hurt anyone but herself until now, but if she let George kiss her then she would be hurting Lisa and Ashlie. George would be hurt too, in the long run. She couldn't do this. If she succumbed to weakness now, then all her fight for independence would be for nothing. She'd never recover from so deep a loss of self-esteem.

Her emphatic denial shocked him. Her eyes stared back at him with fear and revulsion. Had he been so wrong? He'd been so sure she felt the same attraction he did. His stomach ached as though he'd been kicked; her rejection hurt incredibly. It was worse than when she'd walked away from him while he was showing her his turkeys. He felt something strong for Jacey, but she didn't return his feelings.

"Jacey, what is the matter? I never meant to offend you."

Hurt and confusion shimmered in her stormy gray eyes. He swallowed over the lump in his throat. He watched her struggle to keep tears from falling. He hadn't meant to rush her or frighten her. That stupid stunt he'd pulled dropping her into the creek had upset her more than he'd realized. He longed to talk out their differences and get to know each other better. Too many of his questions were still unanswered. He didn't think she'd heard his apology. He'd apologize again as soon as he thought she'd listen to him. She opened her mouth, but no words came out, only an undecipherable whisper.

"Help! George, help!" A scream cut between them.

He whirled about to see Joey Kitsu riding frantically toward them. With one hand he grabbed the child's horse's bridle and the animal skidded to a halt.

"John fell, and I can't reach him," Joe sobbed.

"Where's your dad? Jeremy?"

"They went on ahead, but we wanted to play. Dad said we could until you caught up to us."

"Is John hurt?" The boy solemnly nodded his head.

George reached for Jacey. He boosted her onto her horse, then vaulted into his own saddle. He started them moving while still questioning Joe. "Where is he?"

"The big rocks by the spring." George picked up the pace. He glanced back once at Jacey and she motioned him to go ahead.

"Don't wait for me," she called.

Jacey lagged behind, fearing she might fall and delay John's rescue if she pushed Lady to keep up. She arrived at the spring in time to see George climbing down a boulder-strewn path with Johnny cradled in one big arm. She slid from Lady's back and hurried toward them. Johnny smiled weakly at her when she reached George's side, though his chin quivered. His clothes and skin were dirty, and tears had left shiny streaks down his cheeks.

"He's bleeding pretty heavily," George stated in a calm, matter-of-fact tone. "See if you can find something to make a pressure bandage."

Jacey's eyes flew to where George's hand tightly gripped the child's slender arm. Blood oozed between his fingers, and she could see where it had dripped on the boy's pants and smeared his shirt. She fumbled with the knot at her throat. When it yielded, she handed the bandanna to George. Deftly he fastened the cotton scarf around the cut, then stood with Johnny in his arms.

"Do you think you could hold him while I remount, then hand him up to me?"

"I think so." Jacey looked up at him and held out her arms.

As he transferred his burden to her waiting arms, she saw George's eyes widen. His skin seemed to pale, and his hands convulsed around Johnny's small body. His eyes were focused a few inches below her face.

"Jacey!" Only one whispered word escaped his grimly set mouth.

Jacey's heart plummeted. George's eyes were filled with all the horror she'd expected and more. Others had reacted the same way when they'd seen the raw keloidal scar stretched across her throat, but George's revulsion hurt more.

Chapter 7

"Give him to me." Jacey moved to take Johnny.

George slowly released his grip on the boy and Jacey settled him in her arms. Her face revealed no emotion as she nudged George to action. "He needs a doctor, and he's too heavy for me to hold for long."

With grim determination George vaulted into his saddle. He reached down to take Johnny from her. He avoided looking at Jacey as he tucked the child securely in front of him.

"I can ride by myself," John protested. "I don't need two hands to ride a horse."

"Sh-h, you ride with George this time. Joe can lead your horse." Jacey attempted to soothe him. She reached for his uninjured arm, closing her hand around his smaller one. "Here, these will help to cheer you up on the way back." She filled his hand with brightly colored pills, then dropped more into Joe's pocket.

"What—?" George reached for John's hand before it could reach the boy's mouth.

"Want some?" Johnny opened his hand. Candy! Brightly colored M & M's. He felt a flush creep up his neck. He should have guessed, but he'd assumed the worst. But why on earth did Jacey keep candy in a prescription bottle? He glanced down at her and decided his questions could wait. Her face looked grim and frozen, and he suspected she knew what he had thought. Right now he had to focus on getting Johnny to a doctor.

"Right after we turn the twins over to their parents, you and I are going to have a long talk," he promised. His heels touched the horse's flank and the gelding responded with long ground-eating strides.

His promise sounded like a threat to Jacey. She blocked it out of her mind for the moment and noted how Joe got back on his horse, then followed his example, using a large rock for a mounting block.

They rode single file until they reached the gate. She glanced at the makeshift bandage at frequent intervals and felt relief that no blood seeped through. She struggled to open the gate and close it with just Joe's help. After George rode through it with the injured child, Jacey helped Joe get back on his horse and instructed him to hurry ahead to her house to call his parents.

She couldn't climb back in the saddle by herself. Barbed wire ruled out standing on the fence, and she couldn't see anything else she could climb. She'd have to walk to the cabin, leading both of the riderless horses. Her arms and shoulders ached, and each stiff step felt like it would surely be her last. She could feel blisters on her heels; her boots weren't meant for hiking.

Hard as she tried, she could not wipe from her mind the look of horror on George's face when he saw her scar. She knew in detail the way that ugly red ridge slashed across her throat. Dr. Bellows had promised her a pencil-thin white line that would eventually fade almost away, but that was before the complications occurred which had torn open stitches and stretched the unhealed incision. Radiation had done its part to damage her chances of successful plastic surgery for a time, too. How she hated the thought of George finding her ugly!

From the top of the hill she watched the flurry of activity as George surrendered Johnny to his father and the Kitsus' station wagon left a trail of dust as it departed back up the lane. Johnny no longer faced any really serious danger she knew, but still she felt sorrow for the pain the child would suffer having the arm stitched, and she suspected it would be difficult for him to curb his high spirits while the cut healed. She shuddered remembering the fuss her mother had made and the long tedious hours of boredom she'd endured as a child with rheumatic fever. She wondered how long he would have to be kept quiet and she wondered too, if Joe would stay home with his brother. She'd miss them. Tomorrow she'd see if she could find a bookstore and stock up on adventure stories and games for him.

She saw George remount and start back toward her. Suddenly she felt like sitting down and bawling. She couldn't face him now; she was much too tired. He would ask questions and demand answers she didn't want to give. If her scar was disgustingly repugnant to him now, she could imagine how he would react to hearing the rest of her story. Cancer scared people. She'd been hurt by people who reacted to the word as though she were a carrier of some communicable disease, and she'd been relegated to the status of a non-person by those who pitied her. She didn't want George to avoid her or pity her.

Bitterly, she reminded herself she had prayed for help to avoid getting involved with a married man, and this would surely do it. She didn't have to tell him anything; he didn't have any claim on her secrets. He had no right to expect her to tell him anything she didn't want to. Besides, she absolutely would not tolerate his pity. The past few weeks were too precious to end that way. Never before had anyone treated her so badly, demanded so much from her, or expected her to be so fully self-sufficient. He didn't baby her or treat her like an invalid. He made her angry, but he never ignored her. Not once had he pulled his punches, softened his words, or acted as if he thought her too dumb to understand what he had to say. He took her seriously and treated her like an equal. Even when he got bossy, he didn't assume she'd follow his orders. He made her feel alive and like life was worth living, like she was a participant in the adventure of life. Once he knew the whole story, he'd be kind like Roger and her family, but the magic would end. She squared her shoulders and lifted her chin. Whether she liked it or not, it had to end.

Reining in beside her, George dismounted from his horse. Something in Jacey's bearing told him she wouldn't let him pick her up and carry her to the house, though that was precisely what he wanted to do. He noticed immediately that she had buttoned her shirt all the way to the collar button and turned up the collar. He had a pretty good idea what it cost her each time she lifted one foot to place it in front of the other. Instead of attempting to carry her or set her back on her horse, he dropped his arm about her waist to give her as much support as possible. He suspected fatigue to be the only reason she didn't shake off the support he offered.

When they reached the corral, he pushed her gently toward the house. "I'll take care of the horses. You go crawl in that big red tub, but don't stay too long. In about twenty minutes I'll be through with the horses, then I'm coming in. If you're still in the tub, I'll haul you out by your hair. You and I have some talking to do."

When he entered the house a short time later, silence greeted him. He feared she really had fallen asleep in the tub. Cautiously he opened her bedroom door to find her sitting on the edge of the bed wrapped in her green robe. Her long hair lay in wet tangles about her drooping shoulders. He picked up a towel she had dropped on the floor and moved toward her. She didn't speak, so he sat down beside her and began to rub dry her wild curls. When he finished, he wrapped one arm around her and with one hand on her cheek, pulled her head back against his chest. His chin dropped to the top of her head. He sat holding her until shadows began to spread across the bedroom floor.

Finally George asked, "Can you tell me about it, Jacey?"

Silently she shook her head. After another long silence, George sighed. They needed to talk, but Jacey couldn't handle it right now. "All right, honey. You're exhausted. Let me fix you some lunch, then you can sleep. We'll talk later."

"Go away, George." It was the hardest thing she had ever had to say. "I don't want you to fix me any lunch. Go home to Lisa."

A note of finality rang in her voice. It wasn't only fatigue making her want to be alone. He sensed she was sending him away forever, and his heart ached. He couldn't force her to talk to him, not when he could see her exhaustion. His feet moved slowly as he walked across the room. He didn't think he could bear to never see her again. Something terrible had happened to her, and through his stubborn refusal to look beyond past prejudices, he'd hurt her and made her hate him. He wanted to strike out, fight for the right to stay beside her, but who or what could he fight?

The little rooster woke her at the usual time. She didn't even remember crawling beneath the quilt last night. A glance at her bedside clock radio confirmed she had been asleep for nearly fourteen hours. She felt tempted to snuggle back under the quilt and sleep another fourteen hours. A rumbling in her stomach reminded her she hadn't eaten since yesterday's hasty breakfast, and a tentative attempt to move convinced her she was every bit as stiff and sore as she had suspected she would be. With a groan she turned over and struggled to a sitting position. From there she hobbled to the bathroom.

It was bliss to sink into a tub of steaming bubbles. She leaned back and closed her eyes. Half an hour later she reached for a towel. She would have stayed longer, but the water was no longer hot, and both she and the animals needed to eat.

Toast and juice would have to do until the animals were fed, she decided. The walk to the barn seemed to be twice as far as usual. She left Gus until last. After dumping his feed in his dish, she leaned against the wire enclosure, her fingers weaving through the fine mesh. "Oh, Gus, what am I going to do?" She had drifted into holding long conversations with the bad-tempered bird each morning as she fed him. As usual she got no sympathy, just an aggressive gobble. He cocked his head to one side, fanned his tail, and strutted to let her know how far beneath him her petty troubles were.

"Maybe you're right," she giggled as the turkey made its pompous way around the small enclosure. "I probably should stick my nose in the air and ignore him; it really isn't any of his business." Sobering, she added sadly, "Besides, if he discovers how I feel about him, he'll have one more reason to feel sorry for me. I can't have his love, and I won't have his pity!"

Jacey made her halting way back to the barn to return the feed can. The unmistakable sound of a vehicle approaching reached her ears. She stared in dismay at the oncoming cloud of dust. "Please don't let it be George," she prayed. She couldn't face him yet.

She wasn't any happier when she realized the truck pulling into her yard belonged to the Walkers, and the lone occupant was Todd. Warily she watched him swagger toward her, a sheaf of papers in his hand.

"Good morning, gorgeous," he drawled as his eyes boldly checked the fit of her tight jeans. "Dad sent me over with the papers for you to look over. He said he can meet with you and your attorney to sign them any day, any time, but he'd like it to be soon."

"I'm not reading or signing any papers," her husky voice rasped from between gritted teeth. She kept her hands firmly clamped on the feed can and refused to accept the papers.

"Let's not be difficult." He edged closer. "Maybe you've been away from your fancy lawyer too long and could use a little sweetening up." He stepped toward her and she backed up, which only made him laugh.

"Go away!" She tried to shout, but her words ended on a squeak. Todd took another step, and she raised the feed can in a threatening gesture. Before she could swing it toward him, he captured her wrist and jerked her toward him. The can flew from her fingers. She struck out with her free hand and he captured it too.

"Now what are you going to do?" He grinned and leered at her mockingly.

Fear rose in her throat, but she wouldn't give up. She tried to remember everything she'd read or heard about self-defense. When she was unable to raise her knee high enough to do any damage, she kicked his shin.

"Ow! So you want to play rough." His face turned dark with anger. She kicked him again.

"Why you—!" He released her hands as abruptly as though he'd been burned, and she stumbled backward, lost her balance, and sat down abruptly in the dirt. She brushed her hair from her eyes and glanced fearfully toward Todd. He wasn't looking at her, but slowly backed away. Suddenly he began to run, with forty-plus pounds of ferocious turkey nipping at his heels.

"Get him, Gus," she yelled, and her unwanted visitor ran faster. Todd reached his truck and slammed the door in Gus's face. "And don't come back!" she added.

The big turkey, with his neck extended in gobbling fury, disappeared in the thick dust as the truck tore up the lane. Jacey began to laugh. She hoped Todd got the message. He wasn't welcome on her ranch, and she wasn't selling.

Jacey walked back to the porch and turned to watch for Gus's return. Seeing movement from the side of the porch, she turned her head. There stood Johnny and Joey. Their eyes were wide and for once, they appeared speechless, but not for long.

"Wow!" they chorused. "He really is as good as a watch dog."

"Did you see how fast that man ran away?" Johnny giggled.

"Nobody better mess with me and my turkey," Jacey hammed for the boys. They giggled, and Jacey joined their laughter.

"Are you all right, John?" Jacey eyed the prominent white bandage on the boy's arm. "Does your mother know you're here?"

"Sure, it's no big deal." He dismissed his injury with a shrug. It was obviously yesterday's news, and he was more interested in Gus at the moment.

"Mom said if we didn't get out of the house, she'd throw something at us," Joey added, and both boys smirked. Jacey suspected that Mrs. Kitsu had more than her share of aggravation living in a houseful of overly energetic, teasing males. George had told her Miki Kitsu was an artist, but Jacey wondered how much painting she found time to do.

Gus came dragging up the lane. His tail feathers drooped in the dust, but he didn't seem to have lost any of his dignity. When he reached a particularly dusty patch of dirt beside the porch, he lowered his bulk to the ground, ruffled his feathers as though taking a bath, fanned the dirt into a flurry of dust, then tucked his beak beneath his wing and drowsed in the early summer sun.

"Did you let him out?" Jacey turned suspiciously to the boys.

"No." They crossed their hearts and claimed scout's honor. "He got out by himself."

Jacey wondered if she might have knocked the wooden latch to his pen loose herself when she stood by his cage earlier. However he got free, she decided she was too grateful to worry about penning him up again. She invited the twins in for juice and ended up feeding them pancakes and eggs, which they washed down with the last of her milk supply. While she washed and put away the dishes, she could hear them laughing and whispering. Then suddenly they announced they had to go home, but would be back later. She watched nervously as they left the house at a run, but relaxed when Gus didn't so much as lift his head as they ran past.

Eyeing the dust where the big bird dozed, she realized the dust would get worse as summer wore on. Remembering the tools and garden hose in the shed, she decided to go to town for some seed. Planting flowers might cheer her up; besides, she needed to get more milk.

Gus opened one beady eye as she tiptoed past, but didn't move. She bumped slowly down the lane in the red convertible, raising as little dust as possible. She was beginning to feel more comfortable driving, though she didn't yet feel completely at ease.

She bought several flats of flowers and, feeling adventurous, decided to buy a few packets of vegetable seeds as well. The woman in the grocery store advised her on which varieties were best, how she should fertilize them, how often to water, and invited her to Relief Society homemaking night for a gardening seminar. Jacey loaded her purchases into her car and started back toward the ranch.

From a quarter mile away, Jacey could see that a large sign had been attached to Uncle Charlie's arch at the road end of her driveway. As she got closer, she could read large red letters proclaiming DANGER. Now what? Was she being threatened? She stopped the car in front of the sign to read the rest of the message.

DANGER

Proceed at your own risk!

These premises patrolled by Attack Turkey!

"Well, that explains all the whispering," Jacey laughed, remembering the Kitsu boys' enthusiasm for the way Gus had helped rout her earlier unwelcome visitor.

When she reached the house, she found Jeremy and Nga waiting for her.

"Hi!" Jeremy strolled toward her. "We thought we'd better come check on you. The twins came running home a little while ago and said Gus had chased away a man who hurt you."

"He didn't really hurt me. The Walkers want to buy my ranch, but I don't want to sell. Todd brought over some papers, and when I refused to accept them he got pushy. I kicked him, and Gus chased him to his truck."

Jeremy and Nga laughed.

"Lock your doors at night," Jeremy warned her, in case he's as vindictive as he is arrogant. I can be here in five minutes or less if you need me, so memorize my telephone number."

"I don't think I'll need any more help than Gus."

"He won't be any use to you if you keep him caged."

"I've decided not to lock him up anymore." She must have looked worried, because Jeremy assured her he had known Gus since the day Charlie had acquired him, and that the bird only attacked strangers.

"Gus won't hurt you. He's smart enough to know who feeds him."

Nga insisted that she and Jeremy stay to help her plant petunias and marigolds around the porch. Jeremy suggested that Jacey leave Gus's dust hole alone, because the independent old bird would scratch out anything she might plant there anyway.

While returning the tools to the shed, Jeremy asked if she planned to stay permanently, or if it was only the Walkers whose offer she had decided to reject.

"I really don't know," she admitted. "I have to return to Maryland by the first of September; but whether I'll come back or not, I can't be certain."

"I hope you'll stay. We'd love to have you for a neighbor."

"I thought your father wanted to buy my ranch."

"Well, yes. Actually, I want to buy it," Jeremy admitted. "Right now I'm gone almost six months of the year. I go where the rodeo circuit takes me, and we live in a camper on the back of my truck while we travel. But we'd like a home of our own to come back to, and a place where I can raise rodeo stock later on. Your place is ideal because Dad could keep an eye on it while we're away, and graze his sheep on it until I have enough stock of my own. If you do decide to sell, I hope you'll give me a chance to buy it."

"I'll keep that in mind; but right now, I don't know what I'm going to do."

The sun was going down when George knocked on her door. She'd watched him park his pickup near the barn and knew she faced the toughest challenge of the day. When she didn't answer right away, he knocked again. She wished she could ignore him and he'd go away, but she knew he wouldn't. She'd faced Todd Walker and come to terms with Gus; now she'd find the strength to send George away, too. Reluctantly she opened the door.

"Hi!" He had on clean jeans and a denim shirt open at the throat. He'd combed his hair carefully and he wore a hesitant smile. "May I come in?" he asked when she failed to invite him in.

"Uh, no. I—I'm too tired for visitors tonight." She closed her eyes to the disappointment in his.

"I won't stay long," he promised. "But Jacey, we need to talk. There are things . . . "

"I can't, George. Please leave me alone." She struggled to keep her face impassive until George's massive shoulders slumped and he turned and walked slowly to his truck. She closed the door, then stood with her back to it and let the tears run down her cheeks as she listened to the growl of the truck engine roaring to life, then heard its sound receding down the lane.

He called several times over the next few days, but she kept the conversation brief and declined to see him. She spent her days working in her garden or sitting at her computer. One day Johnny discovered a batch of kittens in the barn, and she played with them as much as their mama would allow. She began taking long walks to visit the horses each day. Some days she saw deer at the far end of the pasture, but the shy creatures ran whenever they saw her coming. Frequently Gus tagged along behind her; she talked and he gobbled, their animosity forgotten.

As she stood stroking Lady's nose one day, the twins joined her.

"Are you going to ride her today?" Johnny asked.

"I can't," she answered. "It would take me all day just to catch and saddle her."

They looked at her in disbelief.

"She's easy to catch," Joey scoffed.

"Look!" John snapped his fingers twice and pointed to the mare's front legs. Lady slowly sank to her knees, head bowed. Both boys wrapped their fingers in her mane and leaped on her back. Their laughter rang in the still summer air as the horse regained her feet. "You just have to coax her to come close, the rest is easy."

"Does George know about this little trick?" she asked

suspiciously.

"Of course. Everybody does."

Jacey's mouth dropped open. Anger made her want to scream, and most of all, kick a certain turkey farmer. She had never been so angry in all her life. When George showed up at her door that night, she slammed the door in his face without saying a word. When he tried to call, she hung up on him without ceremony.

After that, she rode Lady every day. Twice George cut through the pasture to speak with her; both times she nudged the little horse into a gallop and ran away from him. And both times she returned to the house to cry. After that, he stopped trying to contact her. She got over being angry, but it seemed to be taking forever to get over her broken heart. She missed him, and staying away from him was getting harder, not easier.

More and more, she began to wonder if she should go back to Baltimore and put a whole continent between them. But she wasn't ready to go back. She liked running her own house, and she found satisfaction in caring for her animals. She felt herself becoming stronger; but enough insecurity still lingered to make her fear that she'd slide back into her old passive ways if she returned to her family.

July came in dry and hot with a haze that shimmered across the valley. The mountains that had appeared green when she first arrived in the valley now looked dusty and gray. Grain in the fields drooped heavy heads, and the air clacked with the sound of hay balers. A new calf arrived in the field, but even on Lady's back Jacey could never get any closer to the cattle than to the deer.

One day it was too hot to work in her garden, so she wandered inside for a cool drink, picked up a magazine, then put it back down. Impulsively she decided to call Anne.

Her sister seemed rushed and reluctant to talk. She brushed off Jacey's suggestion that perhaps she should return to Baltimore. She reminded Jacey to make an appointment with the Salt Lake doctor Dr. Bellows had recommended. Then she hung up. Jacey worried her lip and wondered if she should call Anne back and tell her about George. She felt reluctant to talk to anyone, even her sister, about her strange relationship with her big neighbor. Anne would know what she should do, but she didn't want Anne to know. Anne would never be stupid enough to fall in love with another woman's man. Maybe love was too strong a word; but whatever she felt, Anne would never have gotten herself into such a mess.

Reluctantly, Jacey picked up the phone again. She wouldn't call Anne, but she heeded her sister's warning to call Salt Lake and arrange to see the doctor in two weeks. After that, she stared morosely out the window to where she could see George's cows resting in the shade of a rocky outcropping. Her eyes blurred as she longed for just a glimpse of the man.

She jumped as a loud knock thundered against her door. Had her thoughts somehow conjured George into making a sudden appearance? Reluctantly, she opened the door.

She had been so certain of seeing George when she opened the door that it took just a moment for her mind to shift gears. It was Lisa—and there was no mistaking the fury spitting from the beautiful blonde's eyes as she glared at Jacey.

"May I come in?" Her voice was glacial.

"Uh, sure. I mean, come in." Jacey stepped back. Other than brief glimpses at church, she hadn't seen Lisa since their impromptu shopping trip. Avoiding George had meant avoiding Lisa, too.

Jacey swallowed uneasily as she anticipated what Lisa's sudden angry visit might mean. Her thoughts turned defensive. She hadn't encouraged George; in fact, she'd done everything possible to stay away from him.

"Sit down, please." She indicated the sofa. "Would you like something cold to drink?"

"No, I wouldn't. I didn't come here to socialize," Lisa snarled as she continued to stand.

Jacey took an involuntary step backward. "Lisa, I—we didn't . . . "

"You self-centered, spoiled brat!" Lisa cut her off. "You're nothing but a greedy, selfish, spoiled-rotten tease. George admired Charles Mathews more than anyone else he knew. Grandpa worked George awfully hard, but every minute he could get away from the farm George spent with Charles, and he never complained because Charles talked constantly about you. All your uncle's plans and dreams were for you. Year after year he made plans for your big visit. But you never came, did you?"

"I couldn't, but I wanted to." Jacey felt confused. What did Uncle Charlie have to do with this, anyway? Perhaps Lisa was angry because she hadn't sold her ranch to George; or possibly she felt that Uncle Charlie should have left it to him instead of her.

"Sure you did." Sarcasm dripped from Lisa's lips. "But you always had more important things to do—like attend your fancy school, fly off to Switzerland, take a cruise to the Bahamas, and attend charity balls."

"I did those things, but—"

"And while you did all those important things, guess who was here for Charles? That's right, George. Charles' last thought was for you; he even charged George with making certain you got that fancy saddle. He told George there was a unique gift waiting for him too, but there wasn't. Charles left everything to you. You couldn't be bothered with him while he was alive, but you didn't waste any time claiming everything he owned the minute he died!"

Jacey's head was spinning. "It wasn't like that," she whispered, her voice sounding raw and scratchy, but Lisa went right on.

"George admits he was hard on you when you first arrived, but even you should be able to see he had good reason. People seem to assume that just because George is big, he must somehow be stupid. Well, he isn't. He graduated with honors from Utah State University, and he's published several articles in agricultural and poultry production journals. People like you don't give him credit for having brains or feelings." Lisa was practically crying. Her voice trembled as she paced back and forth.

"People either fear him because he's so big, or they try to take advantage of him. He's been hurt more than once. That kind of attention has made him shy and uncomfortable around women, and Grandpa's continual deprecation of his worth has been difficult for him to overcome."

"Lisa, don't cry." Jacey wanted desperately to comfort the other woman, even though Lisa's tirade made no sense at all to her.

"In spite of his reservations about you, George has tried to help you. He's even willing to buy this farm, which he doesn't need or want, so you can have your money immediately." She rummaged in her pocket for a tissue. "What he didn't plan was falling in love with you!"

"No, Lisa. He doesn't . . . I don't . . . "

"Yes, he does. He's a kind man, and he never meant to be hurtful. He's always been here for me, but you won't even give him a chance. I can't bear to see him suffering." Her voice caught as she headed for the door. Pausing with one hand on the doorknob, she turned back to Jacey. Her voice was quieter. "No one can force someone to fall in love. Either it happens or it doesn't. But if you don't give yourself a chance to really know George, you'll never know what a truly wonderful person my brother really is." She didn't slam the door, but she did leave.

Jacey stood as though glued to the floor. Numbly, her brain repeated over and over, *Brother? Did she say George was her brother?* Why hadn't she guessed? She'd instinctively trusted him right from the first, and had known that Uncle Charlie and his neighbors respected him; so why had she failed to see his behavior toward her as contradictory to the kind of man she knew him to be?

Because she was a coward. Jacey's knees buckled and she groped for the closest chair. She sank in a heap beside it. She'd set out to become strong and independent. She'd wanted to claim the part of herself that hadn't been taken over by cancer; but she couldn't divide herself into two parts, a cancer part and a part that was just like everyone else. She'd taken pride in learning to run her own household. Confronting Todd Walker, overcoming her fear of Gus, riding Lady, improving her driving skills, evading her father—all had seemed like important milestones. But she'd failed the biggest test. As long as she'd kept herself convinced that George was unattainable, she hadn't had to face the real reason she couldn't have him; she could push the reality of her cancer into the background and pretend she was like every other woman. Love demanded honesty, and she wasn't ready to admit that cancer was the real dictator in her life. Love was a commitment to shared tomorrows, and she didn't know if she even had a tomorrow.

Chapter 8

Holding her makeup mirror in one hand, Jacey twisted sideways. She still couldn't see well. If only she had a full-length mirror like the one in her room back home. She had driven to Manti by herself to buy these clothes, and now she couldn't see whether she looked all right in them.

"Men!" She included dear Uncle Charlie in her exasperation. "Why do they only care what their faces look like? If a mirror is big enough so they can see to shave and comb their hair, they just assume the rest looks great!" Again she twisted and peeked, but still couldn't see how her jeans, her new high-heeled western boots, and the blue denim shirt with pearl snaps looked together. The green silk scarf fluttering at her throat lent a saucy touch—or maybe it looked dumb. Hunching her shoulders, she stared critically at her jacket. She had selected the warm golden-brown suede to match her new hat and boots, but now she wondered if a jacket in July might be too much. She'd never been to a rodeo before, and she wanted everything to be just right.

As she wandered into the main room of her cabin, she shrugged out of the jacket and placed it carefully on the arm of the rocking chair. The room looked vastly different from the one which had greeted her two months ago. She didn't know much about decorating—Mother had never allowed her to decorate even her own bedroom—but she'd had a desire to make the cabin her own since the first day she'd walked through the door.

A large area rug now covered the floor. Southwestern Indian pots sat to one side of the fireplace, and a bristly potted cactus graced the opposite corner. A cool mountain scene had replaced the stag head above the fireplace, and fluffy pillows covered the sofa. A pewter cowboy rode a wild mustang on the mantel. A soft glow of light shone on smooth sand-colored lamp bases sitting on the two end tables she'd sanded and polished to a fine sheen. The room pleased her. She'd retained Uncle Charlie's western tone while blending it with her own softer taste.

With one hand she brushed back the curtains she had recently added to the room and gazed anxiously down the driveway. Would he be there? She tried to ignore the question uppermost in her mind, but thoughts of George were impossible to escape. She had mixed feelings about seeing him again. Every time she drove to town or walked to the pasture she held her breath, wanting to see him, aching to be with him, and fearing she might. What would she say to him? Could they be friends? Deep inside she suspected that being friends would never be enough; but allowing more would be cruel to both of them.

Jacey's heart had been in a swirl of confusion since the day George rescued her car from the mud. While fighting the pull of attraction developing between them, she'd cataloged his faults. He was rude and overbearing, unpredictable, and bossy. He'd laughed at her when she fell in the mud, and no doubt he'd laughed all the times he'd seen her try to saddle Lady. But on the other hand, he did get her car out of the mud, he'd saved her twice from Gus, and he'd fed her animals until she got there, then taught her to do it herself. He'd been concerned when she caught cold; he'd rescued Johnny; and he'd made her feel alive. One minute she'd fumed and called him a bully; the next she felt touched by his kindness and ached for just a glimpse of him.

It would be better not to see him again, not to let her feelings for him grow. Even if, by some miracle, George really did care about her, could she face telling him the truth? Her hard-won strength was new and fragile. She doubted it could withstand seeing his feelings for her turn to pity. George might not want anything more to do with her, anyway; she'd been unforgivably rude and judgmental.

But if he did offer her a second chance, would she take it? There could be no more hiding behind her own cowardice. It would be unfair to let him care for her without telling him of the limitations cancer placed on her life. That left her with two choices; tell him the truth, or stay out of his life. She paced the room restlessly.

The truck had traveled halfway up the lane before Jacey, absorbed in her thoughts, became aware of its approach. When the sound of its engine caught her attention, she gathered her jacket in one hand and hurried to the porch in time to see her new friend beckon to her from the cab.

"I glad you come." Nga squeezed her fingers as Jacey slid onto the seat beside her.

"Hi!" Nga's young brother-in-law, Samuel Heber, smiled from behind the steering wheel.

"Sam drive. I not so good drive mountain road," Nga explained. "Others go station wagon."

Jacey laughed, "I'm not very good at mountain roads either, and I'm glad you invited me to go to the Ute Stampede with you. I've always wanted to go to a real rodeo."

The mountain pass between the Sanpete valley and the little town of Nephi didn't seem nearly as scary with Sam at the wheel. The teenager didn't drive recklessly, but he wasn't intimidated by the narrow curving road as she had been. Jacey laughed and chatted with Nga and Sam, and in less than an hour they were in Nephi. Sam found a parking place as close to Main Street as possible so they wouldn't have far to walk to watch the parade that preceded the rodeo. He pulled the truck into an empty space in the parking lot of a little grocery store. They would watch the parade from lawn chairs in the back of the truck.

Both women jumped at a sudden pounding on the side of the truck, then joined in the laughter as the rest of the Kitsu family joined them. Lee and Miki placed their chairs on the sidewalk, while the boys lowered the tailgate to sit with legs dangling. John and Joe climbed to the top of the cab for a better view, but scampered down when Miki threatened no ice cream during the parade if they didn't get down immediately.

Jacey's heart caught in her throat when she saw a big man in a gray hat across the street. When he turned and she saw a full beard and a sagging stomach, she painfully swallowed her disappointment. It had been like that ever since Lisa's visit. Everywhere she went, she thought she saw George, then she would be disappointed. Neither he nor Lisa had been to church last Sunday, though she had watched carefully for him. She'd even gone so far as to ask Johnny and Joey a few questions about their neighbors— just to be sure that she hadn't misunderstood Lisa. George really was Lisa's brother, not her husband. Drat! Why couldn't she stop thinking about him?

"It's coming! It's coming!" Children all up and down the long street made the announcement to anyone who cared to know.

It was a grand parade with flags and soldiers, floats, dozens of beauty queens and rodeo queens from all the surrounding towns, marching bands, the governor, antique cars, and best of all, horses. There were children's riding clubs, the sheriff's posse, ladies in shimmering veils on Arabians, Spanish dons stiff-backed in their silver saddles, and blushing señoritas riding sidesaddle with their full skirts spread across their horses' backs. There were Clydesdales and Percherons pulling heavy wagons, and ponies trotting before little carts. Indians in traditional buckskin rode painted ponies bareback. There were buggies and Conestogas, too. But best of all were the cowboys and a few cowgirls, who would be riding in the rodeo later. Jacey stood and cheered with the Kitsu family when Jeremy doffed his hat in their direction.

Miki produced a cooler of frozen treats and soft drinks to keep them cool. When the parade ended, Jacey discovered there would be a barbecue supper before the rodeo.

"I ate too much ice cream. I can't eat another bite," she told her friends.

"Ice cream doesn't last," John told her.

"As soon as you smell the barbecue, you'll be hungry again," Joe added confidently.

"They're right, you'll see." Miki laughed and began shepherding her family down the street, where a huge crowd was gathering on a church lawn.

While they stood in line waiting to fill their plates with barbecue sandwiches and potato salad, Jacey found herself anxiously scanning the faces in the crowd for one particular face. A frisson of warning told her he was near, but when she looked around and met only the faces of friendly strangers, she chided herself for being fanciful.

She felt a gentle pressure on her hand as Nga whispered, "Not worry. He be here." Jacey felt herself redden. She felt embarrassed that her friend found her so transparent, and made a special effort to concentrate on her friends and her first outdoor barbecue.

After eating, she excused herself to go inside the church to the ladies room. As she made her way through the crowd to return to the Kitsu family, someone grasped her arm. She jumped in surprise and instinctively attempted to free herself. The hand on her arm tightened, and she turned to see Calvin Walker.

"Evening, Miss Mathews." He tipped his hat a fraction in her direction. "Todd tells me you refused to accept the papers I sent over for you to look at. I've offered a fair price, and I won't go higher. It's time to stop kidding yourself and get down to business. I don't have time to play games. Construction is scheduled to begin August first, and I want the paperwork out of the way."

"Just a minute," Jacey sputtered, so angry she could hardly grasp what he was saying. "I told you—"

"No, you wait just a minute," Walker went on. "My attorney and I will be at your place Monday morning at nine sharp. You see that your lawyer is there, too!"

"I will not!" Jacey's husky voice rose. From deep inside she found the strength to fight for what was hers. "If you or that demented son of yours sets one foot on my property, I'll call the sheriff!"

Walker turned back, a glint of dark anger in his eyes. Jacey stepped back as though she would retreat to the shelter of the church behind her. What had gotten into her to shout at the man?

"Look, lady," Walker's voice was ominous. "Maybe that eastern lawyer you're engaged to doesn't care if you seduce my son or sleep with every turkey farmer in the county, but nothing you do changes the contract he drew up. You and I are signing that paper Monday."

"What are you saying?" Jacey's anger was white-hot. "I didn't seduce Todd. The idiot attacked me, and my turkey chased him away. The Kitsu boys saw what happened. And no matter what you think or say, I own that property, and I'm not selling it to you!"

"I think you'd better leave." George's deep voice cut between them, cold as ice. "Miss Mathews obviously wants nothing to do with you. And you might mention to Todd that if he bothers the lady again, he'll have more than a turkey and two little boys taking him apart."

Jacey stood watching Calvin Walker's angry stride as he disappeared into the crowd. Her knuckles were white where she gripped her hands into fists. She had an uneasy feeling she'd missed something important in that tense exchange. In a daze, she let George led her to one of the nearby picnic tables. She felt a moment's disappointment that he'd arrived when he did. Though unaccustomed to confrontation, she'd been holding her own. For the first time in her life, she'd stood up to someone trying to tell her what to do. But doubt suddenly assailed her. She might not have been doing as well as she thought. George might have guessed that she'd lose the argument and stepped in to protect his own interest in the property.

She glanced toward him, but couldn't fathom the expression on his face. Was it anger or something else? She wondered how much he'd actually heard. Until his intervention, she hadn't been aware of his presence, and his current stiff posture was a little frightening.

"Why didn't you tell me about Todd?" he asked abruptly. Did he think she really had enticed Walker's son?

She outlined the episode as succinctly as possible. "He came to the ranch once, uninvited. When I refused to read some papers he brought, he grabbed me. Either I left Gus's cage unlocked or Johnny and Joey turned him loose. Gus chased him off the place. There was no reason to tell you. The whole thing was over in five minutes, and he hasn't been back."

"You still should have told me," he added belligerently.

"It didn't concern you!" George's anger made her feel defensive. Why did he always seem to assume the worst about her?

For several minutes neither one spoke. She'd been foolish to hope George might really care a little bit about her. Finally Jacey stood up. "I guess I'd better get back to Nga," she said while trying to edge around the big man.

"You weren't hurt?" His voice sounded concerned.

"No, just scared."

"Jacey . . . " He stopped. An irresistible little seed of hope made her pause. "Would you . . . "

"George!" A pretty chestnut-haired woman slipped her arm through his. "There you are. Lisa said she thought you'd come this way."

Jacey didn't wait to hear George's response before hurrying away. After all her agony over Lisa, and the relief she felt on learning he wasn't married, how could she have been so foolish as to overlook the probability that he had a girlfriend? She'd been naive to think he hadn't given up on her by now. She felt tears prick the backs of her eyelids.

Get a grip on yourself, she ordered under her breath. She would not turn into a watering pot. Seeing her friends, she took a deep breath and hurried toward them. She forced a cheerful smile and nodded her head in agreement when the twins urged her to visit the carnival with them until time for the rodeo to begin. Miki's quick, grateful smile told her the twins' mother appreciated her help in keeping an eye on the pair. Lee and Nga said they wanted to find Jeremy and wish him luck. Before Sam and Spencer disappeared, Lee instructed them all to meet him at the north ticket gate in an hour.

John and Joe wanted to ride everything. Jacey couldn't believe they could ride the ferris wheel and the hammer without becoming ill, considering the amount of barbecue and ice cream the two had consumed. Watching them helped to take her mind off the distressing earlier events, but not completely. She jumped each time someone brushed her arm, and she found herself scanning the crowd with longing and trepidation for a glimpse of George.

Jeremy had reserved seats for them in the covered portion of the stadium. The Kitsu boys politely stepped back, allowing Jacey and Nga to enter first, followed by Miki and Lee. Jacey led the way, walking carefully along the long plank seating to the number painted on the board which matched her ticket number. As she glanced down at the number, she saw a large hand holding a gray Stetson resting on the space. She closed her eyes briefly. Did she dare look?

Slowly she moved her eyes past the hand, up a long, muscular arm, past bulging biceps, to a shoulder she would know anywhere. His hair gleamed golden in the fading sunlight, and the surprised expression in his eyes told her he was as stunned as she. He recovered first, picking up his hat from where it sat on the bench beside him and idly twirling it between his fingers.

"Hello, Jacey." His hesitant smile encouraged her.

"Hi!" She managed to greet him without stammering. Her eyes moved involuntarily to the seat on the other side of him. She hated to admit it, but she was glad to see the space next to him occupied by a rangy, sunburned gentleman well past sixty. Realizing that everyone else was seated, she hastily sat down too, then felt as though she were drowning. He was so close she could smell his aftershave and feel his arm brush hers.

Suspecting she had been set up, she turned accusingly to Nga, who shrugged her shoulders nonchalantly while still managing to look like a bashful doll.

"Jeremy say stubborn Swede, shy lady need all help can get."

Jacey felt the mortifying red creep up her face, but a glance in George's direction convinced her she wasn't alone. He was red to the roots of his hair! They looked at each other; a small smile twitched George's lip and a giggle escaped Jacey's mouth. Suddenly George roared with laughter, and Jacey leaned weakly against his side as tears of laughter streamed down her face.

The night took on a magical quality as the crowd stood to salute the American flag, carried into the arena by the rodeo queen riding a flashy quarter horse, flanked by her princesses carrying state flags and rodeo banners. An emotional lump lodged in Jacey's throat as the crowd stood to listen to the national anthem. When the first bronco rider burst from the chute, she clutched George's hand. She hadn't expected to feel every buck and jolt along with the cowboy. She had no idea eight seconds could last so long.

Jeremy was the fourth rider out on a stringy buckskin bent on sunfishing his rider clean out of the arena. He bucked and twisted, landed straight-legged with a bone-shattering jolt, plunged forward, then reared backward. Jacey screamed as the crowd surged to their feet. When the buzzer sounded, Jeremy still clung with one hand to the horse's bucking strap while his other arm flew in the air. His teeth gleamed as he flashed the crowd an exultant grin.

Jacey didn't think the pickup riders would ever get to him, but of course they did. He picked up his hat from where it had dropped to the arena floor, slapped it against his leg, then casually strolled toward the fence while the crowd roared its approval.

"How can you stand it?" Jacey turned to Nga. "He could be thrown or trampled. I had no idea it would be so rough!"

"Jeremy very good rider. Best cowboy! Long time I shut eyes. Not now. Maybe hurt some day. Many cowboy hurt. Jeremy all time want to be cowboy. He train. He happy. I happy too."

Jacey shuddered. "You're awfully brave. I don't think I could live with someone who had such a dangerous job. What if something should happen to him?"

"Jeremy rodeo man. He happy ride bad horse. I happy be with Jeremy. He do something else, he not so happy. He not so happy, I not so happy. Better be happy little time, than sad long time."

The philosophy sounded good, but Jacey couldn't buy it. Jeremy's choice involved more than a safe, unexciting career versus excitement ending in death. What if brief happiness was followed by years and years of pain and suffering? Would Nga feel bitter and cheated if Jeremy spent forty years in a wheelchair? Could Jeremy bear seeing Nga take on the responsibility for his daily care and watch her grow old in a shadowy land where she was neither wife nor widow?

Suddenly, Jacey saw too many correlations between Jeremy's career and her own illness. She didn't want to think about that. Not tonight. For a few hours she'd subscribe to Nga's philosophy and enjoy herself.

George explained to Jacey how points were awarded for a good ride. Just staying aboard for the requisite time limit meant points; but how hard the horse bucked, and whether the rider kept one hand in the air counted, too.

She liked some events better than others. Sympathy for the

calves during the calf-roping elicited a chuckle from George, and she greatly admired the barrel racers. She laughed as Jeremy and his partner attempted to milk a longhorn cow. She was impressed with his roping skill, but thought him crazy to try to wrestle a young steer to the ground. She breathed a sigh of relief when Nga and George informed her that Jeremy didn't ride bulls. As a little girl she had loved clowns, and the ones at the rodeo were outrageously funny. But it didn't take two bulls before she understood that here they served a purpose far more serious than entertainment. They were masters of speed and intelligence as they distracted the heavy beasts away from riders who had been catapulted into the dust. They made it possible for the pickup riders to reach a cowboy when his ride ended, and they helped to chase the bulls back into their holding pens.

Before the rodeo ended, the night air turned chilly and George helped Jacey put on her jacket. He placed his arm around her, holding her close to his body. A breeze sprang up, chilling the air further, and she burrowed into George's side. He wrapped his arm more tightly around her and pulled her closer. Later she would pay for this happiness. There would be no childish avoidance of the truth from now on.

When the rodeo ended, George asked if he could take her home. She nodded acceptance, and he let the Kitsu family know. The long talk with Jacey he'd planned weeks ago could not be put off any longer. He didn't know why she'd avoided him so long, but something had changed and he intended to take advantage of that change. As they slowly made their way through the crowd, they spoke of inconsequential things. They laughed quickly and easily, and they held hands.

On one level, George was aware of the twins pleading to be allowed to ride the carnival rides again; Sam and Spencer leaning against the arena rail talking to a couple of girls who had competed in the barrel race; Lee telling Nga to stay with Miki and the boys while he helped Jeremy take care of his horses. He responded to greetings from friends and acquaintances. But on a deeper, more intense level he was aware only of the woman walking beside him, of his arm holding her close, of the tang of lemon and flowers and something intangible that was part and essence of Jacey alone.

On the ride home, he scarcely thought of the winding mountain rode. In fact, he found it difficult to think of anything but the woman seated beside him. It felt so right to sit close together, speaking quietly of the rodeo and laughing about their friends' effort to get them together. Sometimes they were quiet, and the silence felt right, too. Although he had questions, he didn't mention the ugly scene earlier with Calvin Walker, and Jacey didn't bring it up, either. They were almost to the dirt lane leading to her cabin when he finally said softly, "There are things we need to talk about."

He dimly made out the movement of her head as she nodded in agreement. "I know."

The porch light lent illumination to the interior of the vehicle as George halted his truck. Turning to her, he placed his hands on either side of her face to angle it so he could see her eyes.

"I know I've been hard on you since you came. Throwing you in Salt Creek was a stupid thing to do. Saying I'm sorry is terribly inadequate, but I am sorry. Will you let me make it up to you?"

"Oh, George, I got over that a long time ago." Trying to smile and not burst into tears, she added, "Finding out that Lady is a snap to saddle, and you knew it when you watched me struggle to saddle her that first time, was a lot harder to get over."

"Yes, well . . . I'm sorry about that, too." He squirmed uncomfortably and remained quiet for several moments. "I started out with some preconceived notions about you, but as I got to know you better, I knew I was wrong. These past weeks, when you wouldn't speak to me, have been pretty difficult."

"They've been hard for me, too," Jacey admitted. "I wanted to see you, but I was afraid."

"Afraid I would hurt you, or because there's someone else?" He heard the hesitation in his own voice, but he hadn't missed Walker's reference to a fiance back east. He had to know.

"No," she answered the second question first. "There's no one else. I was engaged to a junior partner in my father's law office, but I broke it off before I came out here. He's been a good friend all of my life, but I don't love him, at least not the way I should if I were to marry him. Right now I'm terribly angry with him for negotiating to sell my property when he has no right." She paused, then continued haltingly. "I'm not afraid of you, at least not the way you think. Actually, I'm embarrassed now to tell you."

"Embarrassed?" Why should she be embarrassed? Slowly he stiffened. "Because a turkey farmer doesn't measure up to a fancy lawyer?"

"No! No, that doesn't matter." She hesitated, and he held his breath, still suspicious. "You see, I thought you were married. I thought Lisa was your wife."

George's head jerked back. He stared at her, wondering if he'd heard her right. "You thought I was married?"

"You have the same last name; you live in the same house; Lisa has a baby; and no one explained your relationship to me. Everyone speaks of you as a couple—George and Lisa this, the Lindquists that." Her voice rose as she attempted to defend her assumption.

"Do you really think I'm the kind of man who would kiss another woman if I had a wife and child at home?" Anger roiled to the surface. How could she have misjudged him so badly? Disappointment in her lack of faith in him gripped his heart. Fidelity and trust were important to him—even more so since Lisa's husband had betrayed her.

"I'm sorry, but it hasn't been very pleasant for me, either. I've hated myself for wan . . . ah . . . feeling attracted to you. I've always believed myself to be the kind of woman who would never look at another woman's husband, yet I let you kiss me and hold me. I was so ashamed of myself, I thought the only thing I could do was stay away from you."

"Why didn't you come right out and ask me if I was married?"

"Because I'm a coward. There are things about me I didn't want you to know, and as long as you were someone else's husband I had an excuse not to tell you." Her fingers toyed with the scarf at her throat, telling him the scar it hid was connected to those things she didn't want to speak of.

He admired her honesty even as he struggled to bring his own pain into perspective. He'd misjudged her, too; he was sure of that. Whatever her reason for not visiting Charlie, it hadn't been because she was shallow and selfish.

"Oh, Jacey. I want to get to know you and have you know me. There have been too many misunderstandings between us. I hope you'll soon trust me enough to tell me what is still troubling you." He kissed the corner of her mouth. He meant to keep it light, but the moment his lips encountered even that little bit of her sweetness, he longed for more. She turned her head slightly, almost an invitation, and his mouth met her faintly parted lips fully.

Suddenly an ear-shattering horn blast broke the still night air.

Jacey jerked away and George grinned sheepishly. "It's all right, honey." He attempted to sooth her startled wariness away. "I'm too big for romance in a parked car. I accidently bumped the horn."

Smouldering blue eyes stared uncomprehendingly for just a moment, then she began to giggle. "I think that's my signal to go in."

"I won't ask to be invited in." He smoothed her hair away from her face, then his fingers settled on the scarf at her throat. He'd have to put off a little longer finding the answers to the rest of his questions. "Right now my brain isn't even functioning. All I can do is feel and want. If I were to go in with you tonight, we wouldn't talk, and we've put off talking too long."

Neither one made a move to open the door. They sat quietly, each absorbed in thought, until George shifted to place his arm around Jacey's shoulders. "Jacey, will you spend the day with me tomorrow? We could leave right after I finish morning chores. I'd like to take you to a place I know in the mountains. We'll have all day to ourselves."

"All right," she whispered. "I'll fix a lunch."

Their footsteps lingered as he walked her to the porch. At the door she placed both arms around his waist and leaned into him as his mouth took hers. It would be heaven to invite him inside, but she sensed he was right. They were both on an emotional high that could lead to greater intimacy than they were ready for. She owed him a full explanation before encouraging their relationship to deepen. She couldn't allow any more caring, any more involvement until he knew.

Chapter 9

George turned the truck off the main road onto the Mt. Nebo loop and drove slowly, allowing Jacey a view of the mountain, towering nearly 12,000 feet high. Stark and bare, the massive bold rock face rose majestically above the deep summer green, appearing purple and gray against the vivid blue sky. A wispy vapor trail cut across the sky, accentuating the contrast of worlds seen by the ancient stone mountain as it had stood sentinel over the Sanpete valley for thousands of years. George had camped and hiked in the area most of his life, and had developed a kinship for the mountain. It was part of him, and he'd looked forward to sharing it with Jacey. Introducing her to Nebo was just the beginning of the things he'd like to share with her.

As scrub brush gave way to maple and quaking aspen, the foliage became too thick to see more than glimpses of Nebo and its lofty neighbors. Layered rock cliffs appeared as crumbling castles of the gods. Side roads led to campgrounds, where trails subtly beckoned the travelers to stay and explore, perhaps drifting back in time to an unhurried life closer to earth and sky. George took his eyes from the road momentarily to watch Jacey's face. He smiled in satisfaction at the rapt expression on her face. He wanted her to love this land, too.

"Why is it called Nebo?" The question came out softly, as though she didn't want to offend the mountain with a personal question.

"It was named by early pioneers for the hill Moses stood on to survey the promised land. I don't know if you could call the Sanpete area a promised land, but those early settlers thought it was, in spite of how hard they had to work to turn it into one."

Jacey asked questions about the history of the West and repeated some of the stories Uncle Charlie had told her so long ago. She exclaimed at the spectacular vista seen from the windows of the pickup truck as they followed the narrow, two-lane road higher into the mountains. Peace settled in George's heart. He was with the right woman, in the right place. When he'd first glimpsed her throat, horrible images of her being attacked or experiencing some terrible accident had filled his mind. A botched suicide had occurred to him, but had been quickly ruled out as too bizarre and out of character for Jacey. She had faced something terrible in her past; but whatever had happened, he felt sure they could put it behind them. Soon they'd reach the destination he'd planned; and they'd have the time and privacy to speak of the past, get to know each other better, and discover where their dreams might lead them.

Along the way, George pulled off at a lookout point to allow Jacey to get out of the truck to view a deep canyon. As she stood in the still mountain air, breathing deeply of the tangy sharpness of pines, he placed his arm about her waist.

Jacey leaned back against him and felt a deep peace, a rightness almost unfamiliar to her. It was a feeling she had experienced only once before. As a twelve-year-old girl, she'd come up out of her own baptism and felt this peace wrap around her like a warm quilt. She didn't want the feeling to end. She thought of last Sunday's Gospel Essentials lesson, and she wondered if this was the way the Holy Ghost let her know something was right. Was the Spirit telling her that being with George was right, or assuring her that telling him of her illness was right?

Spread at her feet was a view of valleys and trees like she had never seen before. In places the soil showed tan, turning to a deep, rich brown, contrasting with hills and broad slashes of rust red. Trees and brush ranged from the dusty gray of sagebrush to the deep winter green of spruce and Douglas fir. Green meadows were dotted with wildflowers of every hue. The land spoke to her in a way cities and seashore never had. It would be easy to call this land of stark contrasts home. She stirred uneasily. Lovely as the scenery might be, it wasn't the land as much as George that drew her. She felt tempted to linger over the scenery and stretch out the time they had together, but she wouldn't. She'd promised that there would be no more avoiding the truth.

A few miles beyond the summit, George swung the truck onto a little-used road. After bumping for some distance along a narrow trail hanging precariously to the side of the mountain, he pulled to a stop in a grassy glen overlooking a shimmering mountain lake. There he spread a blanket in the shade of tall conifers for their picnic, and she unwrapped the lunch she'd packed.

Jacey hadn't had time to fry chicken; instead she produced sandwiches made from thick slabs of leftover roast beef, deviled eggs, tossed salad, and an assortment of fresh fruit. She poured orange juice in plastic stemmed glasses. George raised one eyebrow, but said nothing. They ate quietly, but it wasn't a strained silence—more the comfortable ease of two people who have passed that stage, made the necessary choices, and now only wait for the right moment.

When the remainder of their lunch was packed away, George sat down on the blanket and held out one hand to Jacey. Without hesitation she took it and sank down beside him. Placing his arm around her shoulders, he drew her back against his chest. They sat like that for a little while before he asked, "Why didn't you ever come? Didn't you know how much it meant to Charlie? How much he dreamed of having you here in this place he loved?"

Jacey tensed. The time had come, and she had promised to face George with the truth about herself. "Yes, I knew, but for years I was a child and my father wouldn't let me come." It wasn't the answer, but only the beginning of the complicated explanation she'd prepared.

"Why not? I know your family is affluent. You could have afforded to come."

"It's difficult to explain. Uncle Charlie was really my grandfather's brother. At one time he was engaged to marry my grandmother. I think they were very much in love, but Grandfather cared for her, too. The two families had been friends and had summer homes in Maine next door to each other until Grandmother's family joined the Church. Soon after, Charlie was baptized too and trouble began between the two brothers. Charlie decided to leave the family business and move to Utah. In a year he would return for grandmother and take her to Salt Lake to be married in the temple. But Grandmother was afraid of the risks and didn't want to leave her home and family. She married Grandfather before the year was up."

She paused briefly to gaze pensively across the lake. "Uncle Charlie didn't seem to hold her defection against either of them, and occasionally he returned to Lakeport or Baltimore to visit. He eventually married someone else, but she died shortly after and none of the family ever met her."

"Grandfather, however, continued to need to justify marrying his brother's fiance. She suffered from a weak heart, which caused her to nearly die giving birth to my father. Following Daddy's birth, Grandmother lived the life of a semi-invalid; and Grandfather was highly vocal in his belief that life with his brother would have killed her early on."

"I suppose your father simply carried on his father's animosity toward Charlie," George speculated aloud.

"No, it was more than that." Jacey picked up a leaf which had drifted onto the blanket, twisting it in her fingers as she talked. "I was born prematurely, a weak and sickly baby. My parents, with the help of the best medical professionals they could find, nursed me carefully, but I improved slowly, then succumbed to every childhood illness, cold, or flu that came along. The year I turned twelve, I had a particularly serious bout of chicken pox. Just as I was recovering, Daddy had an important conference to attend in Europe and plans were in place for an extended tour of the continent. He'd planned a family trip, but I was contagious so they decided to leave me with my grandparents. That was the summer Uncle Charlie also came to visit. It was the most magical, special summer of my childhood, but it ended unhappily for Grandfather and Uncle Charlie. They quarreled, and Uncle Charlie never came again."

She swallowed deeply before going on with the story. "Unfortunately, the following winter I contracted rheumatic fever, and Daddy became convinced it was because of the vigorous activities Uncle Charlie had encouraged during the summer. To complicate matters, I happen to look a great deal like my grandmother; and my family became as protective of me as they've always been of her."

"Did the rheumatic fever leave any permanent damage?" The concern was evident in George's deep voice.

Slowly nodding her head, Jacey admitted that the disease had left her with a mild heart murmur. She hastened to assure George that it wasn't terribly serious, but it did mean she had to watch out for strep infections. It didn't really hamper her life under normal circumstances.

It wasn't necessary to continue, George thought. He could easily imagine how Jacey's father had become protective of her health, although he couldn't see that visiting Charlie could have caused her any harm. Possibly her resemblance to her grandmother had been part of what drew Charlie to her, too.

"What about later? Why didn't you come when you were old enough to do it without his permission?"

She didn't answer at once. Instead her eyes sought the soothing comfort of the still mountain lake, the quiet constancy of the stalwart mountain peaks.

"I could have, if I'd had the courage," she admitted sadly. "But I contracted what was believed to be a serious thyroid disease in my mid-teens, and somewhere along the way I lost the ability to fight for what I wanted. I became accustomed to letting my parents decide what was best for me. They hired tutors to help me keep up with school, and later they sent me to an exclusive private school. They never allowed me to exhaust myself with sports or the usual teenage activities; consequently I graduated from high school early and immediately plunged into college work. I received my bachelor's degree at twenty."

"But Charlie told me you traveled."

"Uncle Charlie and I made plans to celebrate my graduation with a trip west, but my parents surprised me with reservations for a cruise and European tour with them. I was far more dependent on my parents than most twenty-year-olds; besides, I thought I could do both. It never occurred to me to disappoint my parents."

"You went on the cruise, but you didn't come here!" George stated the facts with a touch of accusation in his tone. "When

Charlie told me you weren't coming, he had tears in his eyes. He was so choked up he could barely speak."

"I went on the cruise, but I didn't finish the tour of Europe. I collapsed in Switzerland and was rushed to a hospital. From there we flew straight home so I could be evaluated by a team of specialists at Johns Hopkins. Our family doctor, Dr. Bellows, broke the news to us." Her voice turned flat, its huskiness almost a whisper. "He told me I had cancer. A malignant tumor had been found on my thyroid gland."

Stunned, George slowly sat up. Cancer! He couldn't possibly have understood Jacey right. His arms tightened convulsively around the slim girl. Memories of his own grandmother's slow, agonizing death from cancer superimposed themselves over the beautiful young woman he held. *No!* Everything within him revolted at the thought of losing her. Surely no one so young and lovely could have cancer. But he knew better. Cancer snatched its victims indiscriminately from the arms of their loved ones every day without regard to age or beauty. Sheltering her against his huge body as though he might shield her from an advancing enemy, he crushed her to him until a faint whimper reminded him to loosen his hold.

How could this happen? All his life he had felt an emptiness, a loneliness that only went away when this woman had entered his life. Was he too late? Had he found her, only to lose her? His broad fingers stroked her silky hair until they encountered the silk scarf knotted at her throat, then they stilled. He felt a sudden shame that his first reaction had been one of self-pity. Suddenly he wanted to take her to the top of the mountain and let her see all of the world before it was too late. He wanted to fulfill every fantasy she had ever dreamed.

"George?" He had been still so long. Her worst fears had been realized, Jacey thought sadly. He wouldn't run, as many do when they hear the terrible "C" word, but his attitude would change. He'd be kind to the "poor little sick girl," he wouldn't yell and threaten or toss her in the creek anymore—and he wouldn't think she was beautiful and desirable anymore, either. He wouldn't think of the future when he thought of her.

"I want to know all about it. What treatment is being used,

what the next step is, everything." George's voice sounded gruff and demanding.

Drawing back from his commanding tone, Jacey hesitated.

"Oh, Jacey." He hugged her more gently this time. "I would give anything if I could take this from you. I feel as though Clyde had suddenly turned on me, kicking me full in the chest, and still I know this pain is nothing to what you have endured. I feel humbled by your strength and courage."

"You're wrong, George. I'm not strong, and I'm not brave."

"It took great courage to come here by yourself and establish a life totally alien to the one you knew before. And my own actions didn't make it any easier for you, either." Turning her in his arms, he leaned forward to place a tender kiss on her temple.

She felt dampness on his cheek. Awareness flooded her mind, shocking her with the realization of the depth of feeling she felt for this man. To think this great, strong man could shed tears for her!

"Jacey, I need an answer to my question. Please, I need to know it all."

Taking a deep breath, Jacey attempted to recover her thoughts. This was something she knew she had to finish. Something too strong existed between them to entrust him with anything less than the full truth.

"From a medical point of view, the surgery went well. The tumor was removed, along with most of my thyroid gland and the surrounding lymph nodes. A few weeks later I underwent radiation therapy to kill the remaining thyroid cells. But emotionally, I was devastated. I became more dependent on my family for everything. They made certain I didn't need to lift a finger. They waited on me, showered me with presents, and sheltered me from the world. Eventually Dr. Bellows urged me to get out more, to get a job, in effect to start living again. So Daddy found me a job, and Mother bought me a suitable wardrobe. Though I had majored in elementary education and had planned to teach kindergarten or first grade, they said exposure to young children and all their colds and childhood diseases would be too dangerous. Daddy convinced an old friend at the college to hire me as a research assistant."

George squeezed her hand, encouraging her to go on.

"I hated my job, but knew if I complained the alternative

would be staying home day after day, doing nothing. I became more depressed, and my energy level dropped to almost nothing. Uncle Charlie urged me to come visit him, but I couldn't push myself to take action. I know that makes me sound weak and spineless, but the simplest exertion exhausted me and the depression sapped my will to try. "

"Oh, Jacey," George said quietly, "Charlie was so alone when he died. All he had was me and the people from the ward, no relatives, no family. He talked to you in his sleep and about you when he was awake. No matter how fierce the pain, his thoughts were always of you and of this great plan he had for you to come to Utah. He kept telling me everything would be all right once you came, that I'd see; but I thought I could never forgive you for turning your back on him, especially when you refused my calls."

"I didn't know you called. I told you last night I didn't even know Uncle Charlie was ill. It was six weeks after his death that my family finally told me. I wrote to him twice after I left the hospital, and if my letters were returned they didn't find their way back to me."

"But why, Jacey? Why didn't they tell you?"

"They were protecting me from anything unpleasant."

"Charlie and I were close. He told me a lot about you, but he never said you were ill. Didn't he know?"

"Yes, he knew, but I don't know why he didn't tell you. He never mentioned you at all, except in the most general terms which I've only just begun to realize were references to you. He told me more about your house and ranch than his own, but in a round-about way."

"He wanted you here for Christmas. He was hurt when you didn't come."

"He knew I couldn't come. In the last letter I wrote before I learned the cancer had recurred, I told him that I'd like to come for Christmas. But then Dr. Bellows noticed a thickening near where the tumor had been removed. I returned to the hospital for a checkup and a complete analysis. Again I went through a biopsy, x-rays, ultrasound, and every other test ever invented. Uncle Charlie didn't have a telephone, so I sent him a telegram telling him I couldn't come for Christmas because the cancer had returned. Then on Christmas Eve he called my hospital room from a pay phone, and we talked for a long time in spite of his dislike for telephones. He told me about the saddle he'd made for me, and encouraged me to trust in God and hold on to my dreams."

Jacey traced the pattern in the quilt with a fingernail and remembered how Uncle Charlie had understood her romantic fantasies. He'd encouraged her to stretch herself and take on new challenges; and she could see now, from a more distant perspective, that over the years he had worried about the family's insistence that she was just like her grandmother.

"Jacey, did you have to have more surgery?" George brought her mind back to the present and the need to continue her story.

"Yes, I had surgery again. I was so frightened I was half out of my mind, worse than the first time. The tumor was smaller, but it lay across the major nerve leading to my larynx, requiring a careful scraping. After the surgery, I awoke feeling totally disoriented. Even my voice had changed to a harsh whisper."

"I like your voice."

Looking at George uncertainly, Jacey went on. "The worst part was waking up. I was expecting sympathy and comfort, but instead I found a celebration in progress. While I was still unconscious, Roger had placed a huge diamond solitaire on my finger. My whole family was thrilled. I threw up."

A smile flickered across George's face, then tightened to a grim line.

"Everyone expected me to be happy and excited. Even Dr. Bellows was optimistic about my prognosis, but I remained depressed. When radiation therapy began, I was run down, exhausted, and pretty indifferent to pain. When I noticed a sore throat, I didn't say anything for several days. Once I told Dr. Bellows about it, he wasn't particularly concerned, since sore throat is a common side effect of radiation."

"Did you lose your hair?" Picking up a handful of shimmering curls, George let its silky texture run through his fingers before lifting it to his face. He breathed deeply of its essence— of Jacey.

"Radiation therapy doesn't cause hair loss, nausea, or a host of other sad side effects like chemotherapy does. It only requires the patient to remain in absolute isolation for four days; not even the medical staff can touch you or come near. Everything in the room has to be burned or isolated for a long period of time following the treatment. I was cautioned to stay away from children, pets, and pregnant women for a week or two afterward. The treatment was basically painless, but lonely. A sensitive mouth and a sore throat were the worst physical side effects I experienced. I don't know if anyone knows about long-term side effects."

"That doesn't sound pleasant, but I remember my grandmother had to have chemotherapy, and she was terribly ill. Radiation sounds a little easier to me. Why didn't you have chemotherapy?"

"Cancer treatment is tailored to each individual patient and type of cancer. Thyroid cancer is a slow variety of cancer that responds well to surgery followed by radiation. It's usually enough to keep it from recurring."

"In your case, it wasn't enough to keep it from coming back."

"No. And it could return again, and spread to the brain stem or larynx."

George closed his eyes and pulled Jacey closer. Without a thyroid, she was dependent on synthetic hormones. He remembered the pills he'd seen Jacey swallow, and mentally kicked himself for his earlier suspicions. Then he remembered she'd mentioned a sore throat, and before that rheumatic fever. "Was your sore throat a strep infection?"

"No, it wasn't strep. It was a viral infection, however, which turned into pneumonia. Before I got well, I ripped open half-healed stitches in my neck and required an emergency tracheotomy to help me breathe. I was ill for months, and I think Dr. Bellows feared more for my emotional state than my physical condition."

"Oh, Jacey." George reached for her and rocked her in his arms as he struggled to come to terms with what she had told him, and with his fear. "Charlie said you'd come when the time was right. I was so sure you only came to sell Charlie's land and collect the money."

"Actually, I came because Uncle Charlie's death penetrated the thick cocoon of apathy I had wrapped around myself. It made me realize that my life was being lived for me, not by me."

"Now what do you plan to do? Will you stay?"

"I hope so, for a time anyway. Tomorrow I have to see a specialist in Salt Lake City. Dr. Bellows made the arrangements. A lot will depend on the specialist's findings. If there are no problems, I will stay until September. Then I have to return to the clinic for thorough testing. I've been afraid to think or plan beyond that."

Leaning against the trunk of a tree with Jacey in his arms, George remained quiet for a long time. He knew now the reason for her seeming drug dependence and her failure to visit her uncle. Charlie had known of her illness, but, in typical Charlie fashion, had been unable to give up his dream of bringing Jacey west. There was more he wanted to know, but could not ask. He wasn't certain if she knew the answers. Did she have a chance? What kind of life could she lead? Or did she measure her life in months instead of years? Had her protective family given her all of the facts? His thoughts reeled in a spiral of turmoil.

In the distance, they watched a car wind its way along a dusty road on the far side of the lake. It followed the shore until it reached an open picnic area. The moment the car stopped, four doors popped open and they heard the squeals and laughter of excited children. Two little boys ran to the edge of the water, followed by a toddling baby in pink shorts. Before the baby reached the water, a tall young man scooped her up, hefting her onto his shoulder. A slender young woman, her long hair in a pony tail, came up beside them. She reached up to take the little girl's hand as the boys came running back with some treasure they'd found to show the others.

George's mind played tricks on him. For just a moment, he saw Jacey in the young woman below. The boys took on his own sturdy build, and the little girl's eyes changed from green to blue. He wanted children. He couldn't remember a time when he hadn't assumed that someday he would have a son to share all those things he missed sharing with his own father, a boy who would turn to him as he had turned to Charlie. Suddenly he wanted a daughter too, with eyes like Jacey's. Could Jacey be the mother of those children? And if she couldn't? Could he be happy without having children? He loved Jacey. He knew it with soul-deep certainty; and if children were not to be a part of their future, he would grieve, but together they could still make their lives rich and full. Contemplating losing Jacey caused pain to twist in his gut like an ancient weapon of torture.

"Come on." He stood, bringing Jacey to her feet. "I want you to see the rest of the loop." By unspoken consent, they didn't speak again of illness. Instead they discovered a common interest in history, compared favorite popular singers, and discovered their political views were similar as they followed the twisting, narrow road around hairpin curves and down steep slopes, until they reached a place where water plunged in cascades of mist into a roaring mountain stream. Stopping beside the road, they walked the short distance to the water, reveling in the refreshing coolness of the shadowed nook. Jacey tried to speak, but her voice couldn't be heard above the roar of the water.

George reached into his pocket for a chocolate bar. He broke off a piece and popped it into Jacey's mouth, letting his fingers linger against her lower lip. She smiled a lost, sad smile as she licked the creamy chocolate from his fingers, and he felt a spark jump in his heart. Without taking his eyes from hers, he slipped a chunk of the dark candy into his own mouth, then handed Jacey half of the remaining chocolate. Side by side, they leaned back against the mossy rock face as they slowly savored the rich flavor melting in their mouths. George threaded the fingers of one of her hands through his own fingers and stood lost in thought. He could feel the fine cool spray at one level, but on another his mind sent silent screams to God asking why.

Jacey couldn't tell where the roar of the water left off and the roar in her head began. George was too quiet. She'd told him everything, and she knew he was upset. Something had changed between them. She'd have to be patient, give him time to think it through. And she'd have to prepare herself to let him back away if that was what he wanted.

With a shudder, George lifted his eyes to meet hers. He smiled sadly, and with one finger he traced a tear that had escaped to slide down her cheek. Then, with one arm about her shoulder, he hugged her to his side and retraced their steps to his truck. When they were both inside, he leaned forward to place a tiny kiss on her lips, his touch so light she ached. She didn't want

George to treat her like spun glass.

"Forgive me?" he asked, apprehension and pain mingling in his eyes.

"There's nothing to forgive," Jacey replied. All their misunderstandings seemed so far away. "The past couple of months have been terrible and wonderful. I thought at first I hated you because you were so mean to me, but at least I knew I was *alive*. I've learned to do a great many things for myself, and I've learned that I'm not as helpless as I thought. I'm still afraid to confront my family, but I'm getting stronger."

Raising his hands to the steering wheel, George started the engine, pulled back onto the road, and began to point out interesting sights and explain various plants and formations they passed as they continued onward to the little town of Payson. His attempt to entertain her and avoid speaking of anything personal both touched and hurt her. She knew that his reluctance to mention her illness didn't stem from a misguided attempt to spare her, but from his need to grapple with his own feelings.

Jacey spoke little on the drive from Payson to Nephi and back to Ephraim. She sat close to the door, reluctant to press George into a closeness he likely wished to avoid at this point. He hadn't reacted the way she'd worried he might, and she felt gratitude that he hadn't offered her platitudes or rejected her physically. His reaction was closer to what her own had been that terrible day when she'd first been told she had cancer. Shock, denial, grief. He'd need time to work it through in his own mind.

The closer they got to her cabin, the more deeply lost in thought he seemed to be. He pulled the pickup to a stop beside her red convertible and came around to open the door. He startled her by taking her arm in his hand before she could step down. "Jacey, I'm driving you to Salt Lake tomorrow."

"I can drive myself." She didn't look forward to the drive, but she didn't want George to feel any misplaced responsibility for her. She couldn't stand it if George became one more person who thought he had to take care of "poor Jacey."

"I know you don't like driving on mountain roads, but I'm not taking you for that reason," he insisted. "I'm doing it for me. There's no way I could mow hay without cutting off a leg, or oil automatic feeders without catching my arm in a belt or something. My mind is going to be with you, so my body ought to be there, too."

A smile briefly lit her face, only to disappear behind a cloud of doubt. "All right. Be here at eight."

"I'll be here." Before she could turn to walk into the cabin, his hand touched her arm and he bent to softly brush a kiss across her cheek.

She pressed her fingers to the spot where he'd kissed her, and watched bemused as he climbed back in the truck, backed it up, turned, and drove away.

Chapter 10

"Gus, what am I going to do?" Leaning against the fence, Jacey curled her fingers through the wire. The gate wasn't locked. She never locked it anymore, but she still put his feed in the cage every morning. "I think I love George. Yes, I know I'm being selfish, but if there's any chance he loves me too, what can I do? I want to take hold of this wonderful feeling with both hands, but I don't want to ruin his life. And I don't want either one of us to be hurt."

Gus concentrated on his breakfast, steadfastly ignoring Jacey. She watched him for several minutes, then sighed. "Maybe turkeys aren't as dumb as everyone says. You, at least, are smart enough not to fall in love."

Cocking his head, sending his wattle shaking, Gus centered one eye on his mistress, then lowered his head to resume pecking at the grain in his dish. With another sigh Jacey wandered back to the house, where she settled on the top step of the porch. Being too nervous to sleep or read, she'd been dressed and ready for an hour. The cats joined her, and she appreciated their company. Mama calico settled herself contentedly in Jacey's lap, while the kittens tottered playfully to capture the petunias blooming around the step.

Stroking the bundle of fur in her lap, she tried to keep herself from thinking about George or worrying about visiting a strange doctor. How she hated being poked and probed. She cringed at the thought of more needles. Glumly she admitted to being a boob. She didn't want George to see her reaction to simple blood tests, yet she felt a need to lean on his strength. Her throat felt dry and tight, and it wouldn't take much to make her cry.

During the long, sleepless hours of the night she had faced the truth. She loved George. And he cared about her; she knew he did. Perhaps he didn't love her, but he might if she were strong and competent. Would budding love turn to pity now? Sharing a long, happy life with George, if she were strong and well, would be the most wonderful thing she could imagine; but letting him care about her, under the circumstances, would be cruel. How could she do that to him? Her cancer had come back once; it could recur again.

By now she knew what George's way of life entailed, including the long hours of physical labor in all kinds of weather, and the endless feeding and watching over his birds until they were ready for market. He lived a rugged life and he worked hard. To share that life would require strength she didn't have. Perhaps if George loved her enough, he wouldn't care if she weren't a full partner. But *she* would care. She couldn't bear being a burden or a disappointment to him.

She remembered George's face as he watched the children at the lake. She had seen a kind of hunger there. It was only natural that he would want children, and she wouldn't ever be able to give him a child. She blocked out her own pain on that score. She should have stayed in Baltimore and married Roger. He didn't expect her to be his partner, and he didn't care about children. All he'd ever expected from her were the social connections that came with her family name, and that she dress well. He wanted a luxurious condo and all the prestige and trappings of a successful career with the most prominent firm in Baltimore. He cared about her and would never be deliberately unkind, and he could afford the best medical care in the world for her. She wouldn't expect fidelity from him, and he'd always be discreet. She didn't love him, but perhaps love wasn't for her. If she'd married Roger as planned, she wouldn't have met George. And her heart wouldn't be breaking right now.

Seeing a plume of dust approaching along her driveway, she

lifted the cat from her lap and stood to brush off her skirt before going inside to gather up her purse. She returned to the porch in time to see George climb out of his truck. He whistled as he strolled toward her, and she wondered if her black and white skirt might be too short. She wondered too if he would kiss her, but he stopped several feet away.

Jacey avoided meeting his eyes and quickly suggested that they take her car, since a skirt made climbing in and out of a truck a little difficult. George agreed.

"I would have driven my Mustang, but Lisa wanted to visit friends today and Ashlie's infant seat is attached to the back seat of my car."

"*Your* Mustang? I thought it was Lisa's car." Jacey wasn't sure why she had assumed the battered blue truck was George's only means of transportation.

Reaching over to help her secure her seat belt, George continued speaking. "Lisa's divorce settlement gave her the baby, half of their bank account, all of the bills, and no car. I told her she could use mine until she was ready to buy her own." He paused, then added with a trace of disgust, "Craig also got her farm. That's why she's living with me."

"Lisa had a farm?" If George wanted to talk about his sister, Jacey didn't mind. She didn't want to talk about herself, and discussing Lisa might keep her mind off George's proximity in the tiny car.

"Grandmother inherited the farm next to Grandfather's, and instead of combining the two farms, she rented hers to different farmers. For the past twenty years or more, Rulon Olsen farmed it. When Grandmother died, she left her farm to Lisa. Rulon continued to farm it until Lisa married his son, then Lisa and Craig moved into the house."

"Craig, Lisa's ex-husband, isn't much of a farmer. He isn't much of anything," he added sarcastically. "His father continued to do most of the work, and since Craig and Lisa broke up, Rulon has taken over the farm completely. He's supposed to hold it in trust for Ashlie until she's twenty-one. The Olsens tried to get the farm outright as Craig's part of the settlement, but fortunately the judge ensured that Ashlie will get it eventually. The bounder did get

Lisa's Corvette, however." George didn't attempt to disguise his distaste for his former brother-in-law.

As George talked, Jacey realized that Lisa hadn't been the only one hurt by her divorce. George and Lisa were close, and George shared his sister's pain. Lisa's divorce had obviously upset George as much as Lisa had been upset by Jacey's supposed ill-treatment of George. Laying her hand on George's knee, she sought to console him.

"Were they married long?" she asked quietly.

Shaking his head sharply, George laughed bitterly. "No, less than two years, but they shouldn't have married at all. Two people should never marry unless they're both prepared to commit equally to making that marriage work."

Jacey sat very still, scarcely hearing George's voice as he continued. He had given her the answer without even hearing the question. But she hadn't really expected any other, and in her heart she knew he was right. Marriage did require an equal contribution from both partners. She'd been childish and naive to dream of sharing George's life when she wasn't strong enough to help with the farm or give him children. She had money of her own, but would it be enough to avoid bankrupting them if the cancer returned? She was assuming too much, anyway; she and George didn't know each other well enough to even discuss marriage.

"I think the Olsens saw their marriage as a way to acquire the farm. Lisa was miserable, and I doubt that Craig was much happier. Between him and his mother, they beat Lisa's self-esteem into the dirt. Craig was his mama's darling, spoiled-rotten little boy. He could do no wrong. Even when he took off with someone else when Lisa was six months pregnant, she blamed Lisa for not being enough of a woman to keep him happy. Sometimes I wish I could get my hands on him for just five minutes!" He drove on for several miles before speaking again. "I'm sorry, Jacey. I've never talked to anyone before about Lisa. I didn't mean to get so worked up, but maybe it was time to let off a little steam."

"It sounds like Lisa's had a pretty hard time." Jacey struggled to hide her own emotional turmoil. "Did you know she came to see me one day and ripped into me for being so mean to you?"

"She *what?*" George was astounded. "I'm sorry. She's gotten some funny ideas in her head since the divorce."

Jacey smiled. She had no hard feelings toward the young woman, who in her anger had let Jacey know that George was her brother. "She loves you."

George grinned at Jacey. "I love her too, and I worry because she's carrying around a pretty heavy load of anger and bitterness. She feels like love made a fool of her, and she doesn't want me to suffer the way she has."

"I hope we can be friends; I really do like her."

"Lisa needs friends. She stopped going to church after the divorce, and getting her to start going again has been difficult. She feels out of place around her old friends, who are now all parts of couples. That's why I was glad to see her friend, Darla, at the rodeo. She's single and wants Lisa to help her run a small lodge in Jackson Hole, Wyoming. Lisa's excited about the opportunity, but worried about investing money she might need for Ashlie."

"Doesn't she get child support from her ex-husband?"

"No. Craig has disappeared, and Rulon doesn't turn over any of the farm's profits to her."

"You're still upset that her marriage cost her so much." She felt troubled by the anger she sensed behind his words.

"You're right. I didn't mean to let it show." He looked sheepish. "It's not the money I'm upset about as much as the damage they did to Lisa's self-confidence. She doesn't trust anyone anymore. The best thing she could do now would be to go away and build a life for herself and Ashlie someplace else, but she's being stubborn about letting me give her the money to go into partnership with Darla."

"Maybe she really doesn't want to go away."

"I think she does, but it'll have to be her decision." Jacey's respect for George increased as he acknowledged his sister's right to decide for herself.

Jacey looked up and noticed that they were approaching the city. She was glad it was George, and not her, maneuvering the car through the traffic. Anxiously she twisted her hands in her lap as they took the Alta View exit. Silently she prayed she'd be able to stay calm and not make a fool of herself. She'd made numerous trips to hospitals, clinics, and doctors' offices, but they still had the power to frighten her.

It seemed no time at all until George held the door for her to step inside the medical offices next to Alta View Hospital. Linking his fingers with hers, he led her to the door bearing Dr. Gifford's name. She took a seat in the crowded waiting room and twisted her purse strap between her fingers while she waited to hear her name called. Uneasily, she recalled that she'd never visited a doctor alone. Her mother had been with her all those other times. She wondered if she might be using George as a crutch, a substitute for her mother. That thought added to her discomfort. Fortunately, she didn't have long to wait.

"Do you want me to go with you?" George asked, his eyes watching her face carefully.

"I don't know. I'm not certain they'll allow it." She wouldn't know what to say to the strange doctor, but George would. What was she thinking? Of course they wouldn't allow it. She'd have to undress, and . . . She could feel red creeping up the sides of her neck.

Standing up, George smiled down at her. "I'll just hold your hand, and if the doctor tells me to leave, I won't argue."

Jacey let George take her hand, and together they followed the nurse down the hall to a small examining room. She should have told George to wait in the waiting room. What had happened to her determination to act like an adult? She'd come a long way this summer; but, confronted by a doctor and nurses, she was reverting back to the helpless ninny she'd been ever since she learned she had cancer.

In a few minutes they were joined by a short, smiling man in a white jacket who looked to be a couple of years older than George. He introduced himself as Dr. Gifford, then sat down as though casually beginning a chat with friends. He didn't resemble Dr. Bellows at all. She had always loved Dr. Bellows, but he was older, a kind of father figure, who teased her and joked with her parents.

Jacey stammered when Dr. Gifford asked questions about her treatment. She didn't know anything about blood counts, lymph nodes, and dosages. She looked around helplessly. Of course George didn't know the answers, and Mother wasn't here; but shouldn't answers to all his questions be in the records Dr. Bellows sent him? The young doctor seemed to disapprove of her answers. He glanced at Jacey, then at her chart, and frowned. Jacey's heart sank. Something was wrong.

After a few minutes, Dr. Gifford suggested that George remain behind while Jacey went with his nurse to the lab for a few tests. George found himself pacing the floor of the tiny room while he waited for Jacey to return. Jacey had been reluctant to answer the doctor's questions. More than reluctant, she didn't seem to know the answers. What had her family and doctor kept from her? He wished he could reassure her. The first chance he got, he'd let her know she didn't have to fight this alone.

He closed his eyes to block out a sudden picture of Jacey being stuck with a needle. He never had liked hypodermic needles, but he wished he could exchange places with her. As the minutes passed, he began to understand why her family had protected her so fiercely. Seeing someone they loved hurt had brought out the same protective instinct he now felt.

Almost half an hour elapsed before the nurse escorted her back to the room. Though pale, she smiled, which greatly reassured him and made his heart swell inside his chest.

Dr. Gifford followed her into the room a few seconds later.

"Everything looks great!" he smiled at the pair. "It will be a few days before we have results on all of the tests. Call the office in a week, and I'll be able to tell you more."

George heaved a sigh of relief before he saw the skeptical look in Jacey's eyes. Obviously, something was troubling her. She didn't believe everything was fine.

Seating himself informally on the edge of the examining table, the doctor asked them if they had any questions. Jacey didn't speak up and George wondered why. He knew she felt uncertain and confused, so why didn't she question the doctor? George had a lot of questions, but wasn't certain whether he had the right to ask. He didn't want to upset Jacey by interfering. When neither of them said anything, Dr. Gifford turned to Jacey.

"I think you're wise to concentrate on building up your overall body strength. You're living a more physically active life now than you're accustomed to, and that's good. Your general physical condition has improved greatly over your last checkup."

"It has?" Jacey sounded surprised.

"A sedentary lifestyle can be dangerous and lower your resistance to illness. You told me you were riding and walking every day. Keep that up. Avoid rich, fatty foods. Your heart murmur is insignificant, and that muscle will only benefit from an aerobic exercise program. When you've become accustomed to walking three or four miles a day, try running for short distances. If you enjoy running, increase your distance gradually. I won't encourage you to run marathons," he added with a little laugh, "but if you want to eventually try a few 5Ks, I won't object."

"Run? But I—"

"If you find you don't enjoy running, go back to walking."

"I thought I was supposed to conserve my strength and avoid strenuous activities!" Jacey gasped in bewilderment.

Frowning slightly, Dr. Gifford asked if that had been Dr. Bellows' advice.

"I guess so. Daddy said I should live quietly."

"Mm-m." Dr. Gifford paused. "Is your father a doctor?"

"No, but he and Dr. Bellows are friends, and Daddy told me they'd discussed my situation thoroughly."

"Haven't you discussed your activities with your doctor?"

Jacey shook her head, looking lost and confused. George reached out to take her hand, but he didn't join the conversation.

"You should be discussing your condition with your doctor directly, rather than through your father. I treat quite a few cancer patients, and I always encourage them to get involved in their treatment. Cancer patients often feel they're dominated by an invisible power running out of control. If they have a say in choosing their treatment, they reclaim some of that power." Dr. Gifford appeared annoyed. He started toward the door, then paused with one hand on the doorknob. He looked right at George.

"You can return to the waiting room. I'll send Jacey along in a few minutes."

When they were alone, Dr. Gifford asked Jacey, "Has Dr. Bellows discussed birth control with you?"

Jacey sucked in her breath and rose from her chair. Shaking her head, she murmured, "I don't need—"

"Jacey, sit back down a minute. I don't mean to embarrass you or imply anything about your morals. You're not a child, and neither is that man I just sent out of here. Before you make any decision concerning marriage or any other personal relationship, you need to be aware of the risks. There's no physical reason to avoid an intimate relationship, but pregnancy is something else. You need to give yourself time before having a child. I usually suggest that my patients wait five years to begin a pregnancy, but that can vary if the woman's overall health is good."

"A child! But Daddy said I mustn't ever have a baby. It would be too dangerous."

"Do you want to have children?"

"Yes, but . . . could I really have a healthy baby, and would I be able to be a mother to it?" The idea was too astounding. Emotion threatened to shatter her composure. Her parents wouldn't lie to her, but had they been wrong?

Dr. Gifford rubbed his hand across the lower portion of his face and down his jaw before speaking. "Ordinarily, I encourage young people to listen to their parents. Most parents give their children pretty sound advice, but in your case I'd say it's time you grew up. It's your body and your decision to make. I have a patient who had the same surgery you did ten years ago, and she's now expecting her third child. Once you decide to manage your illness rather than let it and well-meaning relatives manage you, you'll find all kinds of possibilities open to you." He reached for his prescription pad and hastily scribbled a name and phone number. He tucked the paper in her hand. "When you're ready, here's the name of a good gynecologist."

Jacey tried to smile as she rejoined George, but didn't quite make it. She moved in a daze, scarcely aware of her actions, and jumped when George spoke to her. She had a feeling he'd already asked the question once before.

"Would you like to go somewhere for lunch?" She nodded her head absently, her mind on Dr. Gifford's words. She didn't need him to tell her to grow up. He didn't know how much she wanted to, how much she hated being protected and coddled. But had she done enough? Was it her fault she'd never learned to be strong and competent like her sister? She'd never doubted she'd received the best possible medical care. Her parents loved her, and they had never denied her anything she needed. What kind of daughter could reject honest love and concern? Not once had it occurred to her to question the care and advice they'd given her. Had they been honest with her? No, she didn't question their honesty; but in their zeal to protect her, had they made false assumptions and gone overboard?

Dr. Gifford seemed to think she could have a baby someday. A baby! She felt the corners of her mouth lift. She'd never let herself think about having children. She'd never let herself hope. She'd dreamed about many things, but a child had been too much to dream about. She closed her eyes, remembering the afternoon her parents had told her.

She'd made some flippant remark about them being grand-parents one day. Her mother had gone very still and sniffled. Daddy had sat down on the side of her bed and held her hands in his. "Jacey, my mother nearly died giving birth to me, and she spent the rest of her life as an invalid. That's been a terrible burden to carry all my life. You not only look like your grandmother, but you've inherited her weak constitution. Between a weak heart and cancer, you mustn't ever entertain any thoughts of bearing a child. The risk of losing you is too high."

"Jacey, are you all right?" George sat across from her at a table set for two. A candle flickered in a shallow red bowl. She didn't remember leaving the car or entering the dimly-lit restaurant. "I thought you'd be happy. Dr. Gifford sounded pretty optimistic." He placed his hand over hers where it lay on the table. "A few minutes ago you looked happy, but now I can see you're worried again."

"I don't know what to think. Dr. Gifford said—" No, she couldn't tell George what Dr. Gifford had said, not here in a public restaurant, and not before she had time to carefully go over every word in her mind. She had to hold that thought, ponder it, and treasure it. She couldn't share it yet. Not with anyone, and especially not with George. In her heart she too readily pictured George as her baby's father, and that was presuming too much. "I—I don't think Dr. Gifford liked me much."

"What! Of course he likes you." George squeezed her fingers. "Why don't you tell me what he said that troubles you so much."

"I can't." She groped for a tissue. "Please, I can't talk now."

"All right. We'll eat dinner and play tourist for a while. When you're ready to talk, we'll talk." Jacey smiled her gratitude. She wiped her eyes and struggled to appear normal.

"Are we going to visit the lake?" She tried to act interested in playing tourist.

"No, it's farther out of town than most people realize. Besides, I try hard to avoid large bodies of water."

"Why?" She suspected him of trying to tease her into a happier frame of mind.

"It's the Navy's fault. Four years with Uncle Sam convinced me there was a good reason I was born in a desert. The day I got my discharge, I swore I'd never go near a body of water larger than a bathtub again as long as I live."

"Seasick?" Jacey smiled sympathetically.

"Night and day. With my feet solidly planted on the beach, just watching waves come in makes waves start coming up."

Jacey giggled. "My own sailing career didn't work out, either. Long after I considered myself completely over the rheumatic fever, I got tired of reading books and attending polite little luncheons. I wanted an adventure, so I sneaked down to the boat club and signed up for sailing lessons. I failed knot-tying and every other aspect of the course. I even managed to lose my life jacket. No one wanted me to crew for them after I capsized a boat and knocked my partner into the water. It was almost a relief when Daddy found out and canceled the lessons."

Following lunch, George took her to nearby Liberty Park. They strolled through the aviary hand in hand. Stopping in front of the buzzard cage, Jacey pointed out how much the big black birds looked like his turkeys except for the color. Pretending to take offense, George swung her up in his arms and threatened to toss her to them for lunch.

They left the city late in the afternoon. While George concentrated on the traffic, Jacey snuggled down in her seat and thought about George. She liked being with him. She liked everything about him—almost. Sometimes he got too bossy. Definitely a take-charge kind of person, and she had enough take-charge people in her life. But he made her feel alive and whole. George and her father were alike in some ways. They were both direct and forceful. She frowned as she considered the two men. Her father intimidated her, but George challenged her.

Her thoughts returned again to Dr. Gifford's words, as they had over and over since she left his office. What did he mean when he said she should "manage" her illness? How could she control cancer? She recognized the need to grow up and take responsibility for her own life; she'd come west to do just that. But how could she take charge of a disease that doctors and scientists didn't know how to cure? They couldn't even tell her whether she was cured or just waiting for it to strike again.

Before today, she had believed she had enough decisions to make before she returned to the clinic in Baltimore in September to give her plenty of practice at making up her mind and taking charge of her life. She ticked off the major questions she needed to resolve. Would she quit her job at the college and look for a teaching position? Should she sell the ranch, and if so, to whom? And what about George? Now added to the list were the questions Dr. Gifford had raised in her mind. She would never again be content until she explored the idea of being an active participant in her treatment. And once the possibility of having a baby entered her mind, she'd known motherhood wasn't a decision she could leave to her parents anymore. Thankfully, she had two months to explore all these possibilities.

George glanced over at Jacey. She seemed to be asleep, and he didn't want to wake her. He'd fallen for her hard and fast, but he didn't have a doubt in his mind that the way he felt about her would last for eternity. Learning she'd had cancer had shaken him badly, but it hadn't changed the way he felt about her. If anything, it had reinforced his feelings. He wanted Jacey beside him forever, and that meant marrying her in the temple. More of his early training had taken root than he'd realized. He'd always assumed he'd marry someday, but he hadn't known how deeply he felt about temple marriage.

He squirmed uncomfortably. He didn't know if he could even get a temple recommend. He'd resisted the Church all through adolescence, and when other boys his age began leaving on missions, he'd joined the Navy. He'd done things during those four years he knew his grandparents wouldn't have approved of and which were contrary to Church standards. He'd regretted his actions, and with Charlie's encouragement had straightened out his life after he'd come home. But he'd never talked to his bishop about those years.

He'd only gone back to church because Jeremy didn't want to give up his CTR class during the rodeo season, and he'd gotten a promise out of George to substitute for him before George quite knew what he'd agreed to. His lip lifted in a reminiscent smile, remembering how old Charlie had helped him cram for those first lessons. The old boy had taught him a lot more then he'd ever manage to teach that rambunctious bunch of eight-year-olds he shared with Jeremy. He chuckled. He had a testimony the gospel was true, and he didn't even know when the conviction had sneaked up on him.

"What are you laughing about?"

He turned his head to see Jacey watching him.

"My grandmother. I wish she were still alive so you could meet her. If it hadn't been for her and your uncle Charlie, I don't know what might have become of me."

Along the long freeway stretch between Salt Lake and Nephi, George told Jacey about his grandmother. "She was a big, comfortable woman," George reminisced. "She always wore her long hair in a braid wrapped around her head like a coronet. Grandma was the only person I knew who ever stood up to Grandpa and got away with it. They both had strict ideas about how the gospel was supposed to be lived. Grandpa tried to make me go to church and do everything his way, and Grandma would say, 'Now Ethan, you know God doesn't force any man to heaven, and you shouldn't either. The boy knows what's right, and he'll come around as soon as you stop butting heads with him.'"

Jacey laughed. "Were you really so rebellious?"

"I was," George admitted. "Whichever way Grandpa pushed, I went the other way. I got in so many scrapes, I think the whole town hoped I would drown when I ran off to join the Navy. At first I took great satisfaction in breaking every rule Grandpa had pushed down my throat, but after a while I missed Grandma and Lisa. Grandma's death hit me hard, and I wished I'd tried harder to get along with Grandpa. When I came home, it was your Uncle Charlie who helped me see that the old man really loved me, and that I'd hurt myself as much as him."

"It's hard to have someone else tell you what to do," Jacey ventured softly.

"Charlie was a big believer in free agency. He said I gave mine up every time I rebelled against Grandpa. He said if I'd thought out what Grandpa told me, then disagreed, that was my right. But when I disagreed just because it was Grandpa telling me what to do, I was abdicating my free agency—just plain giving it away."

"I wish I'd known Uncle Charlie better." Jacey sounded wistful.

"He was a good man. Recently I've realized that I'm coming closer all the time to accepting most of the things he and Grandma tried to pound into my head. I've finally realized, too, that what Grandpa wanted for me wasn't wrong; it was the way he pushed it that was unacceptable."

"It looks like we've both been guilty of not living our own lives—you through defiance and me through acquiescence," Jacey reflected wryly.

George glanced ahead. The sun had set and long shadows stretched across the highway. He kept an alert eye out for any deer that might wander onto the road, and watched for the turn-off. He'd been calm all day, but now felt nervous.

Jacey appeared deep in thought, unaware of her surroundings, when the car slowed and turned off the main road. He knew the moment she recognized the dirt road where they'd first met. She glanced around without saying anything for several minutes. When she turned to look his way he grinned, feeling as foolish and uncertain as a boy with his first prom date.

"Brings back a mixed bag of memories, doesn't it?" George made an effort to sound calm and at ease.

"I don't know whether to laugh or cry," Jacey responded. "I was so angry. No one had ever treated me the way you did that day."

"I really am sorry." He reached out to take her hand. "But I wanted to bring you here today because this is where I first saw you. You were the one who landed face-first in the mud, followed by a cold dunking in the creek. But I felt like you did the same thing to me that day. You knocked me flat the moment I saw you. Then, when I realized you were Charlie's niece, I felt like I had been dumped on my head in a snowbank."

"We started off pretty badly."

"I haven't been able to get you out of my head, Jacey, since the moment I spotted you fighting with a cow over a pair of panty hose. I'm not sure I believe in love at first sight, but if it wasn't first sight, it was surely second. I love you, Jacey. Will you stay? Will you be my wife?"

She was quiet for so long that his big heart sank. Her head dipped against his shoulder, and he sensed she was battling to hold back tears. Placing one hand beneath her chin, he lifted it so he could see her face. "Would it be so terrible? Do you care for me at all?"

"Oh, George," her voice dropped to the barest husky whisper. "I don't know what to do. I'm not ready for marriage. There are so many things I have to think about. Just before I came here, I discovered I had no control over my life. My family and former fiance anticipated all my needs before I even asked. I don't know if my family was at fault, or if I withdrew and let others run my life as an escape mechanism, and they stepped into the breach. But I discovered I don't want to be helpless anymore. I want to be in control of *me*. Today Dr. Gifford made me understand that it's not enough to become independent; I have to learn to take charge of my illness, too. Until I feel confident of myself as an individual, I can't consider marriage."

"I love you," he argued persuasively. "I want us to share our lives."

"I don't know if I have a life to share. I don't know if I can give you children. I've believed for a long time that I'd be unable to have a baby, but today Dr. Gifford held out hope that I might. I haven't had time to absorb that possibility. It's too soon for me to plan for a future."

"Jacey, everything Dr. Gifford said today gives us reason to hope, and even if I knew we would only have a year, ten years, or just today, I'd still want to spend it with you. Whether or not we have children doesn't change the way I feel about you."

"It wouldn't be fair to you." Her shoulders shook and he wrapped his arms around her, holding her while she cried.

"Let me decide what's fair," he whispered against her hair. "I won't pressure you. Just don't tell me no."

"I won't tell you no, but I can't say yes either."

"It's all right." He kissed the tip of her nose. "I'll give you all the time you need. Just promise me you'll think about it; and when you decide, ask Heavenly Father if it's right for us to be together." He didn't say anything further as he backed and turned the car. He ached with disappointment, but he'd keep his word. He'd give her time as long as he stood a chance.

From the antler gate, George spotted a strange car parked in front of the cabin. An uneasy premonition roughened his voice. "It looks like you have company."

Jacey lifted her head to look. He heard her stifle a giggle and followed her line of sight. Gus, with tail spread in all its glory, paced back and forth beside the strange car. He marched in proud dignity, his wattle shaking, his beady eyes glaring toward the tightly enclosed vehicle.

George unfolded himself from the confines of the little convertible. Before he could reach the passenger door, Jacey had opened it and joined him on the driveway. He walked a couple of steps ahead of her as they approached the other car. Gus, seeing reinforcements had arrived, retired to his dirt hole, pausing briefly to send one last baleful stare at the intruder.

Slowly the car door opened. Roger stepped out, and Jacey knew what she'd missed when Calvin Walker approached her before the rodeo. He'd been in touch with Roger again, and now Roger knew where to find her.

"Hi, sweetie."

"What are you doing here?" The words sounded squeezed from her lungs.

George stood, unable to move, as a handsome stranger in an expensive tailored suit wrapped his arms around Jacey.

Chapter 11

"Don't look so surprised, darling." Roger brushed her lips lightly with his own.

Jacey jerked backward in a startled movement, her hand groping for George's reassuring presence. George frowned at the man who now extended his hand.

"Roger Blake, here." Roger smiled congenially while George ignored the outstretched hand.

Remembering her manners in spite of the warring emotions chasing through her head, Jacey completed the introduction. Putting her hand on George's arm, she introduced him to Roger.

"Do you think you might call off your dragon and invite me inside?" Roger asked Jacey with a familiar teasing glint in his eyes. For a heartbeat, she didn't know whether he referred to George or Gus. George certainly looked close to breathing fire.
"I saw the sign on your gate, but I thought you were kidding until that old bird let me know otherwise," Roger chuckled good-naturedly.

"I'm sorry," she apologized, "but Gus really isn't very sociable."

Jacey led the way inside, still clinging to George's arm. She invited both men to be seated, then hurried to the refrigerator for cold drinks. Her hands shook as she pulled the tabs on the cans and poured root beer over ice. When she handed Roger's drink to him, he closed his hand over her fingers still holding the damp glass, then casually lifted her hand to his mouth. She jumped, nearly spilling the drink, then nervously glanced at George. She wanted to tell him she hadn't invited Roger. She hadn't realized he'd found her.

George hadn't spoken to Roger yet. That added to Jacey's nervousness. He remedied that now.

"Are you the lawyer who's been trying to sell Jacey's farm?"

"It's not any of your concern, but yes, I am her attorney. Also her fiance."

"You are not!" Jacey choked. Neither man looked at her.

"As one of the potential buyers who submitted a bid, I suppose you feel you have a right to know the status of your proposal. I don't mind telling you, we have received a much higher bid, which has been accepted."

"No, Roger!" Jacey interrupted, so angry she could hardly speak.

Looking directly at George, Roger continued blandly, "The papers will be signed in two days, then Jacey will be returning home with me. I understand we owe you some compensation for the time you cared for her animals. Arrangements have been made for their disposal too, so if you'll draw up a bill, I'll see that you are paid immediately."

"Roger, I am not selling my home, and my animals are not going anywhere! You are not my attorney! And you are not my fiance!" Jacey's voice nearly failed her completely as she tried to make Roger listen to her.

Roger stood, a smile on his face. "Your help has been appreciated, Lindquist, but I haven't seen Jacey for several months and we would like to be alone."

Slowly George rose to his feet. He didn't believe Roger, and surely he wouldn't leave.

"Don't leave me alone with him," Jacey wanted to shout, but her voice wouldn't cooperate. Only a strangled whisper escaped her throat.

George looked down at Roger with grim determination. Roger glared back, then suddenly seemed to become aware of how much bigger than himself George happened to be. He took an instinctive step back. His hesitation only lasted a second before all his arrogant self-confidence surged to the forefront again. Jacey didn't know what to do. She didn't want them to fight, verbally or physically.

Looking down at the smaller man, George spoke slowly and clearly. "Mr. Blake, you haven't been listening to the lady. If you had, you'd know you made a trip out here for nothing."

"No, Lindquist, you seem to be the one who isn't listening. Everything was decided months ago."

"I didn't have any part in that decision, Roger," Jacey protested. "You and Daddy did all of the deciding."

"Don't worry, honey. I'll take care of everything. As soon as Lindquist leaves, we'll go somewhere nice for dinner, and I'll tell you all about it."

"Roger!" Jacey wailed.

"That's enough!" George snarled. "You'd better get in that fancy car and leave. You seem to be a little thick between the ears, but you should have been able to figure out by now that Jacey doesn't want your interference."

"Speaking of interference, Lindquist," Roger said, his voice taking on the icy tones he used to intimidate courtroom witnesses, "it seems to me you have no part in this discussion. I was told you were spending too much time with my future wife, and that you've been trying to influence her to back out of the arrangements I've made for the disposition of this piece of property. It would be best if you left now, before trespassing charges are brought against you."

Never before had Jacey experienced such anger. The rage she felt at George's earlier tricks diminished to nothing compared to the fury she now felt. Letting Roger make decisions for her had been a habit, but no more. She couldn't blame him for thinking she'd let him have his way; she always had before. But this time he wouldn't wear her down or override her wishes. She wasn't the same person he'd last seen in Baltimore two months ago.

"Calvin Walker told you where to find me, didn't he?"

For once, Roger responded to her question. "It's a good thing he did. Look at this place! This is no place for you. You don't belong in this kind of crude setting."

"Roger, if I speak to you in simple two-syllable words, do you think you might be able to understand me?" Jacey's voice dripped ice, finally drawing Roger's attention. "I don't want you here, and nothing you say will make me sign anything. You are not my attorney; Anne is. I signed papers giving her limited power of attorney before I left Baltimore. I gave you back your ring—which, by the way, you never asked me if I wanted in the first place. Under no circumstances will I ever sell this property to Calvin Walker. So please go back home and leave me alone."

"Jacey, you're tired, and so am I." Roger smiled, putting a thousand megawatts of little-boy charm behind it. "Send your big friend home, and we can discuss this sensibly later, when we're more relaxed."

Jacey had the strange sensation that she'd ridden a carousel too long. George hadn't spoken for several minutes, and she didn't know what he was thinking—probably that she was inept and weak. She *felt* inept and weak. No matter what she said, Roger didn't hear her.

"For once you're right; Jacey is tired." George's voice cut through her despair. "She's had a long day, and it's time she had a little peace and quiet. If you want to speak to her again tomorrow, she'll probably agree to that. I'm sure she's anxious to hear about her family; we'll be happy to meet you at your motel at whatever time is convenient. If you haven't made reservations, I'll call the manager for you."

"Don't trouble yourself. I'm sure there's plenty of room here for both of us," Roger answered suavely. "I'm quite accustomed to taking care of Jacey."

"That's where you're wrong, mister." George folded his massive arms across his broad, solid chest. "The only man taking care of Jacey from now on will be me." The two men stood glaring furiously at each other. Jacey looked from one man to the other and wondered what to do. She didn't want to fight with Roger. No matter how angry she was with him now, she remembered all the years he had been her devoted friend, bringing her little gifts and taking her places her father would never have let her go alone. She had looked up to him and admired him most of her life.

She didn't want to be alone with George right now, either. If he stayed, she would be in his arms; from there it would be too easy to shut out every other concern, and in her weakness agree to be his wife. She couldn't marry him because she needed a buffer between Roger and herself. If she married George to escape Roger and her family's domination, she'd never know if she had the strength somewhere inside her to take care of herself. She found herself rubbing the pressure points above her nose where pain was building. Soon she would have a full-scale headache.

"I don't want to have to remove you forcibly," she heard George growl at Roger. "We don't need you here. I'll give Jacey any help she needs."

"Would you both please leave?" In minutes she'd be crying, her headache had worsened, and she felt miserable—like a bone caught between two growling dogs. Suddenly she couldn't bear the sight of either man. She wilted into the chair behind her and buried her face in her hands.

George wanted to go to her, but sensed it would be a mistake. She'd been on an emotional roller coaster all day. He didn't doubt she needed some peace and quiet, and he hadn't helped matters any by letting jealousy run away with him. Patience wasn't a virtue he'd ever laid claim to, but he'd really blown it today, proposing prematurely then reacting like Gus when he found a snake poaching on his territory. He glanced toward Roger, who had dropped to one knee beside Jacey and was trying to coax her to look at him. The man was irritating. Real irritating.

"After you." George held open the door and stared at his rival. Looking disgruntled, Roger attempted to take Jacey in his arms. George reached out a hand and propelled the other man out the door. He walked to his pickup and waited with his arms folded until Roger's engine roared to life, then he started the blue truck and followed him down the lane.

Rocking slowly back and forth, Jacey held her aching head between her hands. What could she do? Now that Roger knew where to find her, if he didn't manage to drag her back to Baltimore, he'd tell Daddy, who would come to get her. No, she wouldn't go.

A couple of Tylenol tablets and a long soak in the tub helped to ease the headache, but not her worries. During the long hours of the night, she lay awake wondering if she should give up and go back home. Twice she climbed out of bed to kneel and ask God to give her strength and help her know what to do. She considered that George might be better off without her, and in time he would forget her. But that thought was unbearable and started a fresh river of tears.

It seemed she had barely drifted off to sleep when the rooster crowed. Stumbling out of bed, she hurried to feed her animals. She laughed in delight when one of the banty hens strutted into sight trailed by a dozen balls of brown and yellow fluff. When the kittens began to pay them too much attention, she shooed the little chickens into their pen and locked the door.

She fed Gus and carried on her usual one-sided conversation with him. "I don't want to leave. I've been happy here." Feeling sad and afraid, she gazed off over the fields. The past two months she'd learned a lot about herself, and no one here challenged her right to take care of herself. That made trusting her own judgment easier. But would her convictions hold up against a lifetime of accepting her family's decisions? They, and Roger too, loved her. She owed them a debt of gratitude she could never repay; so how could she tell them they no longer had any say in her life? After a few minutes she walked back to the barn and picked up Lady's bridle and a bucket of oats. Lady trotted toward her when she entered the pasture, and Jacey quickly caught and saddled her.

Letting Clyde trail behind them, she reined the little mare toward the canyon. Opening and closing the gate had become easier each time she had done it over the past months, and in moments Lady was galloping along the dirt road leading to the meadow. The early morning sun sang through the trees, and the air rushing past her face brought the tangy aroma of cedar. Breathing deeply, she sucked the mountain air into her lungs. Its pure freshness seemed to stimulate her mind as all the dark, sleepless hours hadn't.

When she reached the spring she slipped from Lady's back. She sat on a large rock and bowed her head. She wished Uncle Charlie were still alive. He'd know what she should do.

"Winners ain't quitters, girl. Stay in there and keep fightin' and prayin'."

Great . . . she was hallucinating now. For a moment, she

thought Uncle Charlie had spoken to her. Of course, advising her to pray would be just what Uncle Charlie would propose if he were here. He'd talked a lot about praying and hanging on to her dreams in all those letters. Well, she'd tried praying, but nothing happened. Maybe she hadn't done it right. She'd keep praying until she did get it right. As for fighting, she knew less about that than she did about praying. But she'd learn! And whatever happened, she vowed, Charlie's animals wouldn't lose their home.

She wished Roger had stayed in Baltimore. If he had, she wouldn't have to make decisions now that she didn't feel ready for.

Lady nickered and nudged Jacey's shoulder, reminding her they'd been stopped for too long. Jacey looked around the peaceful valley before remounting. Time alone had shored up her faltering confidence. Maybe she didn't need to decide everything now. If she could find a way to persuade Roger he was spinning his wheels, perhaps she could gain a little time.

She heard the telephone ringing as she opened the door to her cabin. Rushing across the room, she rasped a breathless hello.

"Jacey! What's wrong?" Roger's agitated voice came over the line. "I've been trying to call you for an hour."

"I have animals to feed, and I went horseback riding."

"Riding? What's the matter with you? You know it's not safe for you to do things like that. I was afraid that big goon, Lindquist, had abducted you or something. It never occurred to me that you would do something so foolish as to ride a horse."

Bristling at his insulting reference to George, Jacey lashed out. "His name is George, or Mr. Lindquist. And if you're going to yell and be insulting, I'm hanging up."

"All right, honey." Roger modified his voice, letting it become silky and soothing. "I'm coming right out. We can talk everything over, and I'll help you pack."

"No, Roger. I'm going to talk, and you're going to listen, or I won't see you at all."

"Whatever you want, baby. You know I only want to make you happy."

"I don't know any such thing. But I am serious, and you'd better be prepared to take me seriously." She slammed down the phone, then shook her head. Talking back to Roger on the phone and getting him to listen to her in person weren't the same thing.

Next, Jacey called George. She told him she had agreed to see Roger, and she thought it best if he didn't come over until after Roger left.

"I'll give you an hour, then I'm coming."

"George, I have to talk to him alone. You know I do."

"I don't like it."

"George . . ."

"All right." He sounded terribly weary. "I won't interfere, but please don't leave with him. I don't think I could watch you drive away with him."

"I won't, George. That's a promise." She'd made two promises, two commitments in one day. Maybe she'd become stronger than she'd thought.

Jacey paced the floor while she waited. Hearing a car in the driveway, she went out to keep Gus from attacking her visitor. She thought how strange it all was as Roger bounced cheerfully up the steps. He was one of the most handsome men she'd ever seen, and she felt nothing but fondness for him, although that was wearing thin. He was dressed casually in a dark blue sport shirt and white slacks, his curly hair falling across his forehead and the dimple in his cheek flashing like a teasing wink. But it wasn't enough. He wasn't George.

"Hi!" He grinned and stooped to plant a quick kiss on her mouth. Prepared, she turned away, letting the kiss land on her cheek.

"Still mad at me, sweetie?" he asked in his most charming fashion. Jacey was too familiar with his charm to be taken in.

"Sit down, Roger." She indicated the sofa, then took her own place in the rocking chair.

"Walker can come over today, if you'd like to get everything tidied up at once. We can pack and be out of here before dark." He smiled winningly.

Jacey struggled to hold her temper. "Roger, that is the first thing I want you to do. Go to the phone and call Mr. Walker. Make it very clear to him that you are not my attorney, you do not represent me in any way, and under no circumstances will I sell this ranch to him."

"Come on, honey. You can't be serious. He made a very good offer."

"Roger, I am very serious."

"Jacey, does this go back to that silly hang-up you have about furs?"

"Only partly. This place means a lot to me. I want cows and horses and Gus to live here, not animals that are being raised to die for something so vain as fur coats. Animals raised to feed hungry people serve a purpose, and I can accept that."

"You're being awfully dramatic." Roger smiled indulgently at her and winked. "You'd think Mr. Walker intended to use your horses for mink feed. He offered to haul them to an auction at his own expense and turn over whatever they brought to you in full."

"There's more involved than that." Jacey wondered if Roger was capable of understanding her point of view. "This ranch is mine, and I don't want to sell it to him. That's all the reason I need. The Walkers are thoroughly obnoxious people; I don't want them here. What happens to this property is my concern alone, Roger, and you have no right to go behind my back to sell it."

"You heard your father assign me to take care of it."

"This ranch isn't Daddy's."

Roger stood up. Thoughtfully he walked toward the fireplace. Leaning against the stone with one hand, he turned sideways to look at Jaccy. "Jacey, I wish you would look at this in a more mature fashion. I've loved you since you were born. In all that time, I've always done everything I could to make you happy. I live in Baltimore; my practice is in Baltimore. There's no way you can take care of animals and run your little ranch from there. After we're married, you'll have to sell this place anyway. Wouldn't it be easier to get it over with now?"

Jacey stood and faced him. "How can I make you understand? Roger, I care about you. You've been the best big brother a little girl could ever ask for. But I'm all grown up now, and I don't need a big brother to fight my battles."

Roger left his spot by the fireplace, swept Jacey up in his arms, and settled with her in the rocking chair. "What's happened, baby?" he questioned in a patronizing tone.

Jacey struggled to free herself, but Roger wouldn't release her.

He soothed and patted her hair as though she were a small child. Hearing a sound outside, he suddenly stiffened.

"You've been listening to Lindquist. He's the reason you suddenly don't want to marry me. Surely you don't want him! Honey, he's a farmer. He needs a wife who can drive a tractor and help him plow, not a darling little doll like you!"

With a final angry lunge, Jacey managed to free herself. Tears streamed from her eyes as she turned on Roger. "I know I'm not the kind of wife George needs, but I'm the woman he wants. He doesn't see me as a pretty toy, and he doesn't care how rich and famous Daddy is. At least he sees me as a real person with rights and feelings!"

"Jacey, come here." Roger held out his arms.

"No! I have something to say, and I want you to listen. If and when I decide to sell my ranch, I'll do it myself. I won't consult you. If you want to continue to play big brother, I won't object, but don't pretend you love me any other way. I know better."

"And how do you know?" Roger asked suspiciously. "Has that gorilla touched you?"

"I'm not a little girl anymore, Roger. What has or hasn't happened between George and myself is none of your business. All you need to know is that I love him."

"I'll kill him!" Roger stormed toward the door. He halted when he heard Jacey laugh.

"Getting physical isn't your style," she reminded him. "Besides," she added with a grin, "you'd better take a second look. In case you haven't noticed, George is a bit bigger than you. I'll put my money on him any day."

"Me too!" came a throaty purr from the doorway. "If you mean that sexy hunk who just climbed out of the white Mustang."

Jacey turned so quickly that she nearly lost her balance. Roger put out a hand to steady her, but missed. He too gaped at the figure in the doorway.

"Anne?" Jacey couldn't believe her eyes. Her sister stood in the doorway, wearing white shorts and a tank top as casually as though they were her usual attire and she'd just dropped in from next door. Roger, for once, was speechless. Deliberately ignoring him, Anne concentrated her attention on the big man approaching the porch. She made no attempt to hide her admiration.

"What are you doing here?" Roger didn't sound pleased.

Without taking her eyes off George, Anne answered as though the matter was of little importance. "When I discovered you had left town, I decided I'd better get out here to protect my little sister."

Jacey's heart sank. She thought Anne believed her to be capable of taking care of herself. Standing up to Roger wasn't easy, but she'd thought she was making progress until Anne arrived. How could she fight Roger and Anne both? Besides, she didn't like the way her sister was ogling George. Why did he have to come so soon? A whole hour hadn't passed yet. Turning to Anne, she asked with more belligerence than she intended, "What are you doing here?"

Anne chuckled, "I think baby sister is staking her claim."

"Nonsense," Roger cut in. "What would Jacey see in that muscle-bound cretin?"

"Plenty!" Anne sighed.

"I didn't know you went for that type," Roger mocked. "Speaking of animals, how did you manage to get past that beast of Jacey's?"

"You mean that big brown Thanksgiving dinner on the hoof? Why, Roger, dear, he's no dumb turkey; he recognizes authority when he sees it. When he came out to meet me, I just told him who I am and he said, 'Excuse me, your honor,' and I waltzed right by."

"Tell me another one, darling. Or is this your oblique way of telling me you got the appointment?"

"I thought you'd never guess."

The two were so engrossed that Jacey slipped past them and outside without their even noticing. She felt George's big arm settle around her shoulder as they stood on the porch, watching the exchange between Anne and Roger.

"Congratulations!" Roger sounded sincere, then spoiled it by adding, "But won't you have a difficult time giving up your designer labels for a one-size-fits-all black tent?"

"Miaow! Miaow! I do believe Roger baby is jealous."

"Darn right, I'm jealous. But seriously, much as I hate to admit it, you'll be good." Stepping forward, he hugged his colleague and swiftly kissed her.

A strange light flickered in Anne's eyes, and Jacey watched her warily. Anne had something in mind other than protecting her little sister. She felt George squeeze her shoulder and turned questioning eyes toward him. His eyes were on Anne, and Jacey watched as a slow grin spread across his face. The two people she felt closest to were acting strange, and she didn't like it.

"How about introducing me to the pretty lady?" George's voice came out in an exaggerated drawl. Looking askance at him, Jacey cleared her throat. She didn't like the smug expression on his face.

"Uh, Anne," she said, "I'd like you to meet my neighbor, George Lindquist."

"Wow!" Anne's eyes carefully raked him from head to toe, leaving no doubt that she liked what she saw. "I see why my little sister doesn't want to come home."

George's ears turned red as he suffered her blatant appraisal. Jacey continued the introduction with her chin jutted forward and a spark in her eyes.

"This is my sister, Anne Mathews."

Anne extended her right hand. "Actually, as of ten o'clock yesterday morning, it's Judge Annelise Gerrard Mathews. But you can call me Anne."

"Anne, that's wonderful!" Jacey threw her arms around her sister.

"Thank you. And it's marvelous to see you again, too." She returned the hug. "You look great. This western life must suit you." After a deliberate pause she concluded, "Of course, it might just be a certain western man who suits you."

The two young women, with their arms about each other, continued talking as they made their way to the sofa where they sat together. Briefly Anne caught her sister up on the news at home, assuring her that their parents were fine.

"You should know something," Anne said, pressing her sister's hand. "Daddy is adamant that I take you back home."

"Anne, I don't know. I need more time."

"Of course she's going home," Roger cut in. "We were

discussing selling this place before you arrived. Celia has rescheduled the wedding for August 28."

"You never heard a word I said!" Jacey smarted from her failure to get Roger to take her seriously, but she wouldn't give up. She looked to George for support, but he seemed locked in some kind of tug-of-war with Anne. Anne nodded her head once, and a satisfied gleam settled deep in George's eyes. Jacey wished she knew what kind of understanding the two had reached.

"What are your plans?" Anne turned innocent eyes to her sister, ignoring Roger as though he hadn't spoken.

"I am considering selling, but not to the buyer Roger has picked. Since you are my attorney, I'll discuss it with you later."

"Now, wait a minute. *I'm* your attorney," Roger cut in. "Leave Anne out of this."

"Oh, I'm very much in this," Anne taunted lightly. "More than you realize," she added under her breath so only Jacey could hear. "You've presumed a great deal on the basis of your previous relationship with my client."

"Previous? There isn't anything previous about it."

"Nor present, either. Now, why don't you be a good boy and run along back to the motel and call your disappointed client to break the news to him that he's not going to get Jacey's ranch." She smoothed a sleek strand of blonde hair behind her ear. "Jacey and I have a few things to discuss."

"I can't withdraw, Anne. The papers have already been drawn up."

"I didn't sign them, and I won't." Jacey made one last attempt to convince Roger that she had the final say and wasn't selling to the Walkers.

"What does it take to convince you?" George slammed his hat against the arm of the couch. "She said no. That's the end of the discussion."

"It's up to Jacey, Roger." Anne spoke softly, minus her usual sarcastic bantering. "You have to let her go." When Roger's only response was to scowl at her, Anne snapped, "I hope you handle your Camden, Mathews, Webber, and Fesch, clients with a wee bit more ethics than I've seen here, darling. Otherwise, I can't wait to get you in my courtroom."

Roger stood. "Sometimes you're just a little too clever. One day you're going to get yours."

"I certainly hope so," she responded so softly that only Jacey, who raised her eyebrows in question, heard the words. "Oh, and Roger," Anne's voice followed him out the door. "Wait for me when you get back to town; we can fly back together. By the way, I have the room adjoining yours, and I'll buy dinner."

Jacey winced at the force with which Roger slammed the door. Perhaps she should follow him and apologize—not for breaking their engagement and certainly not for refusing to accept the arrangements he'd made, but for the cowardly way she'd ended their engagement. She should have had the courage to tell him to his face. He'd always been her champion, and he didn't deserve such shabby treatment. But if she went after him now, he'd think she was backing down. She couldn't risk that.

George touched her hand and she turned to him. He held her while she struggled to untangle her emotions, and she sensed that he understood.

As the dust settled behind the receding car, Anne turned to George. "I'm looking forward to getting to know you better, but right now my sister and I have a lot to talk about. It might be best if you left now, too."

"Are you planning to take up where Blake left off, badgering Jacey to sell this place and go back east?" George didn't look happy with Anne's attempt to dismiss him.

Jacey looked up to meet his eyes. "I'll be all right. I'll call you later."

He brushed a finger down her cheek and walked to the door. Glancing over his shoulder from the doorway, he tossed Anne a funny little salute.

When George was out of sight, Anne hugged her sister again, then got right down to business. She deftly set forth the conditions Jacey specified and drew up a rough draft for a bill of sale, then made a couple of telephone calls. When she finished, Anne looked at her sister speculatively. "He's quite a man," she observed.

"I agree." Jacey smiled, and something in her smile had Anne taking a second look.

"How serious is this?" she asked. "George! I can't believe the little girl who dreamed of knights and princes, and romanticized John Wayne, could fall for a turkey farmer named George."

Jacey giggled. "George really isn't the most romantic name, I'll admit. But it's solid and dependable—like the man."

The corners of Anne's mouth turned down. She hesitated as though it pained her to speak. "Oh Jacey, you're going to get hurt. Loving a man like that is much too dangerous for you."

"Don't you think I've told myself that a thousand times?" Jacey turned stricken eyes to her sister.

"I shouldn't have interfered in your life," Anne said as though the words were being wrenched from her. "It's not too late. If you want to get married, I can send Roger back."

"Anne, I would be miserable married to Roger. I've never seen him as anything but a big brother. I don't want to marry my big brother; I want George."

Tears sparkled in Anne's eyes. "I'll do anything you want with your property, and I'll keep Roger from running rough-shod over you, but I won't let you throw away your life. You're my sister, and I love you. There's no way I can allow you to go on living in this isolated place and tie yourself to a man who raises turkeys for a living. I promised Daddy I'd take you back to Baltimore, and I intend to keep my promise."

"I didn't know you were a snob, Anne. I'll go back to Baltimore, but not because of Daddy or any promise you made. Where I live is my business, not yours. I love you too, but I don't need you to protect me or approve of the life I choose. George loves me and has asked me to marry him, but before I can give him an answer, I have to find some answers for myself. I have unfinished business in Baltimore."

Chapter 12

From the corner of his eye, George saw the horse coming up his lane. Jacey was out early, but she didn't seem to be in a hurry. She was alone, too. He was glad of that; he needed some time alone with her to discuss how Roger's and Anne's arrival might affect her plans for the future. Roger didn't worry him anymore. He was satisfied that Jacey didn't love him; besides, he suspected that Anne had plans for him. Anne was his main concern. For all her defense of Jacey's right to control her own property, she obviously didn't consider Jacey competent to handle the same degree of freedom she claimed for herself. She'd come tearing out here like the cavalry to protect her sister from Roger's manipulation, but he suspected she wasn't above a little manipulation of her own. If her family was trying to run Jacey's life again, he'd set them straight.

George removed his coveralls and left them in the garage as he walked out to meet Jacey.

"Hi! Finished with your chores?" Jacey slipped from Lady's back and looped the reins around a fence post.

"Hi, yourself." He kissed her and assured her that his chores were done.

"Good. Do you have time to talk?" Her fingers creased a pleat in her scarf, smoothed it, and creased it again. George reached for her hand and led her to the bench swing in the backyard. He didn't want any interruptions from Lisa or Ashlie. "Is your company gone?" he asked as soon as they were seated.

"Roger's leaving this morning, but Anne has decided to stay a few days." Jacey didn't meet his eyes, and George began to sweat. Something was up—something she knew he wouldn't like.

"I'm going to sell my ranch and go back . . . "

"No, Jacey!"

"There are things I have to do, George. I've tried to look at this from every side. I've cried and I've prayed. I want to be fair to everyone. So far I've been a coward. I ran away from Roger rather than return his ring in person and tell him how I felt, and I've been hiding from my parents. They don't deserve such shabby treatment. I've been blaming them for taking over my life, but I'm as much at fault as they are. I abdicated the responsibility; I used sickness as an excuse to avoid facing a world that frightened me."

"Going back won't change the past, and it may undermine the independence you've gained this summer."

"I'll never be sure I've overcome my weakness if I don't go back. Don't you see? If I go back, I'll know whether or not I'm strong enough to take charge of my life—or if I'm still a little girl."

"You'll be two thousand miles away from me. Doesn't that mean anything to you?"

"Yes, it does. I don't want to leave you, but staying wouldn't be fair to you, either. When I contemplated marriage to Roger, I didn't expect marriage to change either of our lives. If I thought about it at all, I assumed I would continue to drift along in my quiet half-world, and that was all Roger expected of me. Marriage to you would be different. We would both expect more than that."

"Good grief, Jacey. I don't expect you to plow or catch turkeys. If I need a hired hand, I'll hire one, not marry one."

"I'm not expressing this well, and I'm sorry. There's so much I want to say. I'm not as strong and self-confident as I'd like to be, but I've tasted enough life these past two months to know I want more. I want to run my own home. I want a husband who will share my life and let me share his. I want to teach children. And I want to be a mother. I'm not content to just be alive anymore; I want a real life. But I don't know if I'm emotionally or physically capable of doing those things. I have to return to Baltimore to find out."

George frowned and shifted uneasily. "There were things I had to find out for myself when I joined the Navy. And I suppose even my failures served to teach me who I am and what I stand for, so I can understand how badly you need to prove your independence. But I can't see why you can't do that right here. Are you afraid I'll take over your life?"

"Not intentionally."

"Jacey, listen to me. I'm big, much bigger than you, but I will never use physical strength to force you to do anything. If you're in physical danger and I can help you, I will, but I don't believe in physical threats to sway opinions. You're intelligent and well-educated, and I don't see any reason why your ideas shouldn't carry as much weight as mine. My grandpa tried to force me to live his way, and that experience left me with a deep aversion to any type of coercion. I was ordained an elder a year ago, and I'm aware some people think that when a man holds the priesthood, that gives him some special power over his wife. I don't believe that, and neither does any other man who truly honors his priesthood. I'm a firm believer in equal partnerships." He grinned, hoping to coax a smile from Jacey.

"I believe in equal partnerships, too. That's what I've been trying to tell you. I don't know what I can contribute to a marriage partnership because I've never asked," she continued in a strained voice. "I never questioned my family's assumption that I was destined to live an invalid's life. My parents told me having children would not be possible for me, then Dr. Gifford told me perhaps I can have a baby someday. I've just discovered possibilities I didn't know were open to me, but I should have known. Not knowing, not caring enough to ask questions, and a pessimistic fear crippled me, not my illness. Dr. Gifford made me see that no matter how other people view me, I won't be really in charge of myself until I take back the power cancer stole from me. I have to learn all I can about my individual cancer, then take an active role in my treatment. I might not ever be completely cured, but I can stop allowing it to control me. Until I take back my life, I won't be a whole person."

George was silent for a long time. Arguing would do no good; in fact, it might damage their growing relationship. This was

Jacey's decision, and he'd have to accept it. He wished he could be
certain she would quickly find her answers and return to him; but a
heaviness in his heart reminded him it had taken her eleven years
to find her way to Ephraim this time—and when she got here, it
had been too late for Charlie.

He tried to shake off his gloom by reminding himself that
Jacey was stronger now. He had to have faith in her.

Rain streamed against the windows, a fitting tribute to Jacey's
last night in the cabin. The night had turned cool and George had
lit a fire in the fireplace. Jacey leaned back against his shoulder,
letting the flickering flames hypnotize her. She felt drowsy. Ever
since Anne had arrived, there'd been so much to do.

Only when she thought of tomorrow did the pain become
unbearable. How could she tell George good-bye? She'd spent
little time with him these past few days since their initial
discussion of her decision to leave. Anne had stayed to help Jacey
conclude the sale of the ranch and choose which items to keep and
which to leave with the property. At times, Jacey had suspected
Anne of deliberately looking for excuses to keep her and George
apart; but tonight she'd seemed to understand that Jacey couldn't
be talked out of these few hours alone with him. She had gone on
to Salt Lake City and would meet Jacey there tomorrow.

George's arm tightened around Jacey, letting her know he felt
the same pain. "I love you," he whispered as he touched his lips to
the back of her head. "I don't think I can let you go."

"George."

"I know, it's your decision. I just don't believe this is what you
want, any more than it's what I want."

She could tell him that her father had canceled her credit cards
and closed her checking account, leaving her with only the small
amount left in the Ephraim bank, and it would be true. And though
his actions made her angry and severely damaged the trust she'd
held in him all her life, that wasn't the reason she'd agreed to go
back. George was the reason. She loved him, and she wanted this
chance to prove she could resolve her differences with her family
in a mature fashion. George wasn't the kind of man who would be
happy with a child-bride. He needed a woman, and she needed to

prove, more to herself than to him, that she could be that woman.

Jacey and Anne had talked for hours the day Anne arrived. Then Jacey had invited her sister to stay the night, but she'd insisted on returning to the motel. Jacey had spent the night alternately weeping and praying. When morning came, she'd gone to George. He had a right to be the first to know she'd be leaving. He'd argued and pleaded, but he'd never disputed her right to choose her own future. For that she was grateful.

A log popped, sending a burst of sparklers dancing above the flame. Jacey burrowed closer to the comforting warmth of the man holding her close. George cooperated by tucking her more securely against his side.

"You really don't mind about the ranch, do you?" She sought to reassure herself that he didn't mind her selling the ranch to Jeremy. Roger hadn't spoken to her again before he returned to Baltimore, and she'd heard nothing from the Walkers. She was just glad Roger had gone, and that the Walkers were no longer a threat.

"No, Jeremy will be a good neighbor. He won't block or pollute the stream, and you took every precaution. He or his heirs can't sell it without giving me first refusal. His brothers will take care of your animals when he's out of town, and I don't think it will be many more seasons before he's ready to settle down."

"Thank you for taking the horses. Jeremy would have taken them, but I knew he didn't want to run them with his rodeo string."

"You'll want Lady to ride when you come back, Jacey. She can be getting accustomed to my side of the fence."

"George, it would be unfair for me to expect you to wait for me until I get my life untangled. All my earlier assumptions may be true, and there could be no future for me—for us. I can't bear the thought of you waiting and waiting for what might never be. As hard as it is for me to think about you marrying someone else, I really don't want you to miss out on a family of your own. George, don't count on my ever being able to come back. I want you to get on with your life."

"You will come back! Jacey, you have to believe we have a future together." His big body shook with emotion as he tried to make her see that they belonged together, no matter how much or how little time they might have. "You seem to feel that cancer lessens your value to me, but that's not true."

Tears streamed down Jacey's face as George cupped her cheeks between his big hands. "Jacey, don't do this to us. Go talk to Dr. Bellows. Find out if Gifford is right, if that will make you feel better, and have as many tests as you need, but they don't matter. What does matter is being together. Why can't you see that?"

"Don't make it harder," she pleaded. "You don't know what it's like. When I was a little girl, I saw my grandmother become more feeble each day. At first she got around in a wheelchair, but eventually she became bedridden. Grandfather was afraid to leave town, then he couldn't sail or play golf, fearing she might need him. Finally he grew old just waiting for her to wake up and recognize him. I saw what he and my father went through, watching her die little by little. At the end she couldn't get her breath, the pain was terrible, but I think they suffered more. I saw the terror in Daddy's eyes when I lay in the hospital, struggling to breathe. I don't want to do that to you."

"Do you really think it will hurt any less to lose you now, this way?" He peered intently into the green depths of her eyes. "Honey, I've done some checking. Thyroid cancer has one of the best patient survival records of all the different kinds of cancer. Have some faith that if we do our part, the Lord will bless us with time together. And if that time is short, there's still eternity."

"I want to believe that; I try to have faith, but I don't want to indulge in wishful dreaming." She tried to continue, but the words wouldn't come. Slowly, gently, his mouth lowered to hers. Tentatively he kissed the corner of her mouth. His lips lifted to her eyes, closing first one, then the other. For long minutes he pressed his mouth against her temple. He felt the contraction of her throat as she swallowed convulsively.

His hands slipped to her shoulders, then spread down her back as he pulled her to him. A little sigh escaped her lips as she felt the rightness of his arms closing around her. Why did her first real choice in life have to be so painful? She'd spent so many years drifting whichever way came easiest; and now, when she finally came face to face with placing someone else's needs over her own comfort or desires, she found that this business of shouldering adult responsibility really hurt. It was more painful than she'd ever dreamed possible. She prayed that from somewhere she'd find the strength to do what she must.

George moved one hand across Jacey's shoulders. Her bones were fine and deceptively fragile, but he knew her slender body harbored more strength than she knew. If he believed that returning to her family would give her the confidence she so badly desired, he'd encourage her to go. He wanted her to believe in herself and recognize her own strength, but he feared she'd be outnumbered and lose confidence if the rest of her family were as forceful and aggressive as Anne. He didn't have a good feeling about this at all.

He let his hand continue its exploratory journey, stroking her collarbone, gliding higher, then suddenly pausing as it touched the silken scarf at her throat. He wished he could make her understand. Her cancer didn't matter, not in the sense she thought it did—not in the eternal scheme of things. Grandma used to say that when problems got too big, he should step back and check the eternal perspective. If only he could make Jacey understand that a hundred years from now her illness wouldn't matter, the cost of her care wouldn't matter, whether or not a Lindquist continued to farm this land wouldn't matter. But being together would matter forever.

His fingers worked at the knot. When the strands separated, he gently traced the thick, exposed scar with his finger. Reverently he lowered his head until his lips touched the angry mark flawing her satin skin.

"Don't, George." She tried to push him away. After a moment, he raised his head to look into her face.

"Does it bother you when I touch your scar?"

"It's ugly."

"It's part of you, and I find all of you beautiful."

"There's nothing beautiful about cancer."

"This mark," he drew his fingers along the scar, "is a badge of honor. It proves you fought a brave fight."

"I told you before, I'm not brave."

"Jacey, you have more courage and strength than you give yourself credit for. That's why I don't understand why you're leaving. Your family is against your staying here; they're convinced that marrying me would be a big mistake. They don't believe I can take care of you, especially if you should become ill again. Well, I'm not rich, but I'm not a poor man, either. My farm produces a good living, and I've never even touched my mother's money. Good medical care is available here. Do you think I can't take care of you?"

"No, George. This isn't about money. I have money of my own, and no matter how much Daddy disapproved of you, he wouldn't deny me the money for medical care."

"Then why? I don't know what all Anne said to you, but whatever she said, don't let it be the reason you leave me. Don't forget, your sister is the kind of slick-tongued lawyer who could convince my turkeys that they really are black buzzards. She managed to lull me into believing she was on my side."

Jacey smiled faintly at his words and shook her head. "Anne is on your side and mine, too. She agrees with me that certain risks are not acceptable."

George ran his fingers through his hair in exasperation. He rose to his feet and paced across the room. He turned to glare at Jacey. "Look, you told me you've let other people run your life and make your decisions too long. So don't let your family decide something this important for you." He held up one hand, antici- pating her objection. "I know, you made this decision all by yourself. But Jacey, this isn't the kind of decision you should make alone. You don't need your family's advice, and you don't need mine, but you do need Heavenly Father's."

"Don't you think I've prayed?" Jacey looked pained.

"Yes, I know you've prayed." George's voiced dropped to a gentle plea. "You've prayed and I've prayed, but sometimes more than prayer is needed. Sometimes fasting brings the answer. And sometimes long hours of study and meditation are required."

"George, I have to go." Her tear-filled eyes tore at his senses, making him want to storm and rage. For one insane moment, he considered crushing her to him and holding her a prisoner until she agreed to stay. Instead, he dropped to his knees beside her chair and took her hands in his.

"I know you do," he whispered in consoling tones. "I won't try to stop you anymore, that's a promise. But may I ask for a promise from you in return?"

"A promise?"

"Yes, darling. Promise me you won't make any irrevocable decisions yet. Go back to Baltimore, see your family doctor, study your illness for yourself, quit that job you hate, and think about the future we could have together. Not just the next fifty years, but the next fifty million-plus years. Jacey, when I asked you to marry me, I didn't mean for this life alone. Remember that when you make your decision. The choice you make is one we'll both have to live with for all eternity."

George moved to sit beside her. His elbows rested on his knees, and his hands clasped together to form a resting place for his bowed head. His shoulders hunched, and a fine tremor shook his back once. With one hand Jacey reached out to touch the broad, muscular back beside her. He moved away from her and rose to his feet, moving slowly toward the door.

"George?" she whispered anxiously. "Don't leave me."

He turned to face her. Pain and anger mingling in his voice, he harshly reminded her, "I won't leave you. It is you who is leaving me."

Tears streamed down her stricken face as she acknowledged the truth of his statement. Tomorrow she'd fly away, and she didn't know if she would ever see him again. Her heart questioned whether knowing she'd set him free to live a normal life would be compensation enough.

"I'm sorry." In one smooth motion he gathered her into his arms. "I don't want you to cry or be unhappy. I just want your promise that you'll give us a chance."

Her arms wrapped around his neck, and she leaned her wet cheek against his collarbone and wondered if she could give him the promise he asked for. The first time cancer had been diagnosed, the surgeon had tried to save part of her thyroid; and the next few years had proven that decision to be a costly mistake. A more aggressive approach might have saved years of misery. Wouldn't severing her relationship with George completely be the greater kindness in the long run? She didn't want him to put his life on hold while he waited for her.

"Jacey?" George's hands swallowed up her face as he turned

her head to search her face. His eyes, so full of love and pain, burned into her soul. Slowly she nodded her head. Yes, this one dream she would hold onto. Peace seeped into her troubled heart.

Gradually George felt his body relax its stiff tension, and he leaned his head back against the sofa. Jacey snuggled against his side and he stroked wet strands of hair away from her face. Small sobs shook her slender frame, but eventually she was still and he suspected she'd fallen asleep.

Night sounds drifted through the open window. Sounding eerily close, the long, drawn-out cry of a mournful coyote matched his melancholy mood. A stray rain-washed breeze sent whispers scurrying through the trees, and far down the valley he caught the sound of a diesel engine going through its gears. Closer by, the repetitive chirp of a cricket tapped a lonely refrain in his ear. Silent tears slid down his cheeks, but he didn't release the woman sleeping in his arms to wipe them away.

Just before dawn, George reluctantly separated himself from Jacey. He carried her to her bed and pulled the patchwork quilt over her. For long minutes he stood watching her sleep, with her long hair spread across the white pillowcase. In the faint pre-dawn light there shone a hint of gold in her hair . . . only a promise, perhaps an omen, but a promise he would cling to. Without it he had nothing.

Jacey awoke faintly disoriented. She was in her familiar bed, but everything had changed. She ran her hand across the rumpled sheet and gaped at her crumpled clothes, then sat up abruptly, turning her head from side to side. Of course George had gone, but she didn't remember his leaving. She had meant to savor every minute of their last evening together; instead, she'd fallen asleep. She would only see him once more before she left, on the drive to Salt Lake where they'd meet Anne at the airport. Such a short time to build memories that might have to last her a lifetime.

Drawing her knees up to meet her chin, she gazed around the room. Words formed in her heart, and she prayed for the strength to leave this place where she had been so happy for nearly three months. It would be comforting to know that Jeremy and Nga were living here.

She remembered the promise George had dragged from her,

and close on its heels came one of Anne's favorite phrases. *Promises made under duress are not binding.* Hadn't she learned a long time ago not to dwell on hopes or dreams? But this dream had substance, she argued with herself. She and George loved each other and had a chance at happiness. She mustn't lose sight of her reasons for returning home. Along with making peace with her family, she had to discover her body's true limitations and learn whether or not her hopes for a life with George would fit into the realms of reality.

She swung her legs over the side of the bed. She had things to do. From somewhere deep inside, she had to find the strength to say a last good-bye to this place she loved. And to George.

It didn't take long to pull on a pair of jeans and step into canvas shoes. She picked up one of Uncle Charlic's shirts for the last time and hastily knotted the long tails around her waist before running her fingers through her tangled curls, promising herself a more formal hair-styling after the chores were done. She scowled into the mirror as she contemplated donning city clothes. The sound of metal clanging against metal brought her head up.

She opened her bedroom door and gasped. The sight which met her eyes stopped her in mid-stride. George leaned over the stove, intently ladling spoonfuls of pancake batter in perfect round circles across its shining black surface. His honey-colored hair stood in spiky tufts and fell across his forehead, his jaw clenched in concentration. Bare feet, with little tufts of hair growing between the knuckles of his big toes, were braced firmly on the smooth pine floor. His coveralls and boots lay in a heap beside the door, indicating that he'd come directly to her cabin from doing his chores.

As though suddenly aware of his audience, he turned abruptly, spattering a little row of batter dots across the stove top. Their eyes met, and Jacey didn't know what to say. Behind George's eyes, she could see tightly-leashed anger and hurt. The last thing she wanted to do was hurt him, but if she didn't find out about herself now, she might hurt him far worse. She had never been strong, but she couldn't falter now.

"Go feed your chickens and Gus." George broke the silence with quietly spoken words and a tender smile. "Breakfast will be on the table by the time you're back."

Flashing him a grateful smile, she hurried out the door. She struggled to keep sentimental feelings at bay as the cats wrapped themselves around her legs and the little rooster crowed a lusty good morning. A lump formed in her throat to see the little brown hen trail her line of fluffy baby chicks behind her. She found a record nine eggs, which she placed carefully in her egg bucket. She dumped Gus's feed in his dish, knowing that if she lingered she would cry. Telling him good-bye would be more than difficult.

Breakfast didn't turn out to be stiff and uncomfortable as she had feared. George heaped half a dozen pancakes and an equal number of eggs on her plate beside a thick slice of ham. He drizzled butter and hot strawberry syrup over the lot, then sat down to his own plate, which he'd heaped twice as high. She stifled a giggle when she saw that he had filled water tumblers with orange juice and placed beside them iced tea glasses brimming with milk.

They laughed and swapped memories of their school days and the idiosyncrasies of their families and friends. George said nothing more about her leaving, and she surprised herself by eating half of the food before her. When he pushed his chair back from the table, she noticed he'd cleaned up his huge plate and both of his glasses were empty.

"It'll take me about two hours to finish my chores and get cleaned up, then I'll be back." George touched her cheek briefly before picking up his coveralls and walking out the door.

Jacey stripped the bed and washed the dishes. It didn't take long to pack the rest of her belongings. Most of the things she wanted to keep, including the saddle Uncle Charlie had made for her, had already been boxed and shipped. Jeremy had flown in from Phoenix two days earlier to sign the papers, leaving nothing to do now but say farewell and meet Anne at the airport.

She got out the hose to water her garden one last time. As she stood between the green corn and a straggling row of beans, her eyes lingered lovingly on the little cabin. Her attention drifted across the acres of contrasting green and gray to the mountains she loved. Their towering peaks both challenged and soothed her spirit.

Out of the corner of her eye she caught sight of a hawk soaring in the clear, blue sky. She marveled over the beauty of the seemingly effortless glide of the drifting bird. Wild and free, it caught a wandering air current which carried it lazily across the sky.

Suddenly the hawk plunged at astounding speed. She dropped the hose and ran screaming the instant she realized its target. One of her baby chicks had escaped the wire enclosure. Time took on the grotesque, slow-motion movements of a bad movie. Behind the wire the frantic little brown hen called to her chick, but it ignored the call to scurry beneath a maternal wing. Horror filled Jacey's heart as she saw the invading predator reverse direction and swiftly disappear into the sky with the tiny bit of fluff secured in its beak.

She stood still, staring at nothing. The chick was gone. In spite of the burning heat of an August morning, cold chills brought goose bumps to her arms. Her legs buckled, and she slowly sank to the ground where she huddled, unmoving, for a long time. Why did nature have to be so cruel, so final?

Instead of giving in to the tears threatening to surface, she staggered to her feet and marched to the tool shed. In minutes she returned to the chicken run with boards and nails, which she used to construct a barrier to keep the chicks inside with their mother. While she hammered the nails, she remembered George's warning that hawks would get some of the chicks, and occasionally a skunk or weasel might get in, and even her cats would chase them if they got a chance. She thought of her parents, and freely forgave them for the cage they'd built around her. They had just neglected to open the gate when she was no longer a baby.

She looked up from her hammering to see two solemn-faced little boys watching. When she answered their questions to explain her actions, they volunteered to help and were soon deeply involved in turning the chicken run into a fortress of boards and wire. Reluctantly she turned the project over to them before returning to the house. Her chickens were in good hands, all but the one, and nothing would bring it back.

Seeing Gus fan his tail and strut toward her, she turned aside to speak to him.

"Oh, Gus," she whispered. "Look after the little chicks for me." With a catch in her throat, she added, "And take care of Johnny and Joey—and George, too."

"Are you talking to Gus?" She hadn't heard Johnny come up behind her.

"I always talk to Gus." She gave the boy a lopsided smile.

"Gus is going to miss you."

"I'm going to miss you two." Blinking back tears, Jacey laughed and hugged both of the boys. "I'd hug you too, Gus," she threatened, "if I thought you'd let me get away with it."

The twins roared with laughter, but Jacey knew she really would miss the irascible old bird.

The next half hour passed in a blur as she took her last bath in the red tub, dressed in a silky pantsuit, gave the house a final check, and bid good-bye to the boys. As George's white Mustang carried her down the lane for the last time, she turned to wave a final farewell.

They didn't talk much on the drive into Salt Lake. Jacey didn't question George's choice of the Thistle route rather than the now-familiar Nephi route out of the valley. Leaning back in her seat, she closed her eyes. Her left hand settled on the console between the bucket seats. George reached for her hand, gave it a quick squeeze, then returned his own hand to the wheel.

Three hours later, Jacey sat dry-eyed with her face pressed against the cool glass of a first-class window. Below her she caught a parting glimpse of the Rocky Mountains. They disappeared beneath the wings of the plane, and endless miles of flat midwest farms passed below. She knew they were there, but all she could see was a big man in faded jeans, cowboy boots, and a blue cotton shirt matching the deep blue of his eyes. He reached to hold her in a last bruising embrace that screamed hunger and need. His big body trembled with the emotion he struggled to hold in check. Burned in her memory were the love and despair in George's eyes as he opened his arms to allow her to board the plane. He took two steps backward, and she saw his shoulders slump. Superimposed over George's image she saw herself, standing halfway between the barn and the cabin, watching the hawk carry away her little chicken. And at last her tears came—for the helpless little bird, for herself, and for George.

Chapter 13

"But Jacey, if you don't try it on, Mrs. O'Connell won't know how much to let out the seams."

"It doesn't matter," Jacey nearly snarled at her well-intentioned mother. "I won't be needing it."

"Don't be difficult, dear. You know we only have three weeks."

"Stop it, Mother. There isn't going to be a wedding!"

"Oh dear, do you think September is too late in the season for a garden wedding? Perhaps we should move it inside. The club is out because of the golf tournament. Perhaps one of the hotels . . ."

Jacey ran from the room. She clattered down the stairs and let herself out the front door. Her mother's voice followed her. "Dear, you can't leave now. Remember, you have an appointment with—" Jacey let the door slam behind her. She didn't need her mother to remind her of her appointment with Dr. Bellows. She'd be back in plenty of time.

For nearly an hour she walked aimlessly. Her family was driving her crazy. They seemed to think life should go on just the way it had before she left. She'd come home with such high hopes of making them see her as a real person. Mother was still planning her wedding, for Pete's sake! She'd gone so far as to give the invitations to Anne this morning to mail! Thank goodness Jacey could count on Anne to not mail them.

Anne seemed to be the only one who recognized that she'd

changed. Anne had changed, too. She seemed more subdued, unhappy in some way, and she hadn't given Jacey one word of advice since that interminable flight from Salt Lake to Baltimore. Just this morning, Jacey had walked into the breakfast room and found her sister crying. Anne *never* cried. That's why Jacey hadn't known what to say, but only stood there with her mouth open. When Anne had become aware of Jacey's presence, she'd gulped, "I'm sorry, so sorry," and fled from the room. Jacey wasn't sure what Anne was apologizing for, but it made her uncomfortable.

The squeal of tires caught her attention. She glanced around, startled to discover that she had walked several miles. Almost across the street stood her father's office. There had been an uneasy undercurrent between the two of them from the moment she'd arrived back in Maryland. He'd tried to drive her straight from the airport to the hospital when he'd met her flight from the West. Anne had intervened, and it rankled her that her father had listened to Anne, but not to her. In spite of the fact that Jacey had gained ten pounds and her skin had taken on a healthy glow during her absence, he had remained convinced that she had undergone some great physical ordeal. If she could just get her father's attention, he might listen to her.

Jacey stepped past her father's secretary without a pause in her stride. Her father looked up in surprise when she entered his office and closed the door behind her.

"Why, Jacey. How nice to see you." He looked around, obviously expecting to see someone else. "You're not alone, are you? You know you shouldn't . . . "

"Yes, Daddy, I'm alone; and I'm just fine, except for being very angry. Would you like to handle a lawsuit for me?"

"Who do you want to sue? Has someone hurt you?" He rose to his feet in alarm.

"I want to sue the Frederick Hill Chesapeake Bank of Maryland."

Her father chuckled indulgently. "I don't have time for games, honey, but I'm glad you stopped by. Give me a hug; then, since unfortunately I have work to do, I'll have Marge call a cab to take you home."

"Daddy, if you don't represent me, I'll contact someone at

Morgan, Jewett, and Morgan. I'm sure Mr. Morgan would be delighted to represent me. Even I know there's a law against declaring a person incompetent to handle her own affairs without medical testimony and a hearing before a judge. Mr. Morgan will be very interested to learn that fine old bank is withholding funds from a legitimate, legally-competent depositor on the advice of an interfering third party with no legal claim to the accounts."

"Jacey, you know I only stopped payment on your account to persuade you to come home where you belong. Now that you're here, I'll give Harrington a call and tell him to honor your checks again and reinstate your credit cards."

"No, Daddy, you don't understand. I want my money, every last penny, deposited in a bank that subscribes to a higher code of ethics—one that can't be manipulated by you."

Jacey watched her father's face turn red. He rose to his feet, fury evident in the taut lines of his body.

"Are you accusing me of dishonesty?"

This wasn't going the way she had intended. "No, Daddy." Jacey's voice softened. "What you did was wrong, but I never believed for one minute you were motivated by dishonesty."

Her father took a couple of deep breaths before lowering himself to his chair. "Honey, you haven't been yourself since you returned, and I'm worried about you. When my mother got nervous and upset, your grandfather took her to a quiet little inn on the bay, where she could rest and do nothing but sit in the sun for a few weeks. A few weeks' rest like that would do you good. I'll make the arrangements this afternoon and drive you there myself this weekend."

Jacey stared in horror at her father. "I am not my grandmother, Daddy, and I don't need to go away for a rest. I need you to stop running my life."

"You're getting all worked up, and that's not good for you. Sit down for a minute and I'll have Roger run you home."

"No thank you, Daddy. I'll leave the same way I came." Jacey lifted her chin and walked out the door. She could hear her father yelling into the intercom for Marge to get Roger on the double. Instead of waiting for the elevator, Jacey took the stairs. On the ground floor, she walked out the back door and made her way to a cab stand. When a cab stopped, she climbed inside and huddled in the back.

"Where to, lady?"

Jacey didn't know where she wanted to go. She just wanted to get away from her father. She didn't want to go home, but she had nowhere else to go. She opened her mouth to tell the driver to just drive anywhere when it hit her. She'd go to the bank! Her business was with the bank, not her father. Chagrin stole over her. She'd been acting like an adolescent—the adolescent she'd never been. Fighting with her parents was not the way to convince them she was mature enough to handle her own affairs. She could only encourage them to see her as an adult by taking charge of her own life. She gave the cab driver instructions, then settled back to think.

She couldn't remember a time when her father had ever directed anger toward her, and she didn't like the feeling. She felt small. He'd pampered and loved her—and kept her a child. He had done it because he feared losing her, not because he wanted to hurt her. Jacey knew she was right—but being right didn't excuse her tactics.

In her father's eyes, she had never changed from the little girl he'd protected so fiercely all those years. Now it was up to her to show him that she was ready to move on to a new kind of relationship—one where they were both adults.

The cab stopped in front of the bank where her family had kept their accounts since her grandfather had been a young man. Jacey stared at the gray stone edifice for several seconds, took a deep breath, then clenched and unclenched her hands. She could do it.

"Wait for me. I won't be long." She climbed out of the cab and felt a giggle rise in her throat. She had to handle this right, because if she didn't she'd be in big trouble. She'd left the house without her purse and didn't have a nickel, let alone cab fare.

Minutes later she sat before a tall, thin man with immaculately-groomed hair showing faint gray at the temples. On his desk a narrow gold bar announced in understated tones, *Randolph C. Harrington, Vice President.*

"Mr. Harrington," Jacey spoke carefully, "I have a checking account, a savings account, a stock portfolio, and a trust fund at this bank. I want them all transferred to this address." She printed the name and address of the bank in Ephraim on a note pad on Mr. Harrington's desk. She knew she could trust the people there with her money.

The vice president smiled congenially. "Miss Mathews," he said, "your family has been with this bank for a long time. If you're going to be in Utah for an extended vacation, I'm sure your father will approve the transfer of necessary funds, but there's no reason to disturb all of your accounts."

Jacey clenched her hands and willed herself to stay calm. "Mr. Randolph, I don't need my father's approval. My checking and savings accounts were opened by me with no co-signer. The trust fund arranged by my grandparents listed my father as executor only until I reached twenty-one, which was several years ago; and my sister, Judge Mathews, assured me that she'd made certain the stock is in my name."

"Miss Mathews, your father explained that you've been extremely ill. Why don't I call him . . . "

Jacey rose to her feet. "Did my father provide you with any documentation that I'm mentally incapacitated in any way?"

"No, no, nothing like that."

"Then transfer my funds."

"But your father . . . "

"My father knows better than to interfere with a depositor's account. And you should know better than to discuss my account with anyone other than myself. You were wrong to freeze my accounts without talking directly to me."

"You're right, of course, but we understood you were ill."

"Mr. Harrington, I have been physically ill, not mentally ill. I realize that my father has a great deal of money invested in this bank, and you have served him well. But you do not meet my needs. I want my accounts transferred immediately."

"Yes, Miss Mathews. I'm sorry you feel we have failed you. If there is anything I can do to persuade you not to act hastily, I'll do my best to be of service."

"No, you can't change my mind. I want all but a hundred dollars moved to the Ephraim Bank. I'll take the hundred in cash."

"Very well, Miss Mathews."

Jacey left the bank with a glow of elation. She settled back in the cab with a smile. Now what? There was still the wedding and her appointment with Dr. Bellows. Her euphoria dimmed. She'd taken control of her money, but how could she stop her mother from continuing plans for her wedding? She only hoped she could convince her mother on the way to the doctor's office to cancel everything. Cancel everything? Jacey grinned and reached forward to tap the driver on the shoulder.

"I've changed my mind."

The driver glanced back at her and she gave him the address of Dr. Bellows' office. She would arrive half an hour early, but that would be okay. She had plans for the telephone in the lobby of the medical building. Ten minutes later she paid the cab driver and hurried into the pharmacy for change. She dropped a quarter into the pay phone and dialed. First she called the caterer, then the florist to cancel her mother's orders. They sympathized with her broken engagement, but reminded her that the deposits already paid would be forfeited. She assured them that would be no problem and secured promises that if her mother should reinstate the order, it must be verified with the bride.

When the last call was made, Jacey squared her shoulders and walked slowly down the hall. One part of her recognized that she'd turned a corner. She could take charge of her life. She expected there would still be conflicts with her parents until they felt comfortable with the new Jacey. They would fuss and object when she moved out of their home. But she had to do it. As long as she lived under their roof, it would be too tempting for them—and her—to slide back into the old relationship.

The other part of her was plain scared. All of her tests had been completed almost a week ago, and today Dr. Bellows would review the results with her. She hoped her nerve wouldn't fail her and she wouldn't forget any of the questions she wanted to ask him.

She stepped into the waiting room and glanced around nervously, half expecting to see her parents waiting for her. Relief flooded through her when she saw they weren't there.

"Jacey Mathews!" The receptionist smiled. "Your mother just called to say you wouldn't be keeping your appointment."

"I hope you didn't cancel it." She should have considered the possibility that when she didn't return home, her mother would cancel her appointment, never expecting Jacey to keep the appointment alone.

"No, I haven't done anything yet. Would you like to go back to the doctor's office right now or wait for your mother?"

"Mother isn't coming." Jacey took a couple of steps then stopped. "Would you mind waiting about twenty minutes, then calling my mother for me? I left the house rather hurriedly, and she may be worried. Just tell her I kept my appointment and that I'll be home in a couple of hours."

"Hello, young lady," Dr. Bellows greeted her as he joined her in his office a few minutes later. He'd been greeting her with the same words all her life. Today, she didn't know whether to feel comforted by their familiarity or offended by the gentle implication that she lacked maturity. "You alone today?" He raised an eyebrow as he noted the vacant chair beside her.

"Yes, I wanted to see you alone." She twisted her fingers and groped for the words she needed.

"There's nothing to worry about in any of your tests, Jacey, if that's what concerns you." His bushy eyebrows drew together. "I can go over the results with you now, or if you'd prefer, I can make another appointment when your parents can be here and I can explain everything to them."

"No, doctor." Jacey spoke quickly before she lost her nerve. "I want to know everything about me, about the cancer, my rheumatic heart, everything for myself. I never asked before, and you never told me anything. Everything I thought I knew was filtered through my parents. They sheltered me so thoroughly I became afraid of what I didn't know. In Salt Lake, the doctor you sent me to was impatient with my lack of understanding. He suggested that I ought to grow up and take responsibility for my health."

Dr. Bellows steepled his fingers together and brought them to a point beneath his chin. "It has been my experience that when confronted with a life-threatening illness such as cancer, patients react one of two ways. Some want to be spared the details and are happy to let the medical people do whatever they deem needs to be done. The rest want to see the medical reports, read every book they can get their hands on, join support groups, and insist on playing an active role in deciding what their treatment should be.

The first kind are sometimes a little easier for their doctors to care for, but the second kind tend to survive longer. Your passive behavior has concerned me, but I assumed you fell into the first group and that was the way you wanted it, which was your right."

"I've changed, doctor." Jacey was emphatic. "All my life, I've been the dreamer in the midst of my assertive family. They were all so good at taking charge and getting things done, and I let them. But this summer I discovered I can do many things I'd never thought of doing before, and I found I don't want the same things in life they do. I didn't know how to take charge of my life, and they didn't know how to let go."

"What do you want?" Dr. Bellows watched her with an intent expression on his face, and she sensed that he was really listening to her.

"I don't want a high-profile career like Anne, and I don't want to chair committees and organize charity drives like my mother, or be important like my father. I don't want to live in their shadow, either. I want a life of my own, marriage to a good man, to be surrounded by animals, and to have a close spiritual relationship with God. I want to teach little children and . . . have babies."

Dr. Bellows smiled. "That doesn't sound to me like too extravagant a dream."

"But doctor, are those things possible for me?"

Dr. Bellows reached into the folder lying on his desk and extracted several sheets of paper. "That isn't a question I can answer with a yes or no, but perhaps I can give you some information that will be helpful. One of the difficult things about cancer is never knowing whether or not you're cured. I can tell you that if you get through five years without a recurrence, you have a 95% chance that when you die it won't be from this kind of cancer."

"Is marriage a risk I should take?"

"Depends on the man." Dr. Bellows laughed. "Why do I get the feeling you have a specific man in mind, and he isn't young Mr. Blake?"

Jacey felt her skin flush and she shifted restlessly in her chair. "I met a man in Utah I care a lot about. He's nothing like Roger. George is big, six-five to be exact, and he's a farmer. He loves children and animals, and though he's bigger than everyone else he has a gentle, sensitive side. He threw me in the creek the first time we met."

"What? Doesn't sound like a very sensitive man to me."

"I was covered in mud, screaming, kicking, and trying to bite him and he reacted impulsively. He can't forgive himself, but I can. He taught me a valuable lesson, though it wasn't the one he intended. He came into the creek after me and offered me help. I refused. For the first time in my life, I refused to let someone help me or do what he thought was best for me. I got out by myself, left by myself, and used my own resources to continue on my way."

The doctor chuckled. "Move your chair a little closer, and we'll go over all your test results. Ask questions when you don't understand something."

Jacey moved closer to the desk where Dr. Bellows spread the test results. It took less time than she expected to review them. When they finished, she raised her head and stared thoughtfully at the framed diplomas arranged on the wall behind the desk without seeing them.

"If I understand all this correctly," she said, waving her hand toward the papers scattered across the desk, "there's a bigger chance I won't have another tumor than I will, but there's no guarantee. Right now there's no indication of cancer cells, but because several lymph nodes were affected, I could have cancer cells somewhere in my body we don't know about. How can I make a decision that not only affects the rest of my life, but George's life too?"

"From what you've told me today, I can see the effort you've put into learning to stand on your own two feet. Making choices has not been easy for you, and you'd like a black-and-white world where there's always a right answer and a wrong answer. Not much of life works that way. You're understandably concerned about the effect your health could have on George; you don't want to be a burden to him, or deny him the kind of life he's planned. But you don't want to deny yourself or him this chance for happiness, either. The odds are in your favor. If it were me, I'd take the chance; but you're the one who will have to live with whatever choice you make."

Before she left, Dr. Bellows gave her several pamphlets dealing with nutrition, exercise, support groups, and a fuller explanation of how cancer cells grow and are detected. Jacey left the building still mulling over all he'd said. The backs of her eyes burned. She'd come such a long way from the frightened little girl she'd been at the beginning of the summer; and she'd pinned her hopes, more than she'd realized, on the doctor being able to give her the insight she needed to know whether she should return to George. But how could she decide when even Dr. Bellows said there was no definite answer?

She stood in the middle of the sidewalk and blinked back tears. The sun shimmered through a cloud-like haze, and from deep inside her came a silent prompting to be still and listen. She needed to be alone. She began to walk, and her steps carried her down the street to a little park. She made her way to the swings, and seating herself, she idly kicked back and forth. The park was strangely quiet. No children laughed or played, and the nearby ball diamond appeared abandoned.

She thought about the promise she'd made George. Would she be setting herself up for more heartache and disappointment if she let herself think about going back? Did she have a right to inflict on George all the heartache and expense her chancy future portended?

She felt an urge to pray. She had prayed before, but never felt she'd received an answer. Now she wondered if it might have been because her testimony was weak. Or could it have been because God wanted her to prepare herself?

Jacey dug her toe in the dirt, slowing the swing. She bowed her head and began to pray. She poured out her heart to her Heavenly Father, telling him of her love for George, her desire to be with him, and her fear that by marrying him she would selfishly restrict his life and make him unhappy. When she finished she continued to sit with her head bowed, waiting, listening.

"Jacey." A familiar voice interrupted. She looked up to see Roger leaning against the metal support frame for the swing. Stepping to the empty swing beside her, he sat down. Slowly he scuffed the shiny tips of his shoes in the sand. His dark blue, three-piece suit looked out of place on the playground.

Neither one spoke at first, then they both began at the same time.

"You go first," Roger said, to her surprise.

"What are you doing here?" She heard the defensive note in her voice and struggled to appear calm and in control.

"Your father sent me to find you; he was worried." He stopped her before she could utter the scathing remark that rose to her lips. "I didn't come to invade your privacy, or to march you home like a naughty child. I came because I think it's time we talked, really talked."

Jacey threw him a skeptical glance.

"I know. You don't have much reason to confide in me or trust me to respect your opinions. I can only excuse myself by reminding you that I really do love you." He held up his hand again as she tried to interrupt. "You're right; I don't love you as a sweetheart or wife, but I do love you. As a lonely little boy growing up in a household of important, busy adults, I felt insignificant and unneeded. Then I followed Anne home one day to discover a little girl who needed a big brother to fight her battles and fetch her dolls. I volunteered. When you were so sick, I wanted to be the hero you used to talk about, and I swore to take care of you and keep you safe."

"Roger, I love you, too. No girl ever had a better big brother than I did, but . . . "

"Don't add any 'buts.' I know I carried it too far. It took your big turkey farmer to make me realize that you deserve more than I can give you—and I want more than you can give me."

Jacey stopped the movement of the swing to stare open-mouthed at him. "What do you mean?"

Roger slanted a crooked grin her way. "The light in George's eyes could start forest fires when he looks at you."

Jacey's face burned. Picking up her hand, Roger couldn't resist teasing her a little more. "I'm sure you thought I was blind when I went out there to see you, but I didn't miss your reaction to his smoldering glances. Reminded me of a starving man facing a full-course dinner."

Soon they were laughing together. They were friends again as they had been before their so-called "engagement." Then, as quickly as it had begun, the laughter stopped.

"What are you going to do about George, Jacey?" Roger

asked, the concern showing in his voice.

She bit her lip before speaking. Her voice quavered as she answered. "I don't know."

Roger shoved both fists in his pockets and hunched forward in the child-size swing. "Anne and I have talked about it quite a bit. She made me see how we took over your life by trying to protect you and ended up hurting you. I can only say we did it because we love you, and we meant well. When you think about what to do about George, ask yourself if you're doing the same thing to him."

"What do you mean?"

"What right do you have to decide what's best for George? He's a big boy, and I'm sure he knows the score. If he thinks you're what he wants, who are you to say he doesn't know what's good for him?"

"But—"

"Just think about it. The real reason I came looking for you . . . " Roger hesitated, then started again. "Your mother is still planning our wedding; and though you and I both know we're not getting married, I don't want to disappoint her completely. I've asked Anne to marry me."

"What?" Jacey nearly lost her grip on the swing.

"She accepted, but we've both been a little unsure about how to break the news to you."

"Do you love her?"

"Yes, and this time it's for all the right reasons."

"That's wonderful!" Impulsively she threw herself into her future brother-in-law's arms. "Perhaps I cancelled Mother's wedding plans too soon." She told him what she'd done, and they laughed together.

"Actually, I'm having a little trouble convincing your father which daughter I want to marry." Roger cast her a wry glance.

Jacey laughed, then arm in arm they walked toward Roger's Porsche. Once she was settled in the passenger seat and Roger took his place behind the wheel, instead of starting the engine, he slid his arm along the rich leather of Jacey's seat.

"Just one last bit of advice, then I'll butt out of your life," he murmured. "Go for it—all of it!"

And suddenly she knew. Roger had found the little park where she prayed because her Heavenly Father knew she was ready to make her decision. It would be all right if she chose to marry George. It didn't matter if she didn't have all the answers. She had what mattered most—the strength to meet life's challenges as they came. Her life was hers, and she chose to spend it with George.

* * * * * * * * * *

George frowned. The tractor engine didn't sound right. He'd had trouble all morning with the baler, and now the tractor was acting up, too. At the end of this row, he'd head back to the house. Lisa probably had lunch ready and it would soon be too dry to bale, anyway. Later he'd pull the tractor in the shed and work on it. The engine sputtered, then caught again. He eased back the choke and the engine smoothed out, but only for a moment. A fierce vibration shook the tractor, followed by silence.

George slammed his fist against the steering wheel. Nothing had gone right this whole day. From the time he'd rolled out of bed at four to change the water and begin baling hay, his machinery had acted up, he'd hit several rocks, then he'd had to take time out when his turkey feed delivery arrived a day early. Actually, nothing had gone right since Jacey left. Three weeks, and the pain gripped his heart as deeply as the day he'd watched her turn her back and walk on trembling legs to the plane that carried her away from him.

Three weeks. For three endless weeks there had been no telephone call, no letter. He'd been a fool to agree not to contact her. She had said that she needed time to convince her family she could manage her own life in her own way, and that they'd never accept her declaration of independence if they thought he was influencing her.

Every night he stared at the telephone, willing it to ring. When it didn't, he fought the urge to pick it up and dial her number. Twice he'd punched in the numbers, then hung up before the ringing began. She had to return to him because she *wanted* to, not because of pressure. Besides, he understood her need to think things through and come to her own decision about their future. He'd promised he wouldn't interfere; but he didn't consider it unfair to ask God to help his cause. Consequently, he'd been spending a lot of time on his knees lately.

Her checkup had been a week ago, and he'd hoped she'd call to tell him about it, but she hadn't. Maybe she didn't know the results yet. Her promise was all that kept him going most days. If she prayed as fervently as he did, how could she get any answer other than the one he'd received? They belonged together. He had never been more sure of anything in his life. But back in the deep recesses of his mind one thought crept forward, in spite of his certainty, to torture him over and over. She had never said she loved him.

George sighed and climbed stiffly down from the high seat. He'd have to see if he could restart the tractor and drive it up to the shed. He opened his toolbox and reached for a wrench. After tinkering with the engine for several minutes, he shoved the wrench in his pocket and climbed back up to the seat to press the starter. Nothing happened.

Shaking his head, he climbed down again. He shrugged his shoulders to ease an ache that had crept between his shoulder blades. Before turning to the temperamental engine again, he let his eyes wander down the hill to the fence separating his property from the little farm he still thought of as Jacey's. The hill blocked his view of the cabin, but just thinking of it brought another twinge to his aching heart. He sighed and turned back to the tractor. If he didn't get it started soon, Lisa would be after him with the backside of a skillet for being late for lunch. He didn't want to upset her; she'd been down on Jacey lately, and pretty scathing about his inability to snap out of the doldrums. In some crazy way, she equated Jacey's departure with Craig's desertion.

A few more adjustments, and George walked back to the baler and disengaged it. If he got the tractor started, he wouldn't bother hauling the baler up to the shed, too. He had taken a step toward the tractor, one hand extended to grasp the back of the seat, when a dry rattle at his feet froze him in place. Snake. Not many rattlers came down into the fields anymore, but there was no mistaking this one, and it meant deadly business.

George stood motionless with perspiration running down his back and pooling under his shirt. He studied his options; there weren't many. He could fight or he could run. Neither course held strong promise. He slowly raised his fist, clutching the heavy wrench he'd used to release the baler. His boots came partway up his calves and would offer some protection. With a mighty swing he launched the wrench at the snake, then scrambled backward.

The backs of his legs hit something solid, and his feet flew out from under him. He'd forgotten the baler tongue. His arms flailed futilely in an effort to halt his momentum. There would be no red tub full of hot water to break his fall this time. Then his thoughts exploded in a resounding *thunk!* as his head connected with steel. Light and dark came and went in waves, and he held his breath waiting for the snake to strike.

After several minutes he raised his head a cautious inch, then another. Dots danced before his eyes, but he couldn't see the snake. Maybe it had already bitten him. The back of his head hurt like crazy, and he'd banged up his legs when he'd tripped over the baler tongue. Some of the pain in his legs might be snakebite.

George pulled himself to a sitting position, then dropped his head between his knees. He needed to get to the house, maybe call a doctor. He took a deep breath, then braced his hands against the baler. Once he found his feet, he took a couple of lurching steps to the tractor. He prayed it would start. Pain coursed up the back of his right leg. If the rattler had got him, he wouldn't be able to walk as far as the house. Movement made the blood pump faster, spread the poison faster.

He grasped the back of the tractor seat and strained to lift one foot. The other followed, and the veins in his arms stood out with the exertion of dragging himself onto the seat. He rested his head against the steering wheel as long as he dared before reaching for the starter. The engine caught, and he thanked God before shifting to the lowest gear. He was in no shape to drive, but walking seemed the greater risk. He could handle the slow low gear.

The tractor lurched forward, then began its slow forward crawl. He clung to the steering wheel with all his strength, fighting nausea and the unrelenting waves of blackness. He should turn the tractor around. His house was the other way. It didn't matter. He'd go to Jacey. Jacey would be happy to see him. Had to cross the creek. Should build a gate in the fence; next spring he'd do that.

The tractor nosed down the creek bank and into the shallow stream. Not much water left. Needed rain.

The tractor hit a hole and began to tip. George felt himself sliding, then nothing. Sometime later the cold water revived him enough that he knew a great tire was pinning his shoulder against the muddy creek bottom. He fought rolling waves of pain and prayed that someone would find him. Before blackness settled over him again his thoughts, as always, turned to Jacey. Someone called his name, and a hand touched his face. Jacey had come. No . . . John, or maybe Joe, knelt in the water beside him. Pain screamed through his chest, and he remembered the snake. A woman's voice reached him from far away. He mustn't let the snake get her. "No, Jacey. Stay away. Go back!"

Chapter 14

Jacey heard the telephone ringing as she and Roger entered the house. As she watched her mother pick it up, a strange sensation began to prickle the back of her neck.

"Jeremy? I think you have the wrong number. My daughter doesn't . . . "

Jacey lunged across the room.

"Jeremy? This is Jacey," she practically screamed into the instrument, terrified that she had been too late in wresting the phone from her mother.

Her face turned pale, and suddenly Roger stood beside her supporting her weight, or she might have fallen.

"Thank you, Jeremy. I'll be there before morning." Her voice cracked. Roger took the telephone receiver from her numb fingers, listened for a moment, then carefully replaced it. Jacey turned to him.

"It's George. Jeremy said he was injured in some kind of tractor accident. He's unconscious and in extremely serious condition." Jacey felt her eyes go out of focus, and the room began to slip sideways. Roger eased her into a chair.

"Is Jeremy with him?"

"No, Jeremy's in Denver. He's been in touch by phone with his parents, and he just realized no one had notified me."

"Who are George and Jeremy?" her mother asked, clearly puzzled by the unfamiliar names.

"George is the man I love, and Jeremy is his best friend." Jacey answered mechanically, her mind miles away. She scarcely noticed her mother's shocked expression.

"But Roger . . . " Her mother looked to Roger for help.

Jumping to her feet, Jacey grabbed the telephone again. Ten minutes later, she had a seat reserved on a flight leaving for Salt Lake City in a little over an hour. She slammed down the telephone and leaped toward the stairs. She stopped halfway up, spun around and looked at Roger. "You'll drive me, won't you?"

"Of course!"

"What is going on?" Her mother looked from one to the other.

"Mother, there isn't time to explain everything now. I have to go to George. I should never have left him." She couldn't spare the time to explain further. Roger put his arm around Celia and led her to a chair as Jacey dashed up the stairs. When she returned, Roger took her bag and they headed out the door.

She barely made her connection in Chicago. A two-hour layover in Denver gave her time to find a telephone. After an interminable wait she was connected with the nursing station nearest George's room, but all the nurse would tell her was that there was no change in his condition.

The sun was beginning to cast a faint glow over the Wasatch peaks as a yellow cab disgorged its tired, disheveled passenger at the front entrance of the University Hospital medical complex. Inside, panic lent wings to Jacey's heels as she worked her way through the maze of hospital corridors. When she finally found the right floor, she rushed to the nurses' station.

She interrupted the middle-aged woman in a white uniform, who was intently studying the charts spread on the desk before her. "Please, where can I find George Lindquist?"

"I'm sorry; he's not allowed visitors." The nurse's voice held a hint of starch.

"Is he going to be all right?"

"There's been no change in his condition."

"I won't disturb him. Please let me see him for just a moment."

"Why don't you come back at eight? Most doctors finish their rounds about that time. Perhaps his doctor will approve a short visit then. There's a room just down the hall where you can wait."

Jacey made her way to the waiting room, where she sank into a deeply-padded sofa and buried her face in her hands. She hadn't expected this. It had never occurred to her that she could fly across the continent, be only a few doors away from the man who held her heart, and still not be able to see or touch him.

In a few minutes she was on her feet, pacing the floor. She visited the ladies' lounge where she brushed her hair and applied fresh lipstick, then paced the floor some more. By seven-thirty she stood waiting in the corridor. A different nurse sat behind the desk now. She cheerfully looked up George's room number, and when Jacey turned in that direction her spirits lifted to see the door open and Lisa step out. She was accompanied by a serious-looking young man with a stethoscope dangling around his neck. They were in deep conversation.

"Lisa!" Jacey took off at a run.

"What are you doing here?" Lisa spat the words.

Taken aback, Jacey faltered. "George . . . ?"

"Go away!" the distraught blonde woman shouted. "You're not to go near my brother. Haven't you hurt him enough?"

"I didn't mean to hurt him. I have to see him," Jacey responded with quiet dignity.

"No!" Turning to the man beside her, Lisa said something in a quiet undertone that Jacey could not hear. She thought the doctor might override Lisa's objections, as he appeared to want to argue with her; but in the end, he nodded his head in agreement.

"I'm sorry," he spoke to Jacey, identifying himself as George's doctor. "Lisa is George's only family. As long as he is unconscious and cannot speak for himself, she has the right to bar anyone she chooses from his room. George has mumbled a few words a couple of times that would indicate he might not want you here. You might as well go home."

"I can't go home. I have to see him." Why was Lisa doing this? She had to make them understand.

"I'm sorry, miss. You can't stay here." She glanced anxiously toward George's room, and the doctor added a stern warning. "Orders will be left to call security if you attempt to enter Mr. Lindquist's room without permission."

"Leave! Go away," Lisa hissed.

Blindly, Jacey stumbled backward. "Lisa, don't do this to me," she pleaded. Lisa's jaw set firmly before she turned around and walked back into George's room, closing the door behind her.

"Are you all right? May I call a cab for you?" The doctor gripped her arm as though he thought she might faint.

"No. No, I'm not going anywhere." She pulled away from the doctor's grasp to make her way slowly back to the waiting room. She collapsed on one of the sofas. Her shoulders shook, but she felt too much shock to cry. Was this the end, then? Did George really not want to see her?

"Heroes don't give up without a fight, and neither do their ladies."

Jacey raised her head. She knew she wouldn't see anyone, but she wished the stern, gravelly voice really had come from Uncle Charlie. He'd loved George too, and she now suspected that leaving her his property and making George promise to give her the saddle he'd made was a less-than-subtle attempt at matchmaking. A warm feeling of comfort came over her, and she resolved that no matter what happened, she wouldn't give up.

For two hours she paced the floor of the small lounge. Other people came and went, but Jacey barely acknowledged them. Sometimes she stood in the hall, staring anxiously at George's closed door. Every twenty minutes she stopped at the desk to ask about George's condition, and each time the nurse politely told her she wasn't allowed to give out information about the patient.

At long last, she sank into a deep-cushioned chair and covered her eyes with her hands. She couldn't give up, and she wouldn't go away. George needed her; deep in her soul she knew he did. She could feel him reaching out to her. And she needed him. She didn't need him to take care of her in the traditional sense; the days when someone had to protect "poor little Jacey" were gone. But she needed his love and companionship.

Silently she poured out her heart to her Heavenly Father and gradually felt peace replace the fear. She'd received an answer before, but she hadn't been ready to listen. George had tried to tell her, but she'd had to find out for herself. Understanding flooded her soul, and a still, small voice whispered to her heart, *Daughters and sons of God are sent to earth to act for themselves; that is part*

of the plan of salvation and is the meaning of agency. George is a
choice son of God, as stalwart as the mountains. He has faced his
own refiner's fire and come out ready to serve God. Your trials
have made you strong and taught you to appreciate that you are a
unique daughter of God, a fitting companion to one from whom the
Lord will require much.

Jacey raised her head and looked around the room. She felt a fierce burning in her soul. God had answered her prayer, and her faith blazed strong. He hadn't told her when or how she and George would be reunited, only assured her that their coming together was pleasing in his sight. He was leaving it up to her to work out the details, but she was ready to accept the challenge.

A small hand slipped between her clasped fingers. Glancing up, Jacey's face crumpled at the love and concern she saw reflected in the face of her dear friend, Nga.

"Oh, Nga. They won't let me see him, but I feel strongly that I should. In here," she pointed to her chest, "I know he's waiting for me to come to him."

The sofa dipped slightly as Jeremy sat down on the other side of her. Both Nga and Jeremy wrapped their arms around her. She listened intently as Jeremy told her all he knew about the accident and George's condition.

"He slips in and out of a light coma, Jacey. At first he seemed worried about a snake, but the doctor assured Lisa he hasn't been bitten. He has a concussion, a broken collarbone, a badly sprained ankle, and heavily bruised ribs. When he's awake, he seems to be depressed and doesn't speak." Jeremy gripped her hands tightly. "He could wake up completely any time, and should have by now. The doctor doesn't believe there will be any permanent brain damage, but for some reason George just doesn't want to wake up."

"Doesn't want to wake up?" Jacey repeated in puzzlement.

"He waiting for Princess Charming to wake him." Nga held Jacey's attention with a knowing smile.

"You're mixing up your fairy tales," Jeremy smiled wryly at his wife, "but I suspect you have the right idea." He jumped to his feet and paced thoughtfully across the room, his high-heeled boots adding emphasis to each step he took. "I'm no psychiatrist or a great theologian, but I think this feeling you have that George is waiting for you is something you shouldn't ignore."

"I don't intend to. Will you help me get into his room?" Jacey asked softly.

"Of course," Nga answered immediately.

A wide grin slashed across Jeremy's face; his eyes narrowed to mischievous slits, reminding Jacey of his little brothers. "They can't do any more than throw us out if we get caught," he said.

"Tell us what we do." As Nga leaned forward, Jacey noticed for the first time the rounded mound where the tiny woman's waist used to be. Following her friend's eyes, Nga sighed in resignation. "Doctor think maybe two baby. I get fat really quick." For the first time since she had left Baltimore, a real smile touched Jacey's eyes.

A short time later Jeremy, who had posted himself near George's door, peeked into the waiting room to let Jacey know that Lisa had left to eat dinner and the halls were crowded with visitors. Jacey dashed to the ladies room, where she swept her curls beneath Jeremy's hat and eyed herself in the mirror. Jeremy's spare jeans and satin parade shirt, smuggled in from his truck, fit her quite well. Instead of boots, she wore canvas sneakers. "How appropriate," she giggled nervously, eyeing the shoes before stepping unnoticed into the corridor.

From the corner of her eye she observed the Asian couple leaving the elevator. Nga had accentuated her pregnancy with considerable padding. She leaned heavily against her husband's arm, clutched her stomach, and moaned. Just before she reached the nurses' station, Nga slid to the floor, dropping her shoulder bag as she fell.

Ten dollars' worth of loose quarters, all of Jacey's makeup, and a myriad of pens and papers flew in all directions. Hiding a grim smile of appreciation for her friend's acting skill, which had thoroughly captured the staff's attention, Jacey found the door handle to the room she sought. A quick twist, and she was inside.

Noiselessly she closed the door behind her. She paused briefly to orient herself, then made her way to the hospital bed where George lay with his head slightly elevated. He looked much too big for even the extended-size bed. Her eyes watered as she gazed at his haggard, sleeping face. She noticed an IV drip attached to one hand, and reached tentatively for the other hand lying atop the sheet. Cradling it between her palms, she lifted it tenderly to her lips. Even like this, he looked wonderful to her.

"George," she whispered. "I'm here. They'll try to make me leave soon, but first I have to tell you . . . please wake up and get well. I love you with all my heart, and I want us to be together for however much time the Lord gives us, now and forever." Her tears fell on their joined hands.

Jacey's voice continued softly, though she had no idea whether George could hear her. Over and over she told him she loved him. She told him about the continuing battle with her mother over a wedding that wasn't going to happen. She told him about Roger's and Anne's plans to marry. Gulping back a sob, she told him of Jeremy's and Nga's complicity in helping her to sneak into his room in spite of Lisa's orders. Suspecting that her time was running out, she pressed her lips against his still mouth.

"George, I don't have all the answers I went looking for, and I've learned there's no one perfect moment when I ever will. But I've gained the faith to go on looking and hoping. For too long I've feared my own death so much that I didn't dare to really live. Today, I faced the possibility that you might die. I saw our roles reversed, and knew you were right when you told me that none of us comes with a guarantee. Anyone can die at any time. I know now our love is not for this time alone. I'll take all we can have now, but I want the only guarantee that counts. I want an eternal marriage with you."

Her voice dropped to a hoarse whisper. "I've learned something else, too. I don't have to be alone to be my own person. I'm stronger than I ever imagined I could be—strong enough to accept your strengths as complements to mine, not threats."

For just a moment she thought she felt a broad, calloused thumb press the back of her hand; George's eyelids fluttered, but didn't open. A sense of peace washed over her. He knew she'd come. She felt his pulse beat steadily against her fingers and knew he felt the peace, too. She wondered if she wanted him to awake so badly that her imagination was playing tricks. No, it was no trick. The Spirit spoke softly to her soul. Clear as a voice, she felt the admonition to take heart. All would be well.

She didn't hear the door open, but jumped guiltily when Lisa's fingers closed over hers to wrench them away from her brother's hand.

"I told you to stay away from here."

Jacey didn't move from George's side. Willing herself to stay in control, she spoke in a deliberately calm voice. "Lisa, I'm not leaving. You're frightened. With all the loved ones you've lost in your life, that is understandable. But you're not losing George."

"You don't know anything. If you don't leave, I'll call a security guard."

"You can do that, but when George wakes up he'll be upset. I don't think you want to upset him. What he needs is for all of his loved ones to be praying together for his recovery, not fighting." If only Lisa could understand that she could help her brother more by surrounding him with love and peace than by creating protective barriers.

"He doesn't want you here." Lisa's voice sounded sulky.

Jacey turned to face Lisa fully. The other woman was a head taller, but Jacey took a chance and placed her arms around her. Lisa stiffened, but didn't move away.

"Lisa, George told me you've had a rough time and that you don't have much faith in love. I don't know how to assure you other than by just telling you. I love George, and he loves me; and whether you believe me or not, our future is together."

Lisa didn't say anything and Jacey stepped back, but clasped Lisa's hands. Jacey smiled. "Now, you can either go get that security guard to throw me out and I'll come right back, or you can go get Jeremy and Lee and have them administer to George. The choice is up to you."

Lisa hesitated, then marched out of the room with her head held high. Jacey might not have much time. She turned back to the hospital bed, and blue eyes met hers.

"George, oh George." She bent over the bed at his side. His hand tangled in her curls, and her hand sought his.

"You came." Moisture intensified the shine in his eyes.

"Of course I came," Jacey tried to joke. "Don't you remember? I'm one of those spoiled rich girls who always gets what I want. And I want a certain Sanpete turkey farmer."

George's lips moved in a faint smile, and the smile carried to his eyes. "How soon will you marry me?"

Jacey laughed. "As soon as I find out if Brother Hadley managed to track down my membership record, and if Bishop Thorsen will give me a recommend."

George squeezed her fingers, and she caught the flicker of a grimace cross his face.

"Oh." She jumped to her feet. "I should call a nurse and let her know you're awake."

"In a minute. First I want to kiss you." Jacey leaned toward him and their lips met.

"Jacey!"

At the sound of Lisa's voice, Jacey turned slowly toward the door. She didn't know for sure what she would see, but when she looked past Lisa to Jeremy's broad grin, she knew she'd passed the last test. She could fight for what she wanted and win.

Gratitude filled her heart. The Lord had not only shown her the way, but had given her the assurance that her search for strength had been right. God desired that his daughters be as strong as his sons. Hand in hand with her growing confidence, her testimony had grown too, adding an inner strength to her new sense of competence.

She reached for George's hand and their eyes met. His fingers pressed against hers. Yes, she was ready—they both were—to forge a bond that would meld their strengths forever.

Celia wiped a tear from her eye as she gave her younger daughter a final once-over. Every curl, every flounce and ruffle, was exactly in place. Lifting a circlet of daisies, she carefully positioned it on Jacey's head.

"You look lovely," she whispered, brushing a feathery kiss against her daughter's cheek. A frown marred her serene countenance momentarily. "Are you sure this is what you want?"

"Don't worry, I'm going to be fine." Jacey's eyes sparkled with happiness. "Please go on down. We don't want any delays because the mother of the bride isn't where she belongs." Jacey gently steered her mother out the door.

"Well, all right." Her mother turned reluctantly toward the

door, then stopped. She clasped her hands and looked uncertain. "You're not angry with Anne, are you?"

"No, Mother. I'm very, very happy, and you should be, too. You always wanted Roger for a son-in-law."

"But this new man—he's such a *big* man—I don't know what to say to him."

"George, Mother. George is his name. Just be yourself, and I'm sure you'll soon love him, too." Jacey struggled to keep her laughter from erupting. As soon as her mother was out of sight, she tiptoed down the hall to her sister's room. The sisters stared at each other for a moment, then rushed into each other's arms.

A soft rap sounded on the door and a voice called out, "It's time."

Jacey opened the door and her father stepped inside. He stood still, looking from one daughter to the other for several minutes before clearing his throat noisily. When he spoke, his voice lacked its usual clear courtroom tones, but came out unusually gruff.

"Ready?" He held out an arm to each of them.

"I'm supposed to walk ahead," Jacey smiled and moved toward the door.

"Just a minute, young lady," her father growled in mock severity. "Ordinarily the father of the bride escorts just the bride, but with the kind of wedding you're planning, I won't get to lead you down the aisle. This is as close as I can come to it, so get over here."

Laughter spilled from her lips as she took her father's arm. She could obey this teasing command without feeling any threat to her hard-earned independence. "I'll let you get away with your high-handed tactics today," she scolded in mock severity, "but only today."

Together they moved down the stairs. At the terrace doors, her father gave her waist a squeeze and whispered, "Go ahead, honey."

The music swelled as Jacey stepped through the door. Behind her, she heard her father whisper words of love and encouragement to Anne. She moved slowly down the be-ribboned aisle. Ahead she could see Roger, elegant in a dove-gray morning suit. He winked at her almost imperceptibly, then his eyes moved past her to watch his bride walk toward him.

Jacey turned to face the friends, relatives, and a goodly portion of Baltimore's socially elite who had assembled for her sister's wedding. She felt a swell of pride for Anne, the beautiful bride, her sister, and the center of everyone's attention.

Not quite everyone. George wasn't watching Anne. Jacey's eyes met his, and the wedding ceremony blurred. She pictured herself kneeling at an altar with her hand clasped in his. Theirs would be a Christmas wedding in the historic Manti temple.

Judge Terrington's voice rose and fell, and Jacey's gaze shifted to her parents. Her mother had cried when she and George arrived two days ago from Salt Lake. She'd fluttered around them, never quite certain how to treat this new daughter and the man she'd brought with her. Dad had been stiff and wary, but had gradually relaxed his guard. Jacey suspected that George and her father were well on their way to reaching an understanding.

When she had time to think about it, she'd been surprised that her father hadn't followed her to Salt Lake, or at least called and demanded that she return. Perhaps her new-found confidence showed, and he recognized that his little girl was gone. Perhaps he understood that it was now time to build a new relationship with the woman she'd become.

" . . as long as you both shall live." A tear escaped to run unchecked down Jacey's cheek. She wouldn't hear those words at her wedding; death wouldn't end the vows she and George spoke. She didn't want death to cheat Roger and Anne or her parents, either. Already the hope that her family would someday join the Church was part of her prayers.

The ceremony ended, and the bridal party turned to greet their guests. After the first flurry of hugs and kisses, Jacey slipped away to meet George. He walked toward her; and instead of the soft gray morning suit that fit him to perfection and showed off his broad shoulders, she saw him dressed in white. Her eyes traveled from the tips of white boots, up an incredible length of white pants to a white cutaway coat. She continued to look up and up. There it was, on the top of his head—a white Stetson. A giggle bubbled in her throat.

"I told you to wait for a white hat."

Jacey gasped and looked around. No one stood close enough to have spoken.

"What's the matter, Jacey?" George's arm slipped around her waist.

"Did you hear someone say something?" George shook his head. "It was the strangest thing. I was thinking of our wedding, and suddenly I had the strongest feeling that Uncle Charlie was here."

"I don't know if he's here today or not," George said, tightening his hold on her waist. "But I have a strong hunch he'll be in Manti in December. He told me over and over that his big dream was for you to come to his ranch. But I suspect he had a lot more in mind."

"I suppose you're right," Jacey sighed as she linked her arm through his. "It seems to be a genetic defect for everyone in my family to try to run my life for me, and Uncle Charlie was no exception."

"Do you mind Charlie's maneuvering?" He looked down at her with a gentle smile that made her skin feel warm and shivery at the same time.

"No, I don't mind," Jacey whispered back. "He left me a priceless legacy. Thanks to his scheming, I have a testimony that the Church is true, and I have a wonderful life. Uncle Charlie used the ranch to lure me west, but he left the choosing to me. For that—and for you—I'll be eternally grateful."

About the Author

Jennie Hansen, author of *Run Away Home*, attended Ricks College and graduated from Westminster College in Salt Lake City. She has been a newspaper reporter, editor, and librarian, and is presently a technical services specialist for the Salt Lake City library system.

Her church service has included teaching in all auxiliaries and serving in stake and ward Primary presidencies. She has also served as a stake public affairs coordinator and ward chorister.

Jennie and her husband, Boyd, live in Salt Lake City. They are the parents of four daughters and a son.